A

Bailey wasn't able to admit that Carter was getting to her. But if giving in, just a little, was the only way she could convince him to do things her way, she'd do it. "I'll make a deal with you," she said. "If I let you kiss me, will you stay in bed?"

Carter reached for her and, in an instant, his mouth was on hers. His kiss went on and on and on, until she lost all thought and became disconnected from the world and connected only to him. She did nothing to stop him. Didn't *want* to stop him. Until she got to thinking… his kiss was merely a conquest.

She pulled herself free and jumped to her feet. "You need to keep your hands and lips to yourself," she told him.

Carter laughed. "Okay, honey. But the kiss was your idea, remember?"

She frowned. "I didn't mean *that* kind of kiss."

"I'm not sure I know of any other way to kiss. Would you like to show me?"

"No!"

"Okay. No need to get your panties all bunched up." He patted the empty space next to him on the bed. "If I promise to behave myself, will you come back over here? We'll just sit and talk. I promise."

Liar, liar. "You're impossible," Bailey said. "I'm trying to accomplish something here and you're not taking me, or this situation, seriously." She tossed her hands in the air. "If I come back over there, you'll be all over me. It'll be sex, sex, and more sex. And maybe the next time you kiss me, I won't be able to resist."

"And the problem with that is…?"

"Everything! I don't want to be just some woman you slept with." Only, God help her, she thought that was something she could probably live with…

PRAISE FOR ALEXA DARIN

KISSES DON'T LIE

"A zippy romance that will leave you smiling."
—**Susanna Carr,** author of *Pink Ice*

"*Kisses Don't Lie* is a hunka hunka burnin' fun!"
—**Geralyn Dawson,** *USA Today* best-selling author

"Thanks to Alexa Darin, Elvis lives!"
—**Vicki Lewis Thompson,** *New York Times* best-selling author

"Fantastic! Full of mischief, mayhem, romance, and happily ever afters... one of my favorite books of the year... immensely engaging from the very first sentence."
—**Amanda Haffery**, *Romance Junkies*

"Humorous... delightfully quirky."
—*RT Book Reviews*

LIVE A LITTLE, LOVE A LOT

"Want fun in the sun? Read this book. It's laugh-out-loud funny."
—**Sheila Roberts**, best-selling author of *On Strike For Christmas*

"This book is a fun escape from reality and perfect for a beach vacation."
—*Books by the Glass*

ALSO BY ALEXA DARIN

Kiss Me Twice

Alexa Darin

Top Down Publishing, LLC
www.topdownpub.com

Top Down Publishing, LLC
PO Box 13181
Mill Creek, WA 98082
www.topdownpub.com

KISS ME TWICE
Copyright © 2015 Alexa Darin

ISBN: 978-0-9966306-3-4

Cover design by Kim Killion

Logo designs by Lemoncraft

Edited by Fedora Chen

Print formatting:
By Your Side Self-Publishing
www.ByYourSideSelfPub.com

To Tucker and Sierra.

For all the years of adventure you gave me… you will run by my side forever.

In memory of Chandler.

Peggy,

I thank you for your patience, and for allowing me to feature Chandler in my book.

All my best,

Alexa Davis

Chapter One

Details matter. Or lack of. And that's what bothered Bailey Ventura most about the phone message she'd received regarding her fiancé—*Carter has had a little accident. Please come to Las Vegas.* Should she freak out, thinking the worst? Or should she stay calm and wait until she was able to gather more information about this *little* accident? It was a dilemma, to be sure, especially since it was Carter's sister, Twinkie, who had left the message. She was a showgirl, after all, prone to theatrics. With that in mind, Bailey opted for taking a wait-and-see approach. She tried reaching Twinkie by every means possible, but after several failed attempts, decided to take the first flight Alaska Air offered out of Seattle. By the time she arrived in Las Vegas, her imagination had run wild for approximately seven hours. And for good reason.

"*Amnesia*? What do you *mean*, amnesia?" Bailey asked Twinkie when they were finally face-to-face.

"Shh," Twinkie said. She put a finger to her lips and pulled Bailey off into one corner of the room. Carter was asleep in a Queen-sized bed, looking like Vegas had gotten the better of him. Bad sunburn and a few bruises, but nothing that a good week wouldn't fix. Also, nothing that looked serious enough to result in amnesia. Plus, he hadn't been intubated. That was always a good sign.

"You told me Carter had a little accident. *Little!*" Bailey said, her voice a fierce whisper. "I was thinking fender bender. Or... or anything but this!" She flung a hand in the direction of Carter's bed. "You could have warned me."

Two small, vertical lines appeared at the bridge of Twinkie's nose. "I know. I should have told you, but I didn't think you'd want to hear this kind of news over the phone." She winced. "I'm sorry. You and Carter will have to reschedule your wedding."

Bailey sucked in a breath as visions of melted ice and spoiled food ran through her mind. This was a disaster. Of all the things she'd been thinking could go wrong before their wedding, Carter losing his memory wasn't even on her radar.

Why? she wondered. In three days, she and Carter would have been married. Why couldn't he have waited just one more week before getting himself into trouble? Or how about never!

She took a moment to gather herself. "Are you sure about this? Has he even seen a doctor?" It was a dumb question, as he was hooked up to an IV. "He looks so peaceful. It's just so hard to believe."

"I know," Twinkie said. "And, yes, he has seen a doctor." She paused, looking pained, like she'd just eaten a squid. "You might want to sit down."

Bailey felt the breath leave her lungs. The last thing she wanted was to have one of those *you might want to sit down* conversations. Besides, the only chair in the room was already occupied by some dark-haired beauty that Bailey had never met. That was okay. Twinkie was upset about Carter, and introductions could come later. And, too, the woman was currently slouched in the chair, fast asleep.

"I don't want to sit. Just tell me," Bailey said. "Whatever it is, I'll deal with it."

Twinkie clasped her hands before her and knotted her fingers together. "It's encouraging, actually... just a couple of things. Carter doesn't remember that you and he are supposed to be getting married." She laughed lightly. "Which, I'm sure is no big deal, because as soon as he remembers *you*, your wedding will be back on."

Bailey felt like her hearing might be going haywire. "Say that again," she said to Twinkie.

"Carter doesn't remember you."

"*God*," Bailey said on a gasp. She felt like she'd been slapped. She put a hand to her mouth. This was bad. Maybe not the end-of-the-world bad, but really, really bad. It was all she could do to stay on her feet. She would have sat in the chair, if it weren't for the strange woman.

"Are you all right?" Twinkie asked. She held Bailey's arm to help steady her.

Bailey was still trying to catch her breath. "You said the news was encouraging." Her voice was so quiet, it was almost like she was talking to herself. When she told Twinkie she'd deal with whatever it was, she had no idea it would be something like this. She looked around the room. TV center, nightstands, table and chairs. Typical tourist fare. Couldn't they have at least put Carter in a suite? Or better yet, a medical facility. Even with her short stint in med school, she knew an injury that caused memory loss was significant. He needed medical care. "Why is Carter here, instead of the hospital?" she asked Twinkie.

"He was," Twinkie said. "You know how he can be. He woke up and didn't want to stay put. He said he was leaving with or without a doctor's release." She squeezed Bailey's arm for reassurance, but Bailey wasn't at all reassured. In fact, it took everything she had to keep from crying. Tears formed anyway, and she did her best to blink them away.

"Aww, don't cry," Twinkie said. "You don't have to worry. Carter's in good hands. His doctor drops by twice a day, morning and evening, and a nurse checks in on him three times a day."

"But he has amnesia," Bailey reasoned. Not a common cold.

Twinkie shrugged.

Bailey pinched her lips together. If Carter were any other man, he *would* be in the hospital. The problem was, Carter wasn't just any man. He was special. Like Superman. Only he didn't wear tights. He wore a suit—mostly—and sometimes a leather jacket, accompanied by leather pants. Basically, he led a double life. And both were equally hazardous to his health.

Carter's primary role was head of security for The Oasis resort and casino, where any number of issues might arise that could put him in danger. Intoxicated tourists and disgruntled gamblers were plentiful and they weren't afraid to get their bad-on while in Sin City. Even so, those weren't the types that kept Bailey awake at night. It was Carter's other role, where he paid tribute to the late great Elvis Presley, that worried Bailey most. The King still had plenty of fans and they were always eager to get a piece of him... even if that piece came from a guy who was faking it.

Bailey wondered if that's what had happened. Had some rabid Elvis fan gotten out of control? She was sure it couldn't possibly be some Sin City miscreant who had gotten the better of Carter. He was Security Guy, for crying out loud. It was his job to be aware of potential danger. He would never be caught off-guard.

She moved back up near the foot of Carter's bed. Twinkie stepped up beside her. They stood side-by-side, watching the rise and fall of his chest as he slept. His breathing was strong and steady, and the room was still and quiet, save for the low hum of the air-conditioning unit. Bailey had a chance to think. About all kinds of things. Some of them crazy. Like what if Carter had simply decided he no longer wanted to get married and was using memory loss as a means of escape? It was completely plausible. He'd been married once before, to a red-head named Irene, and his heart had taken quite a beating.

Bailey even remembered him once telling her he wasn't the marrying kind, that he'd had enough of that institution. Maybe she should have believed him. One thing was sure, if Carter *was* faking his amnesia, it was brilliant. No one would expect a man to marry a woman he didn't know.

Bailey settled into a sigh. Sometimes she wondered if marrying Carter was just a fantasy she'd cooked up and no one but she was in on it. At the moment, it seemed so, and she was beginning to have strong doubts that she and Carter would ever take their walk down the aisle. Truth be told, they hadn't been spending much time together lately and she wasn't sure she believed absence made the heart grow fonder. What about out of sight, out of mind? Maybe Carter had gotten lonely and fallen in love with someone else. A sex goddess, perhaps. Las Vegas was ripe with scantily-clad women who weren't at all bashful about letting him know they were interested.

Bailey squinted her eyes in Carter's direction. If he thought she was going to just slink off into the night so he could hook up with some other woman, he'd better think again.

But, no, that wasn't the Carter she knew. She put a hand to her forehead, wondering if she really *was* going crazy. Maybe a little. But, mostly, she was confused. She didn't know what to think. And the only person who could give her any answers was Twinkie. She shot Twinkie a look. "Is it just me, or does this amnesia business seem a little too convenient?" Straight to the point seemed best under the circumstances.

"I'm not sure what you mean," Twinkie said.

Bailey got more specific. "Do you think Carter really wants to marry me?"

Twinkie gave an *ah, I see what you mean* look. "Well, he is a man."

"What's that supposed to mean?" Bailey asked.

"It *means* that I think men are capable of just about anything, especially when they're backed into a corner."

Yikes. That wasn't at all what Bailey wanted to hear. She much preferred hearing that Carter was finally ready to try happily wedded bliss again… that he no longer considered the state of holy union a *been-there, done-that, no-need-to-go-there-again* experience. Wishful thinking perhaps, but certainly not unreasonable.

"What are you trying to tell me?" she asked Twinkie. "Has Carter said something?"

"Easy, girl. Don't get yourself all worked up," said Twinkie. "I was simply remembering how hard Irene was on Carter. I'm sure everyone was surprised to hear he'd decided to give marriage another chance." She waved a dismissive hand. "I wouldn't worry about that. Look at him. Have you ever seen him looking so pathetic? I doubt he could fake that."

Bailey gave Carter an appraising look. Twinkie had a point. He did look pathetic. Still. He was a man… capable of almost anything.

"And so what if you and Carter have to reschedule your wedding. At least he's alive," Twinkie went on.

True. He was alive. And Bailey agreed, they absolutely could reschedule. But if he didn't remember her, there would be no wedding *to* reschedule.

"Don't feel bad," Twinkie said. "He'll get his memory back. Eventually." She shrugged. "Maybe."

Right. Maybe.

Bailey sighed. Her emotions were all over the place. She and Carter had made it through so much. It was finally their time… only, now, it wasn't, and she desperately wanted something or some*one* to blame. She regarded Twinkie coolly. "This is unacceptable. You were supposed to keep an eye on him."

Twinkie frowned, looking frazzled by all the questioning. Or just plain frazzled. It was likely she'd stayed up all night, by Carter's side. Her lips were stained red from remnants of leftover lipstick that had probably once matched the color of her stiletto heels, and her blonde hair swirled lazily about her head, looking like it could use a good shot of Aqua Net. Either that or she was going for the *I just got out of bed* look. She did a palms up. "How was I supposed to know my brother was planning to do something stupid like this? Your wedding is all he's talked about for weeks."

Ha! Bailey knew that was a big fat lie. Carter had never been much for wedding talk. In fact, he'd been so busy the past couple of weeks, he'd left any remaining wedding details all up to her, saying that whatever she wanted was fine with him.

Okay, so maybe it was a stretch to think Carter was faking his amnesia, but maybe if she had more details she wouldn't be forced to make so many assumptions. "Has anyone spoken to him?" she asked Twinkie. "Does anyone know why he was out in the desert? Did his car break down?"

"Detective Forester was here earlier," Twinkie said. "Carter told him he doesn't remember anything. No one knows why he was out in the desert. And as far as his car goes, you know how he is about that car. He keeps it in perfect running condition."

Bailey did know. Carter loved his car.

"Anything else?" Twinkie asked.

Yes, but it could wait. Bailey turned her attention back to Carter, watching for movement of the bedcovers over his chest again, to make sure he was still breathing. He was. In fact, he was stirring and his eyelids were fluttering. She waited for him to open his eyes, but a minute went by and then another minute and he settled again.

Bailey glanced over her shoulder at the woman still sleeping in the chair. How anyone could sleep at a time like this was beyond understanding. Bailey doubted she'd ever sleep again. She wanted to run or cry or throw a tantrum. But she'd do none of those things. She'd stand by Carter and do whatever was necessary to help him recover.

She yawned, feeling fatigued. Maybe she *could* sleep. Later. Right now, she needed something to take her mind off Carter and his suspicious memory loss. It seemed the perfect time to ask Twinkie about the strange woman.

She nudged Twinkie. "Who's the Salma Hayek look-alike?"

"Don't worry about her. She's nobody," Twinkie said.

Bailey had a feeling the woman was *some*body. "Why haven't you introduced us?"

Twinkie cut her eyes to the woman. "She's asleep."

Fair enough.

"No, I'm not," said the woman. She'd finally come alive. "Who can sleep with all this talk about who done what to Carter, and why?" She came and stood next to Twinkie. "Look at it this way, *chica*," she said to Bailey, "at least Carter hasn't lost his *entire* memory. *That* would be unacceptable."

Bailey leaned and looked around Twinkie, giving the dark-haired beauty a more thorough once-over. High cheek bones and large doe-eyes accompanied by handfuls of dark, wavy hair... not to mention a flawless complexion. Plus, she was covered head to toe in black, exuding a sexiness that made Bailey feel not one bit better about having her in Carter's room.

Twinkie introduced them. "Bailey, Maria. Maria, Bailey."

"Pleased," Maria said, flaunting her accent—part Southern Miss, part Hispanic princess.

Bailey mumbled "hello," to Maria, and then slid Twinkie a look that meant *Why is she here?*

Twinkie leaned into Bailey and spoke softly. "Relax. Maria and Carter knew each other a long time ago. She doesn't even live here in Las Vegas."

"What, she happened to be in the area and thought she'd stop by for a visit?" Bailey asked.

Twinkie let her head fall back, like she was tired of being interrogated. She grabbed Bailey's arm and pulled her back into the corner again. "If you must know, Maria has special skills. She was in the army. When Carter went missing, I thought maybe she could help find him. Plus, she's a doctor..." She kept talking, going on about how Maria this and Maria that... blah, blah, blah, blah, blah, none of which interested Bailey. And when she was finished and got back onto the subject of Carter, Bailey began listening again.

"...and that's where she found Carter," Twinkie finished. "Face down, out in the desert, baking to death." She smiled. "Happy?"

Not really. Anyone could see that Maria had special skills. Bailey just didn't want her using them on Carter. "That's all well and good," she said, "but I still don't understand why you didn't call *me* first."

"I'd hoped I wouldn't have to give you bad news. Did you hear the part where I said Maria flew a helicopter out into the desert? Can you fly a helicopter?"

Point taken.

Twinkie put a hand on Bailey's arm. "Don't waste any brain cells thinking about Maria. She's no threat." She looked at her watch. "I gotta run. Good luck with my brother when he wakes up. Coming?" she called to Maria over her shoulder, and then she made a move for the door.

"You're not staying?" Bailey asked.

"Look at me. I'm a fright. I have a show tonight that I need to get ready for. I didn't think you and my brother needed a chaperone."

"A little moral support would be nice."

Twinkie looked back at Carter. "He might not even wake up tonight. His nurse is due to check in on him in a while. I'm sure you'll do fine. I bet if he does wake up, as soon as he sees you, his memory will come gushing back."

Maria was at Twinkie's side. She smiled. "Look at it this way, *chica*, if Carter doesn't remember you, think of the fun you can have getting him to fall in love with you all over again."

Fun. Right.

Bailey watched the door close behind Twinkie and Maria, and then she turned back to Carter. She took a good look at his face. The bruises would fade and any pain he might be in would recede. But amnesia? That was big. Huge. And Twinkie was wrong. His memory wasn't about to come back just from him seeing her. She might be a medical school dropout, but she knew enough and amnesia didn't work that way. When, or if, Carter ever regained his memory, it was likely to be a slow, torturous process.

Oh, Carter. Bailey fought back tears at the idea that when he woke up, he wouldn't know her. Though, probably she should be relieved. Every wedding had glitches and Carter's memory loss was *her* wedding glitch. All she had to do now was get busy fixing it.

Chapter Two

Bailey moved over to the side of Carter's bed and touched his hand. Crazy thoughts aside—that he may have decided he no longer wanted to marry her and that this was all just a big act—she couldn't bear seeing him hurt.

"Who did this to you, Carter?" she whispered. Though it didn't take much thought to come up with a suspect—a man named Frank Zoopa. He was at the top of her list of people who wouldn't lose any sleep over Carter's demise. And vice versa. For as long as she'd known Carter, the two men seemed to have it in for each other. Carter didn't talk much about his past, and she didn't like bringing up bad memories, but she'd overheard plenty of casino gossip and word was Zoopa had caused Carter's parents a world of grief that had ruined them, financially. If that was true, she understood completely Carter's hatred for the man. But she'd never been able to figure out why Zoopa hated Carter.

It was a man thing, she supposed.

Her mouth twisted in disappointment that she hadn't seen this coming. Maybe she could have intervened. Or maybe not. And, anyway, Carter usually had no problem taking care of security issues. For one thing, he carried a gun that he knew how to use. And, too, if he ran into trouble, he had a security team that was always at the ready to lend him a hand.

She smiled, thinking of how things might be if Carter were to turn in his gun for a microphone. She could see it now. On show night, she'd have the best seat in the theater, and then when Carter appeared on stage, belting out songs like "Burning Love" or "Suspicious Minds" or even "Rock-A-Hula Baby," every woman in the audience would lose her mind. Which is exactly what always happened.

"Rock-A-Hula Baby." Now, there was a great song. She'd first heard it as an impressionable three-year-old, listening to one of her mother's old 45s. At the time, she was convinced Elvis was singing "Rock-A-Hula *Bailey*" and, thus, a seed was sown that someday she would grow up and marry a man who could sing.

That man turned out to be Carter.

It was a fun thought... though playing Elvis carried its own risks. And even if it didn't, security was Carter's thing. He would never give up that part of his life.

Oh, if only life were as simple as meeting, falling in love, getting married, and living happily ever after. But it wasn't. And now here she was wondering what the heck came next.

What did come next? She moved even closer to Carter, and got a whiff of a minty medicinal odor. It was the balm on his lips, put there to help them heal, no doubt. She wondered how long it would be before she would feel those lips on hers again. It had already been so long.

Her gaze strayed down to Carter's torso. With gentle hands, she carefully peeled back the sheet and light blanket that were covering him. It wasn't bad, just a few bruises and angry-looking scrapes, but nothing to be alarmed about. In her relief, she rubbed her fingers lightly over his skin, over the roughness of the scrapes. It looked as though he might have been dragged. She was tempted to palpate his abdomen, but decided she'd leave that kind of examination to his doctor. She was happy just to be near him, touching him. He may be bruised, but he was still all hard muscle. And he was all hers. She felt silly to have ever suspected him of faking his memory loss.

She considered what "special skills" Maria had said, how if all else failed, she could try to make Carter fall in love with her all over again. That was the most pleasant thought she'd had all day. And wouldn't that be something, to have a man like Carter fall in love with her twice? Two first times looking into each other's eyes, two first kisses, two first... everything.

She put her fingers to her lips, suppressing a small laugh.

Her phone rang, and she moved quickly to grab it from her bag. Caller I.D. showed MOM, and she wandered away from Carter's bedside to answer.

"Hello?" she said, keeping her voice low.

"I'm sure I've told you this, but it's certainly worth repeating," her mom began. "The groom isn't supposed to see the bride before the wedding. It's bad luck."

Bailey closed her eyes. "Yes, Mom, I do remember you telling me that." At least a gazillion times.

"Did you and Elvis have a fight?" her mom asked. "Did he run off with some showgirl? Those things never last, you know."

Bailey kept her eyes closed and imagined she was on a remote Caribbean beach, listening to ocean waves pound the shore. She wondered if her mother would ever get that Carter was just an Elvis *impersonator*—and only part-time at that. Probably not.

"One more thing," her mom said.

Of course, because there was always more.

"Doc Russo has left town, and your Aunt Fiona, of all people, has gotten it into her head that she's Coupeville's answer to the current health crisis. She's dug out your old medical dictionary and has been taking notes like there's no tomorrow. It's only a matter of time. She'll end up amputating someone's arm or leg and we'll all be sued. I'll lose my house and probably be asked to leave Coupeville. I can't take it anymore. I've put her on a plane with Liza. They should be arriving there any minute."

Her mom clicked off, and Bailey stared at her phone. She couldn't possibly have heard right. Her auntie could not possibly be on her way there to Las Vegas. Certainly not with Liza. Liza was Bailey's best friend. She wouldn't dare bring her auntie to Las Vegas.

Actually, she would. Liza was a slot machine junkie, and she welcomed any excuse to visit Las Vegas in hopes of winning her fortune on the one-armed bandits.

"Lord," Bailey said, reminding herself of her mother. She dropped her phone back into her bag and wondered how she was going to find time to help Carter regain his memory if she was also tasked with keeping an eye on her auntie. But that was something she could think about later… if what her mom told her was really true. Her mom had been in a weird zone lately, so no telling what was what these days.

Bailey had a strange feeling, like someone was watching her. She turned and saw that it was Carter. He was wide awake. She sucked in a breath.

"Giorgio," he said, his voice raspy, like he'd been on a week-long, two-pack-a-day smoking binge. Though Bailey knew better. Working in a smoke-filled casino environment, Carter wouldn't voluntarily add any additional toxins into his body.

"Excuse me?" she said.

"You're wearing Giorgio perfume."

Her stomach did a little flip. She couldn't believe he remembered. "You're right. It is Giorgio." She scooted over close to him. She wanted to throw her arms around him and kiss his face and break out in laughter. Instead, she remained calm and cautious. "Do you know who I am?"

Carter gave her a blank stare.

She smiled a nervous smile. She'd been hoping for something more encouraging. "You're staring. You don't remember me, do you?" She thought she might die if he said no.

"Let's talk," he said at last.

"Of course."

"You start."

"Oh. Okay." But she was caught off guard and had to take a moment to think about what she wanted to—or should—say. It would hardly do to just jump in and tell him she'd decided on raspberry filling over chocolate for their wedding cake. Or that their guest list had grown exponentially since they'd last seen each other. Another route seemed best. "Is Frank Zoopa the reason you're in this bed?" she asked. It wasn't much better, but it was all she could come up with on such short notice.

Carter raised an eyebrow. "You know about Zoopa?"

"I know he's evil."

Carter grinned, looking her up and down. "I imagine a woman like you thinks just about everything here in Las Vegas is evil."

A woman like her? Bailey was curious what he meant, but she wanted to avoid unnecessary conversation that would do nothing to help the situation, so she pressed on. "What happened to you?" she asked. "You promised me that you and that awful man had called a truce. You said you were going to *share* Las Vegas. That you'd stay out of each other's way."

Carter held up a hand, grimacing from the effort. "Slow down. I have no idea about any promises I've ever made to you. I don't even *know* you."

Right. Bailey caught herself. She should have known better than to push him. "I understand how you feel. I know this must be hard. I don't know what, if anything, Twinkie has told you—"

"Everything."

Oh. "Do you want to talk about it?"

"Let's start with the truth. Is this some kind of joke you and my sister cooked up? Is she trying to get even with me for something I did? She's been known to have a sick sense of humor." He pushed the pillow behind his head around some, and his lips tightened with pain.

Bailey was taken aback. She'd never entertained the idea he would think such a thing. "I would never joke about getting married," she told him.

"Good. Now that we have that out of the way." He reached and took her hand and, for a second, she thought maybe they were going to have a serious conversation. But when she looked into his eyes and saw a familiar gleam, she knew better. She drew her hand back.

"I'm not here for *that*," she said, miffed that he was thinking about sex at a time like this.

Carter grinned broadly. "Who said anything about *that*? I'm just trying to get to know the woman who claims she's my bride-to-be. What happened, honey? We get drunk and make each other promises we both knew we'd never keep?"

She frowned. "I never make promises I don't intend to keep. If you knew me, you'd know that."

"That's what I'm telling you. I *don't* know you."

Bailey swallowed. His words made her feel like her stomach had bottomed out. Plus, she was frustrated at herself for being so unprepared. If they kept on this way, she'd only end up crying. Carter hated it when she cried, and she didn't want to manipulate him that way. She had to change the subject. "Could we go back to Zoopa?" she asked. As much as she deplored the man, talking about him was much less hurtful than hearing the man she loved say he didn't know her... or didn't love her.

Carter's shoulders hunched. "There's nothing to talk about where Zoopa's concerned. It doesn't involve you."

Bailey was nonplussed. She could practically feel her blood pressure rising. "You're wrong! If not for Zoopa, we'd be getting married in a few days. Why can't you just forget about him? Would it be so bad to live a life free of murder and mayhem?"

Carter looked amused, like he wasn't taking any of this seriously. "No one's been murdered. And I hate to tell you this, but mayhem and Sin City go together, kind of like ice cream and pie."

Pie? What an interesting comment, considering she baked *pies* for a living. Even so, she didn't want to get off track. They could talk about pie later. "Yes, but just because you live here in Sin City doesn't mean *you* have to be involved in all that mayhem business."

"My job says otherwise."

Bailey pressed her lips tight. This conversation was going nowhere, and arguing was so very tiresome. They hadn't seen each other in weeks and this wasn't at all how she'd pictured their reunion. "Let's go back to us," she suggested, offering him her hand again.

Carter's eyes lost their edge and he put her hand to his mouth. His lips were warm, even through the balm, which was slightly gooey-feeling. But she didn't care. She relished his touch. Though she was no dummy. She knew what he was up to. He was trying to *Elvis* her into bed. And she was having none of it. She knew how to handle him when he played that card.

"Like I said, back to us." She smiled a little smile, wanting to lighten things up. "You know, my mother will be sorely disappointed if we call off our wedding. She's already ordered the cake." Six months ago.

Carter arched an eyebrow. "I don't like cake."

"Yes, I know. You like pie. But *I* like cake. And so do most of our guests. Besides, what's a wedding without a cake?"

Carter grumbled something unintelligible, and she ignored it, preferring instead to get up and let some light into the room. She went over to the cream-colored, hang-over drapes that covered one entire wall and pulled them open. Neon lights blinked up at her from Las Vegas Boulevard, making the Strip look alive. On the sidewalk below, she saw hundreds of tourists bustling along in the relentless heat. Probably, it was triple digits by now. She was glad to be inside—with Carter—though the air-conditioned coolness of the room made her think of home.

Coupeville was in the throes of autumn right now, which

meant that the residents there were already pulling out their winter wear. She loved the crisp weekend mornings. She'd get up early and take her dogs out for their morning walk, and then she might do nothing else all day but sit out on her deck and watch the goings on out over Penn Cove Bay. She'd miss those days... when and if she and Carter married and she moved to Las Vegas.

She turned away from the window, and Carter kept his eyes on her as she moved back across the room. She sat next to him, but kept her hands in her lap for safekeeping.

"What were you thinking about, standing over there at the window?" Carter asked.

"Home."

"You've only been here five minutes. You're already homesick?"

Bailey shrugged. "I don't know what I'm feeling."

Carter smiled. "Okay. What do you suggest we do now, since you've made it so clear you're not here for *that*?" he asked.

Yes, what? She gave it some thought. Though it was easy. "I'd like for us to spend some time together. We could go to a show. Or how about dinner?" Anywhere was okay with her. Better to go out than stay in a room where odds were he'd eventually get her to change her mind about doing *that*.

"You want to go on a date?"

"If that's what you want to call it. Of course, I wasn't speaking of this very minute. How long will you be in this bed?"

"What time is it?"

She looked at her watch. "Nearly seven."

"I'll be outta here by eight."

Bailey frowned and pointed to the IV tubing sticking out of his arm. "I don't think you'll be going anywhere tonight. Not while you're hooked to that. Let me rephrase my question. How long did your doctor say it would be before you could get out of bed?"

Carter yanked the tubing from his arm and tossed it aside. "I'm good to go."

Chapter Three

Bailey's jaw went slack, but then her doctor sense kicked in. "I can't believe you did that! Who's your doctor? I'm calling him right now." She looked on Carter's nightstand for a name or phone number of someone who could get things back under control.

"Never mind that," Carter said. "I feel fine."

"You're obviously feverish, and need more rest. Maybe I should leave. I can come back in the morning," Bailey offered.

"You step foot outside this room, and I'll be out of this bed before you reach the elevator."

She gave him a sharp look. "What am I supposed to do, stay here all night with you?"

A smile inched across his face.

"Forget it." But she was tempted. And he knew it.

"Afraid?"

"Fear has nothing to do with it. You could injure yourself. I don't want to do anything to hurt you more than you already are." Though at the moment, Carter didn't seem all that concerned about pain.

"You sure?" he asked.

No. Even so, one of them had to be sensible. "What if someone were to walk in?"

"Ah, you're modest," he said

He was right. But she'd be damned if she was going to admit it. She hitched her chin. "I'll make a deal with you. If I let you kiss me, will you stay in bed?"

Without a word, Carter reached for her and his mouth was on hers in an instant. She did nothing to stop him. Didn't *want* to. His kiss went on and on, until she lost all thought and became disconnected from the world and connected only to him. But then she got to thinking, and a little voice came out of nowhere, telling her that his kiss was only a conquest. Which she already knew, but the fact that her inner voice was talking to her, telling her this was a bad idea, had so much more impact.

She pulled herself free and jumped to her feet. "You need to keep your hands and lips to yourself," she told him.

Carter laughed. "Okay, honey. But the kiss was your idea, remember?"

She frowned. "I didn't mean *that* kind of kiss."

"I'm not sure I know of any other way to kiss. Would you like to show me?"

"No!"

"Okay. No need to get your panties all bunched up." He patted the empty space next to him on the bed. "If I promise to behave myself, will you come back over here? We'll just sit and talk. I promise."

Liar, liar. "You're impossible," Bailey said. "I'm trying to accomplish something here and you're not taking me, or this situation, seriously." She tossed her hands in the air. "If I come back over there, you'll be all over me. It'll be sex, sex, and more sex. And maybe the next time you kiss me, I won't be able to resist."

"And the problem with that is…?"

"Everything! I don't want to be just some woman you slept with." Only, God help her, she thought that was something she could probably live with.

Carter looked her in the eye. "Are you saying we've never..."

"I'm *saying* since you don't remember me, that for you, it's just sex. But for me, it's how I say I love you." She took a chance and sat back down next to him. "I want you to know I'm not just some crazy female who wants to be able to say I shared a bed with a guy who sings like Elvis. What we have— or *had*—is special, and I'd like it to stay that way."

"I wasn't even thinking about you being a crazy female. But now that you mention it, I hope you're not one of *those*."

"Those?"

"One of those women who teeter between make-believe and reality. I'm not the real deal, honey. I may sing like the King, but that's where the similarity ends."

That's what *he* thought. His resemblance to Elvis was remarkable, even if it was all just an act. Plus, he did dress up well and comb his hair just right on those occasions when he was performing. But probably she should keep it to herself that her mom had trouble telling the difference. Though he'd find out eventually and, well, maybe she should just get it out in the open.

"I know who you are," Bailey said. "But my mom is another story. Until you came along, she was just like all the other women out there who still believe Elvis is living incognito, most likely in Kalamazoo, Michigan, waiting to make the comeback of all comebacks."

"Kalamazoo?"

She nodded. "Whenever my mom has a stress attack, she threatens to run away to Kalamazoo. Not only that, but she's currently involved in a texting relationship with a man she met here in Las Vegas who bears a strong resemblance to Elvis. An old Elvis, that is."

The room became silent, and she wondered if she'd gone too far. She didn't want him to think her mom was loony tunes, after all. Though, really, the theory that Elvis had faked his own death didn't seem all that absurd to her. People, normal citizens, disappeared every day. Why not someone who was fantastically rich and famous?

"Sounds like your mom has it all figured out," Carter said, looking more amused than anything. "Do you think she'll do it, move to Kalamazoo?"

Bailey shook her head. "She wouldn't get any farther than Coupeville's city limits. We Ventura women aren't much for driving, and she'd have to get across the water over to Seattle via ferry first. I don't know of anyone who would take her. It's a bunch of oldsters there in Coupeville."

She'd said enough. She had no idea how the conversation had gotten so far off track. She didn't want to talk about her mom, or whether or not Elvis was alive or dead. She wanted to talk about their future. That is, if they still had one.

"For the record," she said, "I am a fan of your singing, but I want more than a piece of you. I want *all* of you. I want to spend the rest of my life with you, whether you sing or whether you don't."

Her admission left her feeling foolish. Probably he'd heard those words enough times that he all but went deaf around women who were saying them. But when she looked into his eyes, all she saw was pleasant surprise.

She smiled, feeling nervous, wondering where they went from there. They were both quiet for a minute.

At last, Carter spoke. "Why don't you tell me more. About you... your family."

Bailey all but lit up inside. It was a great idea and might be her only chance to give him the full story. "Even better, how about I tell you how we met and fell in love? Then maybe you'll remember me and we can get back to talking about wedding plans."

"Let's not rush things."

She gently pushed him back into his pillow. "I'll talk, you listen," she said.

Carter made himself comfortable, like he was getting ready to hear a bedtime story. Bailey saw that as a good sign. At least he wasn't running.

"It all began when you came to my room to rescue me after I got stuck in a shower here in this hotel. The door was defective..." she began. And she went on with all the details about how she'd won a car on a slot machine, and then talked him into driving it back home with her all the way to Coupeville. Then, when she got to the part about her mom and aunt thinking he was the real Elvis Presley, she paused, assessing the impact of her story. His face was hard to read and she couldn't tell whether he was stifling the urge to yawn, or if he was truly interested, but she decided to continue.

"Little did I know, you'd hidden a diamond in the top of my car. And that's why that awful Frank Zoopa came to town. He wanted his diamond back. Only it wasn't his. He'd stolen it from a man named Mr. Azuri—and you got it back for him."

Carter looked at her for a minute, and she knew he was reading her. He was good at that, reading people. It was part of his job. She hoped he could read how much in love with him she was at that very moment.

He brushed a hand along her cheek. "That's a good story, honey. Hard to make up something like that."

"It's not a story." She looked at him in earnest. "You saved my family from that man. Me, my mom, my aunt... the entire town of Coupeville. You're a real hero to all of us." It was absolutely true.

His look turned guarded. "You being a small town girl and all, it probably seems like quite an adventure coming here to Las Vegas, hooking up with someone like me."

"What do you mean?"

He shrugged. "Intrigue... mystery."

She scoffed. "If you're talking about all that business with Frank Zoopa, you're wrong. That's the part I could do without. It was complete chaos when he and his henchmen came to town, and I was glad to have it over with. Only it's not over, because you and he are still going at it, making life hell for each other. And until it ends, you and I don't get to have our happy ending." Her voice softened. "I want my happy ending."

"I don't know what to say."

"You don't have to say anything." Not right now, anyway. She considered something. "I have an idea. Would you be willing to come home with me?"

"To Coupeville?"

"When you're feeling up to it, of course."

"I have a lot to take care of here. This place doesn't run itself."

"I know… all that madness and mayhem. But you have people who can take care of those things for you."

"I have a better idea. How about you go back home, and if I remember you, you'll be the first to know."

Bailey's heart lurched. "But I don't want to leave here without you. We're supposed to be getting married."

Carter grabbed her and pulled her all the way up onto the bed with him. "I don't know about marriage, but if you're determined to stay, you might as well climb into this bed with me."

She struggled, but only half-heartedly. Having his hands on her made something inside her come alive. She was needy for his touch. Even so, she was still all too aware of his injuries. "You're supposed to be in pain," she told him.

"It's not so bad," he said, and then he kissed her again.

"Ahem," came a voice from the end of the bed.

Bailey froze. They had company.

"I hate to break up your little lovefest, but Mr. Davis needs to eat something, and I need to take his blood pressure," the voice said.

Bailey and Carter stopped kissing and looked at their intruder. It was a robust woman wearing a name tag that said Nurse Sherry. Nurse Sherry was all business. Probably she'd seen it all in Las Vegas.

Bailey felt her cheeks flush at almost being caught in the act. No telling where that kiss might have led had she and Carter not been interrupted. She removed herself from his grasp and slipped off the bed, straightening her clothes.

"Don't worry," Nurse Sherry said. "I'll be out of here in a minute, and then the two of you can go back to smooching and whatever else you were doing."

"Don't waste your time taking my blood pressure," Carter grumbled. "I'm sure it's sky high." He swung his legs off the side of the bed and took to his feet, but his legs were practically useless, so he wobbled more than he walked.

Bailey hurried to help him. She grabbed his arm. "What do you think you're doing? You'll fall and hurt yourself."

"I'm already hurt. Not enough to keep me in bed. I have things to do." He sat back down on the edge of the bed, cursing at his weakness.

"You said you'd stay in bed if I let you kiss me," Bailey reminded him.

"No, *you* said it. I never agreed to that deal."

She felt helpless. She knew it was useless to try and talk him back into bed. Even so, she'd never forgive herself if she just stood by and let him further injure himself.

"Tell you what," she said, lowering her voice, "if you get back in bed, I'll lie down with you for a while." She glanced over at Nurse Sherry. "After she leaves."

Carter stopped trying to stand and looked at her. "You don't want to do that, honey."

"How come I don't?" She knew for a fact she did.

"You've been telling me since I woke up you're not here for *that*." He managed to get to his feet, and then tried walking again, but it was slow going. A layer of sweat quickly formed on his forehead.

Bailey hated seeing him struggle so. "This is crazy," she said. "You should be resting. If you don't get back in that bed, I'll call Twinkie."

"Call her. I'll be gone by the time she gets here."

Bailey looked to Nurse Sherry for help. Nurse Sherry crossed her arms and planted her tree-trunk legs firmly to the floor. "He won't get by me."

Carter looked at his nurse with cool reserve. "Don't make me kiss you, too."

Nurse Sherry huffed, but she backed off. "I'm a married woman. Don't be trying any of that funny business with me." She gathered her stethoscope and sphygmomanometer and told Bailey, "Call me if he decides he needs my services." Then she was gone.

Bailey turned on Carter. "I don't like this. Not one little bit."

"Me neither, honey. But if I don't get out of here, we might both regret it."

Bailey wasn't about to ask why. "Okay," she said, "then I'm coming with you." She was hands on hips, looking like she meant it.

"Not today. I have business to take care of."

"Such as?"

"Business that doesn't concern you."

"Like that awful Frank Zoopa?"

Carter's mouth twitched, like he wanted to smile. "You are persistent, I'll give you that." He put his hands on her shoulders. "Go do something fun. Win another car."

Bailey felt lost. She knew she wasn't going to get anywhere by pestering him to take her along. "Will I see you later?" she asked, frustrated.

"For?" He flashed his practiced-to-perfection Elvis grin.

"Dinner?"

"After that, will you go home?"

She frowned, angry that he was trying to forge a deal to get her to leave town. "You'll have to do more than have a meal with me if you want me to leave Las Vegas."

His grin spread. "I assume you know where to find me."

Chapter Four

Bailey paused at the door to her hotel room for a breath and a little reflecting on what had just happened up in Carter's room. Her blood was still pumping at warp speed from the kisses they'd shared. She pressed a hand to her lips, smiling. Feelings of passion and love were bouncing all over inside her. Need and lust, too. It'd been far too long.

She slipped through the door and stopped short, just inside the entry, when she saw her aunt perusing a magazine. So, it was true. Her mom *had* sent her Aunt Fiona here with Liza. But where was Liza?

"Hello?" Bailey said. She walked into the room and looked around. No Liza. But she did see Twinkie, who was on her cell phone. "You didn't come here by yourself, did you?" she asked her aunt. "Mom said Liza was bringing you."

Aunt Fiona looked up from her magazine. "Liza got the room next door. She's already off playing slots. Myself, I have a hankering to check these guys out." She tapped her finger to an open page of *Vegas Life*. The glossy showed a group of muscle-bound hotties called Thunder From Down Under. "They must get waxed. I've never seen men with chests this bare. I wouldn't mind seeing them up close and personal."

Twinkie finished her call. "I could get front row tickets, if you like," she offered. "That way you can get up *real* close and personal." She looked at Bailey. "All you have to do is say the word."

Bailey considered Twinkie's offer for all of two seconds. The word was, going to see Thunder From Down Under wasn't going to happen. "I need to spend my time here with Carter," she told Twinkie. As tempting as it was to see a bunch of hot Aussies dance around half naked, she was more interested in seeing *Carter* dance around half naked. "I thought you had a show tonight."

"I do," Twinkie said. "But I ran into Liza and your aunt, and thought I'd visit for a few. I didn't think you'd be too long with your auntie here, waiting for you." She stood. "I really do need to go now, or I'll be late getting into my costume. See you later, Fiona," she said to Bailey's aunt, and then she turned to Bailey. "Can I talk to you in private, out in the hall?" Once the door was shut, she turned all serious. "How did it go with Carter? Did he wake up?"

Bailey nodded.

"And?"

"He and I talked, and I guess it went okay. He still doesn't remember me, but I think once we spend some time together, that could change."

"Just be careful," Twinkie said.

"Of what?"

"I just want you to be careful, that's all. I've given it some thought and I think I know who's responsible for Carter's injury. I don't know if you remember, but Frank Zoopa has been in the process of building a new casino. The Majestic. And if it doesn't open on time, he'll take a big hit to his cash flow. Word is someone's been causing problems with the construction. And, of course, he thinks that someone is Carter."

"Is it?"

"Probably. I hope not. Carter's been—was—so caught up with plans to marry you that I didn't think he had time to mess with Frank. I thought it was just talk. Casino gossip." Twinkie shook her head. "I'd hoped after I ended things with Frank that Carter would be willing to let it all go." A tear slid down her cheek and she quickly wiped it away. She'd never been one to let anyone see her being weak. "God, I'm so embarrassed. I'm such a mess. I feel like shit. I should never have gotten involved with that bastard. Carter tried to warn me, but I wouldn't listen." She took a breath and leaned against the wall, like the situation between Zoopa and her brother had become a weight she could no longer bear.

Bailey squeezed Twinkie's hand for reassurance. But Twinkie was right, she should have steered clear of Frank Zoopa. She had no business being with a man like that. As beautiful as she was, she could have her choice of men. Her relationship with Zoopa had never made sense. But it was too late for regrets.

"I'm sorry for all that's happened to you," Bailey said. "And I agree. I think it was Zoopa who got to Carter."

"Is that what Carter said?" Twinkie asked.

"No. He wouldn't say much of anything where Zoopa was concerned. He told me it was none of my business."

"That sounds like my brother."

Bailey smiled a small smile. "Look, I appreciate your warning about Zoopa, but I'm not about to let a man like him keep me from living my life. And you shouldn't, either. Nor should you blame yourself for any of this. Carter has a mind of his own. No one has any control over what he does or doesn't do."

Twinkie dried her tears and attempted a smile. "I just don't want something to happen to you. Carter would never forgive me."

Again? Bailey put a hand to her chest. It would kill her. "Let's not even go there. I just don't understand why Carter can't leave Zoopa to the authorities. If the man is on the wrong side of the law, it's bound to catch up with him, isn't it?"

"It's not like in the movies, Bailey," Twinkie said. "Bad guys don't always lose. For Carter, going after Zoopa has become like a bad habit. He doesn't know how to let go of the past. Or maybe he can't. Sorry," she said, "I shouldn't be saying that. Carter wouldn't want me to put this stress on you. You have enough to worry about with your upcoming wedding."

"Mmm. There may not be a wedding. Which is why I need to spend as much time as I can with Carter." Bailey shook her head. "I don't care about Frank Zoopa. I care about getting my life back."

The door cracked opened and Bailey's Aunt Fiona stuck her head out. "Let's get this show on the road. I hear the best slots are over at the Venetian. I brought plenty of quarters." She hefted up her bag and it made a metallic clinking sound.

Bailey groaned. It was going to be a long night.

Chapter Five

Carter paid the cab driver and stood at the front entrance to Valley Hospice. It was connected to Spring Valley Hospital, which was where he'd woken up just two days earlier. He knew he should be taking it easy, but after being up and out of bed a while, things were loosening up. He was ready to get back to work. But first, he needed to check on something.

He looked at the piece of paper he'd found in his pocket. The name Rosa was written on it and, beneath that, Valley Hospice, Room 413. He knew someone named Rosa. She worked in Housekeeping at The Oasis. But she was much more to him than just a hotel employee. They'd hit it off soon after she was hired and she'd quickly become like a second mother to him, always asking if he was eating right and occasionally bringing him home-cooked casseroles and baked goods. He'd gained ten pounds to show for it. She was an excellent cook.

Admittedly, his mind wasn't at full functioning level yet, and a lot of recent events were still fuzzy, the same as they were with Bailey Ventura, but in his recollection, Rosa hadn't been ill. Maybe a headache now and then, but he'd always suspected that was only on the days when she was needed at home to take care of her grandchildren.

He fought to remember the last time he'd seen her. It was a birthday party. Hers. Some of the other employees in Housekeeping had thrown it to celebrate her turning sixty and they'd invited him, too. It was a fun time for all. Singing, dancing, and plenty of food. She'd looked happy and healthy. Not at all sick.

But her birthday... that was... months ago. Back in March. This was October.

More confused than ever, he entered the hospice and made his way to the front desk, where a nurse sat staring into a computer screen. "I'm looking for Rosa Gonsalvez, Room 413," he told her. She looked up and her eyes lit at seeing him.

"Why, Mr. Davis, it's so good to see you. How are you feeling?" She examined his face closely. "Have they been taking care of you over there at The Oasis? I'm surprised, in your condition, they've already let you out of bed. They should have at least had someone accompany you here."

"I'm good. Just a little headache is all. About Rosa, is she here?"

"Yes, she's still here, though the cancer's been rough on her today. She'll be happy to see you. She's missed your daily visits." She pointed down a long corridor. "You know the way. Follow the wide, blue line."

A fist clenched around Carter's heart as he walked, but he wasn't paying attention to the blue line. Rosa, cancer? How could he not remember something as serious as that?

He paused at the door to Room 413, wondering what he would find on the other side. He listened and heard only quiet. It worried him. What if he was too late? He pushed open the door and stood in the doorway. It was a private room, with a single bed, and the occupant was tiny. Was it Rosa? He thought so. He'd know that dark, wavy hair anywhere. Of course the thick streak of grey helped confirm her identity.

"*Hola*, Rosa," he said with quiet concern.

The form in the bed stirred and pushed the covers aside and a small face, Rosa's, peered over in his direction. She instantly recognized him. "Mr. Carter, I so happy to see you," she said. She reached out with both hands. "I think maybe you forget about me." Then she frowned. "But I hear you have bad trouble."

Carter approached the side of her bed. "Nothing I couldn't handle," he told her, taking her hands in his. "And you know, Rosa, you don't have to call me Sir or Mister anything."

"I know. You tell me that a million times," Rosa said.

He smiled gently and wished he'd thought to bring her some flowers. He'd seen some beautiful bouquets when he passed by the hospital gift shop. But when he looked around the room and saw that no one else had brought any, he thought maybe she wasn't allowed to have flowers in her room. He made a mental note to ask one of the nurses about that.

He sat next to her. "The nurse told me you're not feeling so well today." Though what he really wanted to say was that he was sorry he hadn't remembered about her being sick.

"I die. Maybe today. Maybe tomorrow," she said, smiling a little.

Carter squeezed her hands gently. He knew she was making an attempt to lighten things up. She had such a good heart and didn't want anyone to suffer because of her.

"When I don't see you for a few days," she continued, "I think maybe you give up on me. I take too long."

"Too long?"

"To *die*."

He couldn't smile. He saw no humor in her words. A lump filled his throat instead. "I don't want to hear that kind of talk, Rosa. Just tell me what I can do to help."

"Sing, *por favor*," Rosa answered.

He raised an eyebrow. "Here? Now?"

Rosa nodded.

"And when you're finished singing for her, Mrs. McClusky down the hall has a request," said a nurse who had just entered the room. "And so does Miss Naomi," she added.

"Excuse me?" Carter said.

"Don't look so surprised. You know you're in high demand," the nurse told him. Then she leaned in and lowered her voice. "If I were you, I'd go see Mrs. McClusky first... if you know what I mean."

No. He didn't. He took hold of the nurse's arm and led her out into the hallway.

"I've been a little under the weather," he said. He touched a finger to the side of his head. "I'm having trouble with my memory, and I only just found out about Rosa being here. Beyond that, I'm not sure of anything."

The nurse looked at him and pushed her lips together, thinking. "That's right, I do recall hearing something about you going missing." She smiled. "Good to see you made it back in one piece. But your fans have missed you. And so have all of us nurses. We want to hear you sing." She patted his arm. "That's what you do here. Ever since Rosa arrived, you've been showing up and singing for the patients. Ladies mostly. Maybe you don't remember, but they do. And God bless you for it, Mr. Davis."

She left him and went back into Rosa's room. Carter stood there for a minute trying to conjure up some memory of what the nurse had just told him. He sang for the dying?

Nothing came, so he went back into Rosa's room, glad that he at least remembered her. The nurse finished with Rosa and he sat by her side again.

"You sing for me now?" Rosa asked.

He nodded. "Any requests?"

The slots were cold at the Venetian, and everywhere else, too. So after Bailey's Aunt Fiona finished feeding a good chunk of change to the hungry machines, Bailey decided to take her to the new Vegas production *Water*, where Twinkie was starring in the lead female role. Twinkie had promised they would enjoy it and she had given them tickets to seats that were right up front, though Bailey would have been just as happy sitting *way* in the back. Nudie shows, even semi-nudie weren't her thing. Even so, she was happy to get off her feet and sit in an air-conditioned theater for a while.

A scant minute after she and her auntie took their seats, the extravaganza began and the premise of the glitzy production immediately became clear. A dozen nearly nude women were on a mission to find their Prince Charming among a dozen nearly nude men. For over an hour, much frolicking and gliding across a colorful watery stage ensued. It was sex personified, and the big finale came only after each woman had found her Prince Charming, whereupon one last ritual-type mating dance was performed to seal the deal.

According to the Critic's Section in the weekly issue of *Las Vegas Entertainment*, *Water* was the best show to hit Vegas in years. A show not to be missed. It was all skin, all wet, all the time. Bailey bet the critics were all men. After the curtain closed, she sat looking straight ahead. She was afraid to look in her aunt's direction. She didn't have to. She could see out the corner of her eye that her aunt's lips were stretched wide.

"I hope you were taking notes," Aunt Fiona said. "I bet if you try some of those moves on Elvis, he won't even remember he has amnesia."

"I bet," Bailey said, feeling her cheeks blossom pink.

The cast members returned to the stage to take their bows and the entire audience continued to show their appreciation with plenty of exuberant hand clapping and whistling. Bailey's aunt even got in on the celebration. She put two fingers in her mouth and gave a shrill whistle. It was official—*Water* was a success.

As well done as the production was, Bailey could think of at least one person who hated it. Carter. When Twinkie landed the lead role, he'd ranted for days about how he disapproved of his sister showing God and thousands of tourists her everything. Though in Bailey's opinion, it was a much better way to make a living than what some of the other young women there in Las Vegas did. Poor Carter. He was such an old soul for such a young man.

Bailey and her aunt sat tight, waiting for the theater to clear out. Bailey preferred following, rather than leading, the herd. "I didn't know you could whistle like that," she said to her aunt, making conversation to pass the time.

"Your boyfriend taught me," Aunt Fiona told her. "He said it was something every woman should know. Said I could hail a cab if I was ever in New York City. Or I could even deafen a would-be attacker. I sure would like to give that a try. I imagine it would stop a man in his tracks if he was intent on disrobing me. Unless he was on that crack stuff. Then I imagine nothing would stop him."

Bailey stared at her aunt. She didn't want to think the things she was thinking. Like when would her aunt ever be in New York City hailing a cab? And how did she know about stuff like crack? But, most importantly, to which boyfriend was her aunt referring? The last few years, it had only been Carter and Mark Jefferson. Not that Mark had ever gained boyfriend status. He was simply part of the Coupeville landscape, someone to hang out with when times were desperate. And as far as she knew, neither Carter nor Mark had ever been to New York City.

She was curious, but not curious enough to ask her aunt to specify which "boyfriend." That might only lead to more conversation she didn't care to have. She took her aunt's hand and led her out of the theater. "C'mon, Auntie. Hold on tight. Mom would never forgive me if I misplaced you."

"It'd take a city bigger than Las Vegas to swallow me," her aunt said. "Did I ever tell you about the time I took a train to Miami all by myself?"

Bailey rattled her brain, trying to think of a time when her aunt might have made a cross-country trip, solo. That would be never. But no need to argue over details. She smiled and squeezed her aunt's hand a little tighter. "I'll bet you saw some sights, Auntie."

Aunt Fiona grinned wide and shuffled along. "I say we go back over to the Venetian and play more slots. I feel a lucky streak coming on."

Bailey peeked at her watch. "I don't know, Auntie. It's getting late. Maybe we should head back to our hotel."

"Don't you worry," Aunt Fiona said. "I got something if any of those street hooligans try to accost us." She jiggled her bag that was still half full of quarters.

Bailey had nothing else to do, so she gave in and they headed back to the Venetian, where her aunt quickly won a small jackpot on a *Wheel of Fortune* machine and insisted on being paid in yet more quarters. Her bag was so heavy now that she had to use both arms to carry it like a sack of potatoes.

By the time they ventured back out into the night, the Strip was congested with plenty of colorful people who made Bailey nervous, despite the fact that her aunt was loaded with coin. It wasn't long, though, and she began to relax. The authorities were everywhere, on top of things, their presence dominating the landscape to almost suffocating in an effort to keep Sin City running in an orderly fashion. Probably her aunt had no need for ten pounds of quarters, or security of any kind. Which, as it turned out, was a good thing, because if she and her aunt *did* need rescuing, odds were it wouldn't be her Security Guy doing it.

There he was, already back on the job. Bailey saw him as soon as she and her aunt walked through the gold-framed, glass doors of The Oasis. She couldn't believe it! A few hours ago, he could barely walk, and now here he was trying to keep some woman from taking out some man's eyes. Carter had one hand on the man's chest and his other hand on the woman's shoulder. So far, so good. No blood had been shed.

"Looks like Elvis is back to business, as usual," Aunt Fiona remarked. "Looks like he's been caught in the middle of a domestic dispute. That could be dangerous."

Bailey scoffed. Dangerous was right, for Carter, that is. She wanted to wring his neck. Oh, she knew he'd be back on the casino floor *tout de suite*, but he could have at least limited his activity to simply cruising the gaming floor, making his presence known, rather than being part of the action. That would have been the smart thing to do. But it was also wishful thinking. And, really, Carter didn't look nearly as bad off as he had earlier, up in his room. He'd put on a suit and tie and, now, even with the bruises that were visible, he was super gorgeous. Her heart went pitter-pat just looking at him.

She continued watching him, waiting to see how the situation between the man and the woman would unfold. She held her aunt back, not wanting to get in Carter's way, should things get rough.

As always, Carter seemed well in control. Not a surprise. He seldom needed to raise a fist, or even his voice, to get people to see things his way. Instead, he used calm and firm resolve. He had a gun, and kept it loaded, but Bailey had never known him to use it. Not that he wouldn't—and certainly she wasn't naïve enough to believe he never had—but she was confident that he reserved using the force of a deadly weapon for *really* bad guys. Not obnoxious drunks, or lovers who found themselves in the midst of a squabble.

It took only a minute and it seemed Carter had settled things. He sent the man on his way and the woman... didn't budge. She remained next to Carter, and she and Carter exchanged smiles.

Bailey's stomach lurched. Which was silly. She had no reason to be jealous. Did she?

Chapter Six

Bailey felt her hackles rise. Of course, she had reason to be jealous. Carter didn't know her from any other woman on the Strip, and seeing him smiling at this other woman was too reminiscent of her early days getting to know him. Back then, he'd had the attention of every woman in Vegas.

Get a grip, she told herself. That was the *old* Carter. Not *her* Carter. Her Carter was new and improved. And, really, if he was smiling, it could only mean one thing—that he was feeling better. And if he was feeling better, they could spend more time together, working on retrieving his memory. Only from where she stood, Carter seemed more interested in the woman who was at his side than remembering lost love.

And just who was this creature with the beautiful, controlled hair and eyelashes so impossibly long she probably couldn't even wear sunglasses? Bailey continued watching the exchange between Carter and his lady friend. They'd moved past smiling, and now the woman was leaning into him and laughing. And he was laughing back.

Bailey closed her fists into tight little balls. Here Carter had been an amnesiac for less than two days, and already he was sending out sexual vibes to some other woman. This was time *she* should be spending with Carter.

Aargh! Bailey hated how she was feeling, knowing it was ridiculous to think Carter might be up to no good. He was in no condition to do anything with anyone, sexual or otherwise. Yet, that hadn't stopped him from trying to make the moves on *her* earlier. And here he was, back on the job, like he thought he was Superman or some other hero-type.

She shook her head, trying to gather her wits. She focused on the woman with Carter. Bailey knew she couldn't very well blame any woman for the effect Carter might have on them. Why, she'd even known some *men* to send Carter an adoring glance during one of his performances. All Carter had to do was smile that smile, and they were his.

Still. That was different. Carter wasn't into men.

"You want me to take care of that chickie for you?" Aunt Fiona asked, breaking into Bailey's thoughts.

Bailey jumped. She'd completely forgotten that her aunt was standing right next to her. That's what jealousy did to a person. Made the universe disappear. Made people do all sorts of crazy things. She'd even once heard about some woman who'd gone on a cross-country trek, wearing a diaper to confront her competition. Now, *that* was ridiculous.

"No, Auntie, I can handle this," Bailey said, not at all certain what her aunt meant by "take care of." And what was with her auntie calling the woman chickie? Where had that come from?

Aunt Fiona pulled her lips tight and set her jaw. "Wouldn't be no problem. She's such a skinny thing."

Bailey swung her gaze around to her aunt. "You're scaring me."

"Sorry, cupcake. It's just business."

Right. Business. Bailey shuddered and went back to watching Carter with his gal-pal. They were laughing again and it was almost more than Bailey could stand. She had to do something to break up their delightful conversation.

She took off, moving toward Carter, pulling her aunt along behind her. They were like a single unit, matching stride for stride, Aunt Fiona with an arm wrapped around her bag full of quarters, and Bailey with murder on her mind. By the time they were within three feet of Carter, they were both huffing and puffing and losing momentum. Even so, it was all Bailey could do to refrain from launching herself at him.

Carter must have heard them coming with their heavy breathing, because he turned his head in their direction. "Are you ladies all right? Can I help you?" he asked, looking like he had no idea who they were.

Indignation crept up Bailey's spine. Really? Was he really going to stand there and pretend like he didn't know her?

She looked from Carter to his lady friend and back. She saw nothing but question in his eyes. Was it an act, or did he really not remember that just a few short hours ago they'd shared a passionate kiss?

Her worry meter shot into the red zone. She took a couple of deep breaths. This wasn't Carter's fault. He wasn't purposely trying to hurt her. She needed to cut him some slack. "We're fine," she said. "We were just looking for the ladies' room. My auntie has a problem," she lowered her voice "if you know what I mean."

"Directly behind you," Carter said. He pointed, and Bailey looked and saw a sign that said Ladies.

"Imagine that," Aunt Fiona said.

When Bailey turned back to Carter, his lips were in smirk mode and his gal-pal had one arm hooked possessively through his. His arm slid down and settled at the curve of her waist. It was enough to make Bailey want to cry. She felt her lips quiver. It was time for her and her auntie to make themselves scarce.

"Thank you. Much appreciated," she told Carter, managing a smile. Then she grabbed her aunt's hand, ready to retreat. But her aunt didn't budge. She took her hand back.

"You go on ahead to the powder room," she told Bailey.

"Me and Elvis are gonna have a chat."

"No," Bailey said through her teeth. "Just leave it alone."

Aunt Fiona was having no part of leaving anything alone. "No wonder you and Priscilla didn't last," she said to Carter. "She was too easy on you. You shoulda married that Ann-Margret. She'd have tamed that squirrel in your pants."

Everyone was silent. Bailey closed her eyes, wishing she was anywhere else. But no such luck. When she opened her eyes, she was still standing in front of Carter, wondering what to do next. "Don't mind my aunt," she told Carter. "She's had a long day." She grabbed her aunt's hand again. "C'mon, Auntie, let's go wash our hands. I'm sure you've picked up plenty of germs touching all those slot machines." No doubt that would divert her aunt's attention.

Only it didn't.

Aunt Fiona yanked her arm back and squished her lips around some, like she was forming a thought. "You know what you are?" she finally said to Carter. "You're a punk. I knew it from the first time I laid eyes on you. Bailey's mother thinks you're Elvis, but I got you all figured out. Under all that swagger, you're still just a man. Like all the rest of 'em. If you're breathing, you're cheating."

Gawd! Bailey mouthed an apology to Carter. She glanced around nervously. A crowd had begun to gather. "I really do need to go to the ladies' room, Auntie. Now!" she said. But her aunt wasn't concerned with the crowd. And she wasn't finished with Carter.

"When are you going to forget all this amnesia hooey? You and my niece need to kiss and make up. Stress isn't good for a woman with a bun in the oven. The two of you need to get married and you need to be a good father to her baby." She patted Bailey's abdomen softly and told Carter's gal-pal, "Sorry, chickie."

Bun in the oven? Bailey swallowed. Come to think of it, she had been feeling a little bloated lately.

Everyone stared at Bailey's belly. Even her. Though,

mentally, her eyes were on the ceiling and she was praying for the earth to open and swallow her. But, apparently, God was busy performing miracles elsewhere. Instead, the crowd parted and Twinkie appeared. She'd traded her *Water* attire for something more substantial. Even so, she was still a hot sight on the gaming floor and every man in the vicinity was drooling on his poker chips.

She looked around, not at all in the mood to impress anyone. "What are you looking at? Go. *Play*. Lose your money." Then she turned to Bailey and her aunt. "Hey, ladies. Well, look at you, Fiona. Aren't you fab with that purple boa draped around your shoulders?"

Aunt Fiona's eyes lit up. "I got it 'cause it's purple. I read in one of those Feng Shuey books that purple is the color for prosperity. It might help me win a car while I'm here."

"I bet it will," Twinkie said. She looked at Bailey. "What's going on? What did I miss?"

"Nothing," Bailey said. No way did she want to get Twinkie involved. "Auntie and I were just on our way to the ladies' room."

"And we saw Carter tangled up with this here chickie," Aunt Fiona added.

Twinkie looked at Carter and his gal-pal and her lips curled. "Carter. *Nikki*," she said. Her disdain for the woman was palpable.

Nikki? Bailey's ears perked to attention. Somewhere in the dark recesses of her mind, she recalled Carter telling her about a woman named Nikki Amsterdam who had once helped him out of a sticky situation. Maybe this Nikki and that Nikki were one and the same. And maybe Carter and she were just friends.

Talk about feeling silly for being so suspicious. Of course, Carter had a lot of women friends. That was to be expected. Vegas was full of women. "Nobody was tangled up," Bailey told Twinkie. She leaned, so only Twinkie could hear. "Is her last name by chance Amsterdam?"

Twinkie was giving Carter a sisterly death glare. "That's

her, in the flesh," she answered Bailey. Carter grinned back at Twinkie with his Elvis grin, and that didn't go over well. "Don't play that with me, Carter. I'm your sister. Save the creepy Elvis look for your fans," she told him.

"He's not Elvis. Elvis is right over there," said a woman with slurred speech. She was passing by and decided to break into the conversation. She pointed a finger at an older, white-haired gentleman who was sitting at one of the gaming tables.

Everyone turned to look.

Bailey recognized him instantly. He was that old guy her mother had been texting.

"See," the woman said. "And you thought I was drunk." She waved a hand and continued on her way, bumping into people and slot machines as she went.

Twinkie turned back to Carter. "What are you doing here, cozied up to *this*?" She shot Nikki a hard scowl.

Bailey's aunt shook her head. Her hair didn't move. It'd been secured by plenty of Sebastian Firm Hold hairspray. "That's not cozy you're seeing. That's lust. I know the look. She's got more than a friendly game of Crazy Eights on her mind. Try poker. *Strip* poker." She looked at Bailey. "I know 'cause me and your Uncle Rex used to play—"

"Okay!" Bailey held up a hand. "TMI, Auntie." She didn't need to hear about her aunt's sexcapades with her Uncle Rex. Bad enough she'd grown up sleeping in the bedroom next to theirs. Any further imagery and she'd need therapy.

"No use denying what's in front of your face," her aunt told her.

"Did somebody mention strip poker?" asked a man who'd come up behind Bailey.

Chapter Seven

All heads turned, but Bailey didn't need to look to know who owned that voice. It was Mark Jefferson. And it made her stomach do a sour flip. What the heck was he doing in Las Vegas?

"Mark!" she said. She felt like she was having one of those moments where she was seeing someone she knew, but he wasn't where he belonged, so she wasn't sure it was really him.

But it was.

"Hey, Peaches," Mark said, low and dark. He had a gleam in his eye and evil thoughts on his mind. Bailey knew this because evil thoughts were the only kind of thoughts Mark ever had.

"What are you doing here?" she asked. And why, for God's sake, did he insist on calling her Peaches when she'd asked him at least a gazillion times not to? Peaches was a nickname Mark had bestowed upon her the one and only night he'd seen her in the raw, and she'd done her best to forget that night ever since. But how *could* she forget, if he kept calling her that name? Seemed she was going to have to give him a good talking to… again.

"Liza said you might need some support at a time like this." He did a head nod at a bank of *Star Trek* machines and, sure enough, there was Liza, and she was sitting right next to Mark's twin brother, Brian. "Me and Brian just got here," Mark said.

Mark and Brian, more commonly known as the Jefferson twins, ran Coupeville's only auto shop, where the town's entire population of seniors brought their cars to be repaired. It was a booming business and, for the most part, kept the twins off the streets. Though when business was light, watch out, the twins were trouble times two. Where one went, so did the other. And God help all the single women in Coupeville.

Liza glanced up from the slot machine she was working and blew Bailey an air kiss. Brian tossed her a wave.

Bailey frowned, rethinking Liza's best friend status. Liza should have warned her, so she could be ready for the twins. Scratch that. Liza should never have agreed to bring Aunt Fiona to Las Vegas at the request of her mother. That was a complete breach of friendship trust.

Aunt Fiona nudged Bailey, leaning in and keeping her voice low. "Are you sure you're not interested in this twin?" she asked. "I hear he's been practicing like the dickens, playing that electric guitar of his. Got the amp turned up so high that Charlie, down at Panes o' Plenty, has been over to Mark's house twice to replace windows. And Mavis says she's heard Mark singing 'Love Me Tender' all hours of the night."

"Pfft. That's silly, Auntie. Why on earth would Mark be singing 'Love Me Tender'?" Seriously? If Mark Jefferson thought he had any chance of ever singing his way into her panties again, he'd better do some rethinking. The only reason he'd gotten into her panties the first time was because he'd filled her full of peach schnapps and made her vulnerable, and then she believed him when he told her he could do a pretty decent imitation of the King. As it turned out, Mark didn't even know the words to "Are You Lonesome Tonight?"

"Aren't you even curious?" Aunt Fiona asked.

"Not in the least," Bailey said. No way would she ever be that dumb again.

Ever.

Cross her heart and hope to die.

"You can forget about trying to sing like Elvis," Bailey told Mark. "You can't. Nobody sings like Elvis, except..." And all eyes swung to Carter.

Carter grinned, accepting the compliment. Nikki whispered something in his ear, and then she took off in the direction of the ladies' room.

"Gosh, sure hate to see you go," Aunt Fiona quipped over her shoulder. Then she added, "I could use a minute in the ladies' room, too."

She started off, but Bailey caught her arm. "Where do you think you're going?"

"Can't an old lady take a pee?"

"That depends. Does it include getting involved in things that don't concern you?"

Her aunt clamped down on her molars. "It's a sad day when a girl doesn't even trust her elderly aunt. What could I possibly do to that youngster?"

Bailey pondered her aunt's question for a good ten seconds. "Nothing. I guess." It was a lie, of course. An old lady could do a lot of things to hurt a person—blind them with denture cream, strangle them with support hose, whack them with a bag full of quarters. Not that she was about to give her aunt any ideas.

"So, can I go pee?" her aunt asked.

"Fine. Go. But behave yourself." Bailey waggled a finger at her.

Her aunt *hmmfed* and took off for the ladies' room, wearing a grin that said she'd do anything she damn well pleased. And none of it included good behavior.

"All this talk about tinkling," Twinkie said. "Now *I* need to go." She gave Bailey an I'm-going-with-her-so-you-and-Carter-can-talk look, and she was gone.

Bailey released a lungful of air. At last, she and Carter were alone.

Except for Mark. Urk! Mark! She frowned at him, and he rocked back on his heels, grinning.

"Gee, look!" she said, pointing in the direction of Liza and Brian. "I think one of them just won a jackpot!"

Mark looked. And shrugged. "I don't see any lights flashing."

Bailey set her jaw and managed to keep from slugging him. Either he wasn't getting it, or he was just trying to be difficult. Probably a little of both.

"How's your room?" Carter asked, looking at her. "Comfortable? Anything you need?"

What? So he *did* remember her. Maybe not *remember* remember. But he at least recognized her from earlier. Otherwise, how would he know she was staying there at The Oasis?

"The room is fine," she told him, focusing on his eyes, looking for any sign his memory might be returning.

"What about your guests?" Carter looked at Mark, and Mark slid an arm around her waist.

Bailey felt her brain begin to scramble from the steam that was building beneath her scalp. Mark was definitely taking advantage of the situation.

"We're all fine," Mark told him. "Now that I'm here, I can take care of my girl's needs. No reason for you to worry."

Bailey saw red. First the arm around her waist, which Mark should be glad she'd ignored, but him calling her his *girl*? No freaking way!

"Go. Away!" she told him, through clenched teeth. When it came to the Jefferson twins, especially this one, directness was the best approach.

Mark made a face like his feelings had been hurt, but she knew better. He didn't have the kind of feelings it took to be hurt. Even so, he was smart enough to know when he was pushing his luck. He slunk back over to Liza and Brian, and now she and Carter were finally, really alone.

The corner of Carter's mouth lifted and he gave her his much-practiced Elvis grin. Her heart thumped wildly in response and she couldn't think of a thing to say. Nothing witty, anyway. It was the same as when they'd first met. She was an idiot girl then and she was an idiot girl now. Not that she intended to let that ruin the moment.

She stepped closer and got a whiff of his hair. It was earthy, like freshly mown grass. But she also smelled minty undertones from the balm on his lips. And that's what she focused on. His lips. Some unseen force brought her to her toes. He was going to kiss her again. She was sure of it. She puckered up in anticipation.

"Hey! You're that Elvis fella from the show, aren't you?" asked a woman who was passing by. She paused to get a good look at Carter, but her eyes were doing the droopy-loopy thing, and Bailey doubted she was able to focus on much of anything.

The woman's body tilted to one side, like she might go down any second. She placed a hand on Carter's chest for support and said, "I tried to get one of your scarves, but the bitch in front of me snatched it right out of mid-air."

Bailey stepped away from Carter and his fan. Their moment was lost. Their kiss was lost.

"You have the wrong guy," Carter told the woman. But one corner of his mouth notched up in taunting fashion. He took her hand from his chest and returned it to her, but that was a mistake, because then it found a home on his ass.

Bailey pinched her lips tight. Of course she knew things like this happened to Carter all the time, but, jeez, couldn't his fans at least wait until he wasn't in the middle of having a conversation with someone else? And no matter how often it happened, it never got any easier to watch. So she didn't. She turned her head and stared at the entrance to the ladies' room... something to do to pass the time, until Carter could get his fan under control.

With her eyes focused on the ladies' room entry, she heard Carter utter a curse, and then there was a slight scuffling sound. She didn't think it was anything to worry about. Carter could handle himself. He was Security Guy, after all. And probably his security team was at this very minute preparing to come to his rescue.

Bailey glanced at her watch. It had been a good three minutes since her aunt disappeared inside the hole in the wall. Bailey had seen dozens of women go in and dozens come back out, but no sign of her aunt. Nor had she seen Nikki or Twinkie. What could possibly be keeping them? She didn't know about Twinkie or Nikki, but she knew her aunt, and even if she'd recited the ABC song in Chinese, English, and Spanish, she'd certainly have finished washing her hands by now.

Bailey took a deep breath. She was being silly, of course. Everything was fine.

Probably.

But what if it wasn't? What if something bizarre was going on inside the ladies' room? This was Las Vegas, land where anything could happen. And with the luck she'd been having, bizarre wasn't so far-fetched.

She heard a thump behind her and she surmised Carter had his fan down on the floor in a headlock. No need for her to stick around and save him. She had to go to the ladies' room to see if anyone else might need saving.

Chapter Eight

Relief swept through Bailey when she saw her aunt standing at a long row of sinks, washing her hands. Nikki was two sinks down, pumping soap into her hands, oblivious to the scathing glare coming from Aunt Fiona.

Bailey went over to a nearby mirror, and began applying lip gloss. She wanted to be close, should there be any action requiring a referee. "Where's Twinkie?" she asked her aunt.

"She had things to do," Aunt Fiona answered, and then she turned her focus back to Nikki. "You must exercise a lot to stay so skinny."

The hair on the back of Bailey's neck tingled, but she mentally laughed it off. A little polite conversation between bathroom goers was no big deal. She began applying another layer of lip gloss.

Other than a polite smile, Nikki offered no response to Aunt Fiona's comment. But Bailey kept her eye on them, just in case. "Things to do?" she broke in, by way of getting her aunt's attention focused away from Nikki.

"She didn't elaborate," her aunt replied, tersely. Meaning she was busy, don't bother her.

Nikki moved over to a paper towel dispenser, and Aunt Fiona did the same. They exchanged smiles as they both rubbed their hands dry.

"Must be hard," Aunt Fiona said, "finding time to exercise when you've got a full-time job."

Bailey's senses prickled to attention. She went crazy with the lip gloss. Too much more of this conversation and her lip gloss would be gone. She'd have to start fussing with her hair. That would keep her busy a good while.

Her aunt continued, hands on hips, facing Nikki full on. "Course you probably burn a lot of calories having sex. Sex is a big calorie burner. I should know. My husband and I used to have so much sex when we were first together that I went down three dress sizes before our wedding. Course I didn't have to wear clothes back then. He pretty much kept me naked."

Bailey dropped her gloss in the sink, and she thought she heard someone whisper, "Dear God." She cut her eyes to her left and saw a small, elderly woman, taking in the situation between Nikki and Aunt Fiona.

She looked back over to Nikki. Nikki was still smiling. Sort of. Though when she shoved her paper towel in the waste bin, it was with a lot more force than was probably necessary. Even so, as far as Bailey could see, it was still just a friendly chat between two bathroom goers. Until there was a threat of bodily harm, she had no reason to get involved. But just in case her aunt had any ideas about pushing the limit, she moved over to the mirror space between her aunt and Nikki to create a barrier.

The barrier thing only worked for a minute. Aunt Fiona wanted to see her target. She leaned around Bailey for a better view. "Course you lose some water weight, too, when you have sex. All that sweat from rolling around on the sheets," she said.

Bailey was both mortified and amused. But now the elderly woman three sinks down was huffing her disapproval. She'd obviously come to Sin City for some good, clean, wholesome fun.

"Course if you're having sex with someone who belongs to someone else, then you're probably not eating, anyway," Aunt Fiona continued, brushing off the front of her blouse, even though there was nothing there to brush off. "Guilt does a number on you. Ties your stomach all up in knots."

Bailey said a quiet, "Lord," because she was so becoming her mother. She looked over at Nikki to see if it might be time to step in. It was. Nikki's eyes were narrowed and her jaw was set, like she was resisting the urge to ram Aunt Fiona's head into one of the sinks.

"Auntie! Let's go see if we can win a car," Bailey suggested.

But it was too late. Nikki had suffered enough verbal abuse. She'd stepped back from the wastebasket with her hands fisted at her hips, and she was looking like she wanted a piece of Aunt Fiona.

Bailey did her best to keep from laughing. Poor Nikki. She had no idea what she was getting herself into if she went at it with her aunt. Her auntie might be old, but she was scrappy. And being a practicing hypochondriac, who'd been perched on death's doorstep for years, no way was a scrawny, five-foot-tall, one-hundred pound woman with perfect eyelashes going to take her down. Her auntie would pull Nikki's perfect eyelashes right out of her eyelids.

"Stop beating around the bush," Nikki said. "Just say what you mean."

"Don't play dumb, toots. You're not blond enough to pull it off," Aunt Fiona said.

"Oh, Auntie," Bailey said, half scolding, half laughing. She couldn't help herself. Even so, she did make a real effort at grabbing her aunt's arm to keep her from going at Nikki.

Nikki backed away, out of Aunt Fiona's reach, and said, "Let the old lady get what's eating her off her saggy chest."

Oh boy. Bailey caught her bottom lip in her teeth. Probably she should have taken her aunt back up to their room five minutes ago. She could only guess what was going to happen next.

Aunt Fiona's lips compressed and squished around like they'd taken on a life of their own. "Anyone can see that you've been lusting after my niece's fiancé—Lord knows he's one hot property—so unless someone gives you some incentive, you probably won't stop carrying on with him. Am I right?"

Nikki folded her arms over her chest, holding her ground. "You got it, sister." She smiled smugly, looking like she thought she was so smart.

But Bailey knew better. Nikki was one dumb chick if she thought she could get away with being flippant with her Aunt Fiona. Her auntie took lip from no one. In fact, at the moment, her auntie had a gleam in her eyes that bordered on murderous—and the next thing Bailey knew, her aunt reached inside her bag and pulled out a big black gun. In a flash, she skirted around Bailey and had the barrel pressed against Nikki's forehead.

"How's this for incentive, chickie?" she said, clicking her uppers firmly into place.

The old lady three sinks down squeaked and crumpled to the floor.

Bailey looked. She wanted to make sure the woman was still breathing. She was, so Bailey turned back to the action between Nikki and her aunt. Nikki was concentrating on the gun at her head, probably trying to assess how much damage a bullet might do should it enter her brain. Her aunt remained cool and collected, like assaulting people with deadly weapons was just a part of life.

Bailey swallowed. This was bad. Not totally out of control yet, but really bad. Clearly, polite conversation was over. She chewed her bottom lip until she was on the verge of drawing blood. She had to do something. But what?

Her imagination ran wild. This was her first experience with something like this. What on earth had possessed her auntie to do such a thing? Then she thought about Carter and what he might do to resolve the situation. Probably, he wouldn't even need to draw his gun. It would be a simple case of overpowering the perp—in this case, her auntie—and it would be incident over.

Unfortunately, a gun had already been drawn.

So, now what?

Calm. Carter would stay calm.

"*Aunt Fiona! What are you doing!?*" Bailey screamed. Sometimes "calm" was overrated.

Aunt Fiona lost her focus and Bailey took what might be her only chance. She went for the gun, all the while praying this wasn't one of those times when the person who was trying to fix things ended up being the one who got shot.

She stretched out her arm and just about had the gun in her sweaty palm when her auntie swung it away. She did a side shuffle, putting some distance between them.

"Don't worry, cupcake. I've been practicing," Aunt Fiona said. "She won't get away."

A mental scream lit every brain cell in Bailey's head. *Mother of God, we're all going to die!* And it was all her fault. She should have checked her aunt's bag before they left the room. She should have frisked her.

But that was crazy. How could she possibly know something like this would happen? Her auntie had been acting so normal lately, just a few imaginary illnesses. Certainly, nothing over the top that would indicate she'd do something like splatter gray matter all over a ladies' room wall.

Concentrating like never before, Bailey pressed two fingers to her forehead, wondering what else Carter might do at a time like this.

Negotiate?

Maybe.

But more than likely he'd simply shove the perp to the ground, jam a foot to the back of his or her neck, then wait for Metro to arrive.

Bailey grimaced. That didn't seem like the best idea in this instance. Shoving a woman her aunt's age to the ground could result in serious injury, or even death.

Negotiate it was.

"Auntie…" she began, smiling sweetly. "How about we make a deal? You give me the gun, and maybe I'll take you to see that Thunder From Down Under show, later."

Her aunt gave her a sideways glance. "Really?"

"Maybe," Bailey said weakly. She hated making empty promises. But this was a dire situation and sometimes allowances had to be made. She held out her hand. "May I have the gun, please?"

Aunt Fiona narrowed her eyes. "Front row seats?"

Bailey crossed two fingers behind her back. "I'll talk to Twinkie. I'm sure she'll do her best."

Aunt Fiona held out the gun, and Bailey took it. It didn't feel anything like what she expected. There was nothing cold, or steel, about it. In fact, it felt light and… woody.

She frowned and peered down at the odd-feeling weapon, rubbing her thumb over the barrel. She was right. It wasn't real. She gave her aunt an incredulous look. "This gun is made of *wood*?"

Aunt Fiona grinned and clucked her tongue against the roof of her mouth. "Of course, it's wood. I'm old, not insane. What if there'd been a struggle, and it'd gone off? I'm not about to go to jail for killing some skinny girl who has trouble keeping her panties pulled up around hot men." She skirted Nikki a look. "Course you probably don't wear panties. You probably wear a thong." She got a faraway look in her eye. "There was a time when I looked good in a thong."

Bailey was at the end of her traumatic rope. She so did not want to visualize what her aunt might be wearing for underwear. She turned the wooden gun over in her hand, inspecting it closer. "Where did you get this?"

"Your cousin, Freddie. Ever since that Zoopa fella and his boys brought big city crime to Coupeville, he's been carving up an arsenal. He says even if we can't all afford real guns, he'll make sure us senior citizens are armed with something that at least looks real."

Nikki released a lungful of air and steadied herself against a sink. She took a few breaths and gave Bailey and her aunt a hard glare as she backed toward the exit. "You both belong in a padded cell," she said. And then she ran for her life.

Oh boy. Bailey did a mental groan. Any chance she might've had to reunite with Carter was quickly dissipating. In thirty seconds, he'd know the entire story. Then one of two things would happen—either she and her auntie would be allowed to board a plane and go home, or they'd be thrown into a Las Vegas jail cell. And if by some slim chance they were ever allowed to return to Seattle, it was entirely possible—and likely probable—they'd be banned from ever returning to Las Vegas. For the rest of their lives!

This was so not a good turn of events. And probably Nikki was right, she and her auntie did belong in a padded cell.

With a heavy sigh, Bailey leaned against the wall. This just wasn't fair. All she wanted was to be with Carter and to help him recover from his injury. But if she got thrown in jail, or a padded cell, how would that be possible?

Hot tears clouded her vision at the thought she might never again feel Carter's arms around her. It was unbearable. But after something like this, who could blame him if he never wanted to see her again? After today, he was going to think she was just another crazy fan. He'd never want to marry her.

The elderly woman who'd been relaxing on the floor finally groaned and made it to her feet. Her eyes got big when they focused on Bailey and her aunt, and she quickly shuffled out the exit to safety.

Great, Bailey thought. No doubt the woman was on her way to file some kind of report, the same as Nikki. "Let's go," she told her aunt. She hated the idea of leaving Las Vegas without saying goodbye to Carter, but if they didn't make themselves scarce real quick, odds were they'd both lose their freedom. She didn't know how much trouble one could get into for using a wooden gun to scare someone, but her guess was the authorities wouldn't care much about the weapon's authenticity.

Yes, going home to Coupeville was for the best. With any luck, Carter would get his memory back and he'd be in touch, just like he promised.

"Can we go play more slots?" Aunt Fiona asked.

"No. We're going home. I need to kill Cousin Freddie."

"But we just got here," Aunt Fiona protested. "You've hardly even had a chance to spark Elvis's memory."

"Don't worry, Auntie. It's been sparked. But I'm afraid if we stay, we might end up in jail, or…" Or worse. She didn't know Nikki, but Nikki didn't strike her as the type of woman to let bygones be bygones.

"Or what? We'll become new lumps in the Nevada desert?" Aunt Fiona pulled her lips into a tight line. "I may not have ever told you this, but I'm not afraid to die. You get to be my age and you gotta expect being buried is just around the corner."

Bailey considered that, but at the moment, the last thing she wanted to think about was dying or being buried out in the desert. "It's not the being buried part I'm afraid of, Auntie. It's the getting there that worries me. There are some bad people here in Las Vegas, and they've got ways of torturing you to make you *wish* you were dead. Trust me, you don't want one of them to come after you."

Aunt Fiona *hmmfed*. "That skinny gal didn't look so tough. I coulda had her down on the floor with her arm twisted behind her back in no time."

Bailey stared at her aunt, processing, trying to figure out what was going on in her aunt's mind, talking like that. Something was haywire. Maybe she needed some kind of mental adjustment. First thing, when they got back to Coupeville, she was going to make her auntie an appointment with Doc Russo. No, that wasn't possible. Doc Russo had left Coupeville for parts unknown—lucky guy. Okay, so maybe she'd just have her mom put parental controls on the TV. No more cop shows. From here on out, it was nothing but the

Disney channel for her auntie.

She nudged her aunt toward the exit, first poking her head out to make sure a SWAT team hadn't already been assembled. No gun-toting men in sight. Good. She and her aunt inched out slowly, then stepped up the pace, heading in the direction of the elevators.

"I had her scared, didn't I?" Aunt Fiona said, her eyes full of spark from the adventure.

"Yes, Auntie," Bailey said, giving her aunt a guarded look. "But do me a favor. Don't scare anyone else while we're here. In fact, don't even talk to anyone else, until we get back home."

Bailey steered her aunt around a bank of slot machines that promised a progressive jackpot of more than ten thousand dollars... so long as the reels landed on the right combination. It was a long shot—about 90 million to 1, according to what Carter had told her—but this was Las Vegas, land where long shots happened on a daily basis. She'd found that out when she won her fiery red T-Bird on a Double Wild Card slot machine. Even so, she wasn't about to sit around and try for a jackpot when everything around her was on the verge of crashing down. Or when the odds of going to jail were greater than fifty-fifty.

She and her aunt were nearly home-free. Just one more long row of Double Double Diamond machines and they'd be at the elevator. *Hurry, hurry, mustn't dawdle, mustn't stop to see how much the woman sitting at the machine with the white blinking light just won.*

Then it happened. Just like she had a feeling it would. Carter stepped out from behind a bank of machines. "Let's talk," he said, wearing his Security Guy face—all business and no fun.

Great. How did he always know where to find her? "About what?" Bailey asked, giving him the biggest doe-eyes she could muster. She only hoped her aunt would remember to keep her lips zipped.

"I understand there was an incident in the ladies' room," Carter said.

"Incident?" Bailey continued with the doe-eyes.

"Nikki told me your aunt held a gun to her head."

"I'll tell you everything," Aunt Fiona broke in. "I don't want my niece to go to jail for something I did."

Bailey groaned. She should have known her auntie would stay quiet for only so long.

"Go on," Carter told Aunt Fiona. Anger rode his face, but his lips were soft with amusement, and Bailey surmised that she and her aunt were probably not headed for jail.

"That hussy girlfriend of yours deserved it," Aunt Fiona said. "She all but admitted she was trying to sink her claws into you. I had to protect what belonged to my niece."

Bailey stopped her. "Auntie, why don't you go on up to our room. I'll be there in a minute, after Carter and I talk." She turned to Carter. "She's had a long day. I'm afraid she might've gotten a little too much sun." She punched the UP button and when the elevator doors on the other side of the lobby parted, she ushered her aunt toward the opening.

Carter quickly intervened. He stepped in front of them and spread his arms. "We're inside. No sun in here."

"Don't worry, sunshine." Aunt Fiona patted Bailey's arm. "He won't be mad at you. It's not your fault I wanted to plug that woman." She turned to Carter. "I put the barrel of my Glock to your girlfriend's forehead and told her to keep her skinny mitts off you. Her eyes got real big, like she was gonna faint dead away. But she didn't, thank God. Coulda been a mess if she'd hit her head on a sink. Cherry pie all over the place."

Glock? Cherry pie? Bailey sucked in a breath and grabbed her stomach. She looked for the nearest trash can, mortified that she might actually lose the contents of her stomach on Carter's shoes—though if she did, odds were he'd forget about the gun-in-the-bathroom incident.

Fortunately, her stomach settled quickly. Which meant she

had to continue standing there and endure more questions that she had no idea how to answer.

"Glock?" Carter said, his eyes opening wide.

"Oh. *That*." Bailey waved a dismissive hand. "It wasn't a *real* gun." She reached inside her purse and pulled it out. "See." She waved the hand-crafted wood gun back and forth in front of Carter's face. "It's harmless."

Carter grabbed the gun, muttering a string of expletives, and then looked around to see if anyone had noticed the crazy lady with the gun.

"Jeez, no reason to freak out. It's only a toy," Bailey said.

Carter looked at it, turning it over in his hand, examining it closely. "This is *not* a toy. And it's *not* harmless. I don't care what it's made of. This gun, *any* gun, can be deadly. People see guns, they get scared. Someone gets hurt." He tucked the hunk of wood inside his pocket. "Your aunt is lucky. She could've gotten herself into real trouble here today."

"Thank you, Lord," Aunt Fiona said. She looked at Bailey. "I know your mom would want me to give proper thanks."

Carter pulled Bailey aside and spoke in a hushed voice. "Is she okay?" he asked, tapping the side of his head.

Bailey gave her aunt an appraising glance. Breathing regular. On her feet. Happy. Her auntie was just fine. "She's not used to all this big-city excitement. I'll keep a closer eye on her." She paused and gave Carter one last doe-eyed look. "You're not thinking of sending her to jail, are you?"

He let out an exasperated breath. "Not this time. But I can't guarantee the outcome if she does anything like this again." He pulled his cell phone from his pocket, looked at the front of it, and then wandered off a few steps to take a call.

Bailey waited with her aunt, feeling like she was back in school, waiting for the principal to hand down his sentence. A minute later, Carter returned and said, "We'll talk later." But it was more a warning than a promise and she wondered if that meant he was still willing to have dinner at some point with her.

Chapter Nine

When Bailey woke up the following morning, she had a renewed optimism about her future with Carter. But then reality set in. Yesterday had been about as bad a day as days could get. And not only that, but she had a hunch today wasn't going to be much better. After the gun in the ladies' room incident, getting Carter to spend time with her would be double the chore. Plus, it was highly likely he'd made sure his security team knew to be on the lookout for her and her aunt and had told them to call the police if they saw her anywhere near the control room. Which meant, unless she happened to run into him, she might not see him all day.

That was unacceptable.

She mulled the problem over while taking her morning shower, and she thought about it all through breakfast, and then she barely paid attention to the Kathie Lee and Hoda show. Finally, a reprieve came when someone knocked on the connecting door. It was Liza. She had two pink neon strips of material covering her private parts and a pair of Tom Ford sunglasses in her hand. She wanted to go and lounge, pool side. The twins were destinations unknown, and she didn't feel like spending the day alone.

"Give me forty-five minutes," Bailey told her. Relaxing pool side sounded good. She could use the time to strategize. Maybe Liza could even offer her some advice.

"I'll give you thirty," Liza said and she left Bailey to manage her aunt.

Aunt Fiona didn't need managing. She'd heard the conversation and was good to go. She no longer owned a swimsuit, or a bikini, but she did have a 12-hour girdle and matching bra that Bailey agreed would suffice. A seventy-plus-year-old woman could get away with a lot of things, and wearing her underwear to a public pool was one of them. Once a woman reached a certain age, the only people who cared to look at her had such bad eyesight they couldn't distinguish between sexes, let alone fabric type.

A half hour later, Bailey was also ready to hit the pool. She had on a lime-green swimsuit, technically a bikini, but being that it was three times bigger than Liza's, calling it a bikini seemed overly generous. It was just as well. She was an engaged woman, after all. Or not. Tears filled her eyes. She couldn't bear to think about the possibility that she may have lost Carter forever.

"What's wrong?" Liza asked.

"It's Carter," Bailey said. She sniffled into a tissue. "He doesn't love me anymore. He wants me to go home."

"Hey, now. You don't really believe that. Somewhere deep inside, he loves you. He just doesn't know it at the moment."

Bailey went into a full sob. "With the way things are going, he might *never* know it."

"He's a punk," Aunt Fiona piped in. "Someone needs to teach him a lesson."

Bailey swallowed her tears. That's all she needed, to have her aunt do something else to irritate Carter. "*No*. No one needs to teach Carter anything," she said. "Especially not you."

Aunt Fiona muttered something under her breath and

Bailey ignored her. Sometimes it was best not to know the mess that was going on inside her aunt's mind.

"Let's go," Bailey said. "I need some fresh air."

Go they did, armed with plenty of SPF 30 sunblock, reading material, and a couple bottles of water. Bailey and her aunt meandered along behind Liza, who followed signs that pointed them in the direction of the guest pool. Bailey wondered if there was a non-guest pool.

They made it through the casino without incident, save for every other man who got neck strain from watching Liza strut her stuff. She'd ignored hotel policy that stated women were to wear a cover-up until they reached the pool area. She had a body that might be illegal in some countries and her motto was "If you've got it, show it to everybody." And she most certainly did. Bailey didn't care, though. Let Liza get all the attention. The only man she cared about having gawk at her was Carter.

Upon entering the pool area, the sky, deep blue with purple undertones, opened above them. The air was claustrophobic dry and the ambience uber tropical, complete with Tiki bar, girls in grass skirts, and shirtless men wearing tattoos and not much else.

As soon as Liza made her entrance, a group of shirtless men gave her the once-over. She countered their looks with a toss of her hair and a wag of her ass, then quickly moved past them to look around for the perfect spot. Bailey's perfect spot was different than Liza's. Liza wanted a place to bake, and Bailey wanted a place that allowed easy access to the pool for quick cooling off, plus some shade to prevent overexposure to the sun.

As luck had it, most of the chairs in the shade had already been taken. Bailey kept looking, squinting into the sun to find something acceptable. Her search took her to three chairs in a partially shaded area. It wasn't the best location—between a towel bin and a trio of waste receptacles—but with the sun pushing the mercury upwards of one hundred degrees Fahrenheit, she wasn't going to be picky.

"Let's go over there," she pointed.

Liza looked. "It's near the trash cans. We'll be overcome by the stink of rotting food."

Bailey shrugged. "It's either that or risk a fatal case of melanoma."

"Yeah, in ten or twenty years," Liza reasoned. "Scientists will have a cure by then."

"You hope," Bailey said. "I, personally, am not willing to take that chance." She took off toward the waste receptacles.

Arriving at their destination, a disgruntled Liza chose the end farthest from the source of rotting food. She laid her towel out on her chair and immediately got busy baking. Aunt Fiona chose the opposite end, where the air was most fragrant with the smell of half-eaten, sun-baked sandwiches. "I'll take this end. I haven't been able to smell anything for years," she said. "That leaves you in the middle, cupcake," she told Bailey.

Bailey surmised that.

Once settled in their chairs, Bailey applied sun block to her legs and arms. Then she applied sun block to her auntie's legs and arms. Liza wasn't applying anything. She was busy assessing a group of college-age men who were loitering nearby at the poolside bar. She and the boy-men were passing goo-goo eyes back and forth, and Bailey wondered how long until Liza moved her chair over to their territory.

Ten minutes passed and Liza got bored with the boy-men. She pulled her chair out of the shade so she could get maximum sun exposure and got down to the serious business of broiling her body. She wasn't afraid. She lived by the I'll-worry-about-it-when-it-becomes-a-problem rule. Bailey just hoped Liza didn't get the I-worried-about-it-too-late melanoma.

Five minutes into Liza's broiling, Bailey couldn't keep quiet. "Tan now, pay later," she said. She couldn't help it. She didn't often interfere with her friends' lifestyles and choices, but every now and then her brief stint as a medical student caused her inner doctor to surface, and she had to speak up.

"Don't worry," Liza said, "I put on plenty of lotion before

we came down here. Plus, my dermatologist offers a full menu of treatments that are guaranteed to repair most sun damage."

"Most," said Bailey. "Not all."

Liza ignored her, even going so far as to turn her head back in the direction of her young, male admirers. Of course, *they* didn't think she was getting too much sun.

And why would they? At twenty-seven, Liza could still pass for a well-developed teen. Even her teeth were like those of someone who had never had a cup of coffee, or even a glass of wine. So dazzling white they were that she'd once been let go after being stopped by a biker cop for doing twenty miles an hour over the speed limit. Instead of a ticket, he'd given her his phone number. Bailey surmised that it was possible he'd been so blinded by Liza's smile he hadn't been able to find his ticket pad… which Bailey thought was totally unfair. The only cops who'd ever let her off easy were the ones in Coupeville who felt they were doing her mom a favor. Plus, she'd had to promise them free marionberry pie the next time they dropped in for lunch, where she worked at the Knead & Feed.

"Wouldn't it be more cost-effective, in the long run, if you just skipped the whole process of getting sun damage in the first place?" she asked Liza. "Then you wouldn't even need a dermatologist."

"Are you kidding? Who'd do my Botox?"

Bailey's mouth hung open a beat. "You get Botox?" she asked, keeping her voice quiet. She didn't want to advertise Liza's medical goings on.

"Not yet," Liza answered. "But I will. When it's time. And I want to be ready. I don't want to waste any time searching for a good doctor to fix my mistakes." She smiled pretty. "My doc's name is Greg Shepherd, but I call him Doc Shepherd. He's almost as cute as that Doc Shepherd was on *Grey's Anatomy*. I've been seeing him for five years now and we've developed quite a relationship."

Bailey had no doubt.

"Sometimes, I even go to see him when I have nothing

going on," Liza continued. "And when it comes time I do need Botox, I know he'll treat me right."

Bailey had no doubt about that, either.

Liza arched her back, enhancing her naturally enhanced breasts, and continued baking. And the college men at the bar appreciated it very much.

Liza was a serious sun worshipper, and wasn't at all worried about a future filled with wrinkles and sun damage. Bailey knew continuing to lecture her would be futile. She notched up her sunglasses and left Liza alone to roast in peace.

Peace. What a concept. The only peace she'd have was when Carter was back to normal. Until then, she might as well get caught up on what was happening in the world of fashion and beauty. Maybe she could learn a few tricks.

She cracked open the latest issue of *Cosmopolitan*, and took a test that measured her sexuality quotient. She didn't like the outcome, so she took the test again, and again, and then eventually gave up and moved on to an article titled, "The Secret to Keeping Your Man Happy in Bed." After reading it, she thought, great, now, all she needed to do was find a way to get Carter to remember her, so she could try the secret out on him to see if it really worked.

After several minutes of sweating and soaking up the heat, Liza broke their stretch of silence. "What do you plan to do about Carter?" she asked.

"What do you mean?" Bailey asked.

"What if he doesn't remember you? Ever."

Bailey frowned. Ever was a long time. "I haven't thought that far ahead."

"You should," Liza said. A few more minutes passed and she continued. "You need a plan. We'll call it Plan B."

Bailey rolled her eyes behind her closed eyelids. Evidently, Plan A wasn't worth mentioning.

"You and Mark—" Liza began.

"There is no me and Mark," Bailey felt compelled to remind her.

"There could be."

"But there isn't." Bailey rolled over onto her stomach and turned her face toward her aunt. She watched for a minute to make sure her auntie was breathing. She was.

"Surely, you realize Mark would do anything for you. Or *to* you." Liza said. She laughed devilishly.

Bailey rolled her eyes again. "Yes, I am fully aware that Mark would do anything and everything to me if I were to let him. What are you suggesting?"

"I'm not sure. I just think doing nothing but hanging around waiting for Carter to get his memory back is a waste of time. You need to do something drastic to help things along. Like play nicey-nice with another man. Maybe it'll force a reaction from Carter."

Bailey flipped her head back around. "Nicey-nice? With Mark?"

Liza shrugged. "It's the oldest game in the book. All you have to do is let Carter see you with Mark and, *bam!* The jealousy rod will hit Carter square between the eyes."

Bailey laughed. "I see. You want me to try the old another-guy-is-interested-in-me, so-you'd-better-pay-attention ploy. Do you really think that would cure Carter's amnesia?"

"It's worth a try. At the very least you'd get some pleasure out of it."

Bailey mulled the idea over for a minute, and then said a flat-out, "No."

"Give me one good reason why."

"I'll give you two. First, amnesia doesn't work that way. And, second, Carter already *saw* me with Mark. He saw Mark groping me and he didn't blink an eye."

"That's what you think. I'll bet he was seething. In fact, I'll bet he's still stewing over seeing Mark putting his grubby mitts on you. If I know Carter, he's probably already made plans to dump Mark's body somewhere out in the desert."

Bailey frowned. She mostly doubted it, but the reality was, it could be true. Still, there was no sense in further fueling

Liza's insane fire. "I'm not doing anything with Mark to make Carter jealous," she told Liza.

Liza was quiet for a minute, thinking. "Okay. Then what about Plan A?"

As much as Bailey hated to ask, she was curious to hear all about the prequel to Plan B. "Which is?"

"You could call down to the front desk for help," Liza said. "*Security* help. And make sure to specify that you need Carter Davis to come to your rescue. Then you could have him walk in on you and Brian."

Bailey compressed her lips and wondered if blond might actually be Liza's true hair color. "I just said I'm not doing anything to make Carter jealous."

"Did you hear me?" Liza asked. "I said *Brian*, not *Mark*."

"How is that plan any different from Plan B?" Bailey asked.

Liza grinned. "Maybe you can't tell the difference between the twins, but I sure can. Mark does this thing with his pinkie, and I swear I forget who I am. Then he—"

"Okay!" Bailey held up a hand. "I don't need a play-by-play. I've done the deed with Mark, and I've been trying to forget it ever since."

"I wouldn't mind a play-by-play," Aunt Fiona chimed in. "If your uncle Rex and I ever have sex again, I'd like to give him some tips."

"I thought you were asleep," Bailey said.

"Some men are hard to forget," Liza said, sighing.

"Even when you've got a slight case of Alzheimer's," Aunt Fiona added.

"Tell me about it," Bailey agreed.

Liza pouted. "I don't see why you won't at least give my idea a chance. It's not like I'm suggesting you go all the way with Mark. How about a simple kiss? Something long and slow?"

"How about something short and non-existent?" Bailey said. "I'm not kissing Mark. For any reason." She got up from her chair. "C'mon, Auntie, your daily requirement of vitamin

D has been met."

Aunt Fiona slowly got to her feet, creaking all the way, and Bailey rolled their towels into a big ball and dumped them into a nearby towel bin. "Coming?" she asked Liza.

"I think I'll stay out here a while," Liza said. "I need more vitamin D than your auntie."

"Happy broiling," Bailey said, and she and her auntie left the pool area. Just as they reached the entrance to the dark caverns of the casino, she looked over her shoulder. Liza was already being entertained by one of the college men who'd been ogling her.

Bailey led her aunt through the glass doors and they began their half-mile trek to the elevator lobby. They weaved their way through gaming tables, crowds of people, and cigarette toxins at a good clip. Bailey wanted to avoid any disasters, like what had happened yesterday. Maybe with a little time passing without further incident, Carter would forget.

Halfway to their destination, Bailey stopped before a life-size poster that advertised a show Carter was scheduled to perform in later that night. He was doing his Elvis thing.

"We should go," Aunt Fiona said. "We got nothing better to do. And with a little luck, Carter might even toss one of his silk scarves your way."

Bailey agreed. But not because she was interested in getting one of Carter's silk scarves. She wanted to take every opportunity to be near Carter. That was the only way she was going to stay on his mind.

Chapter Ten

"Elvis" could still pack 'em in. And packed in they were. When Bailey and her Aunt Fiona were shown to their seats, Aunt Fiona took the aisle, and Bailey took the next seat over. The only problem was the seat was already half-occupied by a woman who looked to be a good hundred pounds beyond healthy. She reminded Bailey of a favorite high school teacher who'd also been a hefty gal... who came to a sad ending one day, right in front of her students in Bailey's Programmed Math class. She collapsed, and that was the last any of her students ever saw her. Word was she'd had a heart attack.

With a sigh, Bailey settled into her seat and immediately lost sight of her right arm. It was sucked up by a roll of flesh that belonged to the hefty woman. The woman wasted no time in getting acquainted.

"I just love Elvis, don't you?" she said. "I'm so excited to be here. I paid extra to get these front row seats." Her eyes sparkled under the theater lights.

Bailey simply nodded, not wanting to encourage the woman, in case she was a "talker." She wanted to see every minute of Carter's performance.

"Name's Polly McGee," the woman went on. "From Dayton, Ohio."

Bailey had no choice. She'd been raised to be polite. She smiled a small smile. "Bailey Ventura. Nice to meet you," she told Polly. And then she turned her focus back to the stage.

But Polly wasn't done acquainting herself. She pushed her program over in front of Bailey. "I've seen most of these guys. They're all pretty good." She flipped the pages until she came to the one that featured Carter. "This guy is the reason I'm here. I wanted my daughter to see the real deal." She made a head gesture to the seat on her right. "I promised her I'd bring her here to Las Vegas to see Elvis for her twenty-first birthday."

Bailey looked around Polly, at a young woman who also had a few pounds that needed shedding. Like mother, like daughter was never truer.

"She thinks it's her destiny to become Elvis's bride," Polly continued. "She went to a fortune teller, who told her she had Priscilla's soul, and that she and Elvis were meant to be bound together for all eternity."

Okey dokey. Bailey pressed her lips tight. She could hardly say anything about how ridiculous that sounded. Not when she, herself, had been convinced she was meant to grow up and marry someone who could sing like Elvis.

"I think he's probably had some work done, though," Polly said. "A man doesn't get to be his age and stay looking so fine."

Bailey did a mental groan and slid a glance over the mound of breast tissue that was pressed against her cheek. Polly was one of *those*. She believed Elvis was still alive and about to come out on stage and perform.

"Don't you agree?" Polly asked.

Bailey nodded. Who was she to dash the dreams of an Elvis worshipper? Not her, that's for sure. She'd learned early on that Elvis worshippers took their love for him seriously and that many of them, the same as her mom, still believed he was just waiting for the right moment to make the comeback of the century. About the only thing you could do when confronted by someone like Polly was agree with everything they said, no matter how out-there it sounded.

Bailey closed her eyes and rested her head against the back of her seat. With any luck, Polly would get the hint and let her enjoy the show without any further commentary.

After a minute of quiet, Bailey's eyes grew heavy. The Oasis theater had big, cushy seats so comfortable that she couldn't help but consider taking a nap in them. The head rests were the same... all squishy and pillowy, like a big plump marshmallow.

Marshmallow?

Bailey yanked her head forward and looked over her shoulder. A mass of white—aka Polly's arm—was draped over the back of her seat.

"Excuse me," she said to Polly.

"Sorry, dear, I'm a big girl and you're so slim, I thought you might not mind sharing."

Well, what could she say to that? Nothing, so she went back to relaxing. And thinking. About Carter. And the kiss they'd shared... and how she had to find a way to get through to him. She also revisited the possibility he could be faking his amnesia. What if it were true?

While she mulled that thought over, the MC came out on stage and announced the first performer, a tribute artist named Eric Mead. He was good, singing "Kentucky Rain," but he was no Carter Davis. And then the next performer came out... and the next and the next, until Bailey just had to close her eyes. She wasn't interested in any of the other performers. She was there to see her man. They were obviously saving the best for last.

Finally, the MC announced Carter, and Bailey snapped to attention. Carter appeared on stage, dressed in leather and sexuality, looking so much like the real Elvis that it was like Elvis had been reincarnated. Bailey perched on the edge of her seat. It didn't matter that she'd seen Carter perform dozens of times, it was always a thrill.

The energy was electrifying. The crowd roared, and her heart swelled. Never had she been so proud of her Security Guy. He was Elvis perfect, and wired for sex. Women immediately began tossing their undergarments onto the stage.

She glanced over at Polly. Polly's eyes were focused like lasers on Carter and she was licking her lips. Her puffy sausage fingers were kneading the program and she looked like she might leap right out of her chair to pounce. Bailey wondered if she should be afraid for Carter.

"I don't care if he is a punk, I wouldn't mind being punked by him myself," Aunt Fiona spoke up. She stuffed a hand inside her bag and did some rustling around until she found the object of her search—a pair of pink panties with white lace trim.

Bailey's eyes grew wide. "Those are mine!"

"They sure are," her aunt admitted. "I brought 'em, in case you forgot. I chose pink on account of you two being engaged now. Better to save red for the bedroom. Here," she said, and she tossed the panties into Bailey's lap. "Have at him."

Bailey quickly tucked the panties away inside her purse. She'd never worn them and had no intention of tossing them away, even to the love of her life. And, anyway, they'd only get lost among the hundreds of other articles of clothing that were already on the stage.

"I brought some, too," Polly said, holding up a piece of white fabric that was ten sizes larger than sexy.

Aunt Fiona clicked her tongue against the roof of her mouth. "Get a load of these," she said to Polly. She pulled out another pair—leopard print—and held them up for the entire audience to see. She lowered her voice and leaned in to Bailey. "Gertie gave me these to throw at Elvis. She sewed her phone number inside, in case he gets a hankering for some mature lovin'." She turned out the waistband, exposing a phone number.

Bailey didn't recognize the number as Gertie's. She narrowed her eyes. "Those don't look like anything Gertie would wear. And isn't that Lea Townsend's phone number?" she asked her aunt.

"So, what are you saying?" her aunt asked.

"Auntie, did you steal those from Lea?"

"What if I did? She'll never miss 'em. She has plenty more where these came from."

Bailey groaned. "Don't tell me you took those off Lea's clothesline?"

"Okay, I won't."

Bailey mashed her head into Polly's marshmallow arm. This was her plight, and if Carter ever got his memory back, it would be his plight, too. "Lea is not a threat to your marriage, Auntie," she said.

"Best not to take any chances. The way I see it, Elvis will find Lea's phone number on these panties and he might give her a call. She'd be a fool to pass up the chance for a date with the King to be with your uncle Rex. God love him, but he does have a wild eye. Not too many women would choose a man with a wild eye over Elvis." Aunt Fiona rolled Lea's panties into a tight ball, wound her arm back, and let loose.

Aunt Fiona had a point. Her Rex did have a wild eye. A lazy eye to be more precise, meaning one of his eyes was always off into space. Which eye was always a guess. But wild eye or not, it was ridiculous for her aunt to be concerned about his faithfulness. He wasn't the straying type.

And even more ridiculous was her auntie tossing another woman's panties at *her* fiancé. Bailey watched another piece of material soar through the air. It was about two inches square and the color of hot fire. She'd never seen them before. Probably they belonged to Liza. They landed on stage, just as Carter went down to his knees and he slid toward them. He was in the middle of "Suspicious Minds" and paused just long enough to give them the once over, then he shot Bailey a wink and a lip curl.

Bailey's face flushed deep red. *They're not mine*, she mouthed to him.

He continued singing and the next thing Bailey knew he'd pulled a red scarf from around his neck and was dangling it in front of her face. She reached for it, but then a woman came out of nowhere and snatched it out of mid-air. She pushed it to her face in orgasmic pleasure, while pressing every inch of her upper torso to the lip of the stage. Her proximity to Carter made Bailey squeamish. She was afraid the woman wouldn't be able to resist the temptation to attack.

And then it happened. The woman snagged Carter by the pant leg and held on like her life depended on it. Carter didn't have time to back away. He tried to shake her loose, and when that didn't work, he bent over and tried to pry her hand from his leg. She let go, but not for long. Her hands quickly moved up and around his neck, and she pulled him to her until his face was only inches from hers.

The entire audience went into a feverish chant, "*Kiss her, kiss her, kiss her.*"

"I think he's gonna!" Polly screamed. "He's gonna kiss that woman!"

Bailey held her breathe. She didn't think for one minute Carter was going to kiss the woman, not when he was on the verge of being mauled.

Bailey looked around for some assistance. Where was Carter's security team? Couldn't they see he needed help?

The woman was determined. She was all amped up from the chanting and didn't seem the least bit interested in letting go. Carter was doing his best to escape, but she was winning the battle.

"Are you going to do something?" Aunt Fiona asked.

"What can *I* do?" Bailey frantically looked around again for anyone dressed in black. She saw nothing. She and her aunt continued to watch the action between Carter and his fan. A long tense minute passed and at last Carter was free. He looked exhausted from the fight. Defeated, the woman sat back down and cuddled with the scarf. But now the theater was in total chaos.

"*Elvis! Elvis! Elvis!*" the audience roared.

Bailey saw Polly out of the corner of her eye. She was wringing her big girl panties in her big girl fists and her voluminous chest was heaving so hard, it'd taken on a life of its own. Had Carter finally met his match? Bailey wondered.

"I'm gonna get me some of that," Polly said. Her voice was a purr, deep and throaty.

Oblivious to the new, impending danger, Carter went down on his knees again and wailed right in Polly's face, "Are You Lonesome Tonight?"

That was all the encouragement Polly needed. She shifted her massive bulk, propelling herself out of her chair until the mass of flesh became like a rogue wave, building and growing stronger every second. Bailey could only watch and pray Carter had enough fight left in him to survive another round with a rabid fan.

Polly didn't let the edge of the stage stop her. She hoisted herself up and over the lip with such force that she slid like a baby beluga whale until she crashed into a large speaker. She wasn't fazed. She scrambled around and caught hold of one of Carter's legs.

Carter whipped around, trying desperately to shake her loose, just like he'd tried to do with the other woman, but it was futile. Shaking off two hundred plus pounds of determined flesh was no easy task—as every woman who has ever been on a diet can attest to. Frantic, he shot a look to each corner of the stage. Bailey knew what he was looking for—a little help from his security team.

She looked around, too, but saw zilch. She gave Carter a palms-up.

The action continued with Polly, with the situation going from bad to worse. She had him down and in a few seconds more would be on top of him.

A wave of cold panic shot through Bailey. What if Carter was maimed? What if something freaky happened—though she wasn't sure how much freakier things could get—and he

ALEXA DARIN

was rendered impotent? She couldn't very well sit there and let that happen, not if she hoped to have him father her children one day.

She jumped from her seat and scrambled onto the stage. Aunt Fiona was right behind her.

"You grab her by the hair, and I'll hit her with my purse," Aunt Fiona said. "I've got a ton of quarters in here and she'll feel it all the way to her bones."

"No!" Bailey shouted. "No hitting." Though she seriously doubted Polly would feel anything through all that flesh. Still, she wasn't about to let her aunt hit anyone. Bailey lowered her voice and said, "A little hair pulling, but only if it becomes absolutely necessary."

Her aunt grinned wide and reached into her purse. She pulled out a big black gun. "How about I use this on her?"

Bailey's mouth fell open. Another *gun*?

Aunt Fiona ground her teeth together in a cheesy imitation of Clint Eastwood as Dirty Harry. She pointed the gun at Polly and said, "Make my day, chickie." But Polly ignored her. She was too busy trying to get herself a piece of Elvis.

Screams filled the theater and several voices shouted, "Everyone get down! Some crazy old lady's got a gun!"

It was total chaos.

Bailey didn't know whether she should help Carter, or grab the gun out of her aunt's hand. She had a hold of one of Polly's arms, but getting a firm grip was near impossible. There was so much to grab.

Bailey glanced over her shoulder to see what was going on with her aunt. Nothing much, but at least she hadn't pulled out any more weaponry. Bailey cut a look to Carter. She wanted to tell him how sorry she was about her aunt having another gun, but he was too busy trying to take back his leg from Polly to accept her apology.

In a rush, security finally showed up. They got Polly by both legs and arms and pulled her away from Carter, then dragged her to the back of the stage. Unfortunately, a couple of men also had Aunt Fiona, and were dragging her to the back of the stage, as well. One member of the security team had Aunt Fiona's gun and he was giving it a curious look, which made Bailey feel much better. Obviously, it was the same as the last gun, made of wood.

Getting to her feet, Bailey scrambled after the mob. She followed them down a long, stark hallway, through a couple of doors, and into a small room equipped with a table and four chairs. The men in black went away, slamming the door behind them, and Bailey didn't even have a chance to catch her breath before the door opened again. It was Carter—and he was wearing his mad face. And who could blame him? His leather pants were ripped and the zipper on his jacket was hanging precariously, which was a shame, because it was her favorite Elvis outfit.

He stood there for a minute, red in the face, looking at them.

Bailey thought it best not to say a word... until he gave her permission to speak.

"What the hell was that?" he said at last, jamming a finger in the general direction of the stage. He gave Polly a quick once-over. "And who is this? Another relative?"

Polly offered him her hand. "I'm Polly McGee, from Dayton, Ohio. Can I get your autograph?"

Bailey stayed quiet. His question was ridiculous. Polly didn't even resemble the Ventura women.

"Well?" he demanded, ignoring Polly's request for his autograph.

"You heard her," Bailey said. "Her name is Polly. She's from Ohio."

Carter stared at her, like he was trying to figure out if she was purposely feigning stupidity or if she was simply trying to be a smart ass. Which, to tell the truth, she wasn't sure. Mostly, she was trying to keep things light.

"I thought we agreed, no more guns," he said. He had Aunt Fiona's gun was in his hand and he was squeezing it so hard his fingers were turning purple.

"Well, now, it's not a real gun," Bailey pointed out. "Even kids play with toy guns… spray each other with water pistols—"

Carter slammed the gun down on the table. "THIS is NOT a water pistol."

"But it's not real… is it?" she asked, praying that it wasn't.

"Do you think the police would stop to ask if a gun was real or not before opening fire on someone who's waving it around in the middle of a crowded theater?" he asked her.

She scoffed. "That's just silly. They would never open fire in a crowded theater. Someone could get hurt."

Carter rammed a hand through his hair. "Exactly. My men could have shot her. They could have shot *you*." His eyes lost their hardness and he actually looked pained at the thought.

A ribbon of warmth rippled through her. "You were worried for me," she said.

"It's my job to be concerned for hotel guests."

The ribbon of warmth stopped short. Just when she thought they were making progress.

"I don't hear you yelling at *her*." Bailey pointed at Polly. "*She* could've torn your leg off." Or worse.

"I just wanted to touch you," Polly told Carter. She reached for him and made grabby grabby motions with her fingers. "I couldn't help myself. You were so close, and something inside me just snapped."

Carter backed out of Polly's reach. He gave her an assessing look, like he might be trying to decide how much damage a woman her size could do to a man. "Go on," he told her. "Go back and enjoy the rest of the show."

"But the show is over. You were the last to perform," Polly said.

"Then go to the buffet. Tell them I sent you," he said.

Polly hoisted herself out of her chair and grabbed at him again, saying, "Thank you, thank you, you darling man, you," but Carter wasn't letting her get close. He offered her one of his hands and that was it, and she took full advantage, bringing his hand to her lips. She smothered it with kisses, and then she snagged the blue scarf he had hanging around his neck and jammed it to her nose.

"Take it," Carter told her. "And get out of here before I change my mind and have you arrested."

Sighing and looking all dreamy-eyed, Polly left the room, and that left Bailey and her aunt to deal with Carter.

Carter turned to Bailey's aunt. "And what am I going to do with you?"

Aunt Fiona fluttered her eyelashes. "Why, Elvis, you're quite the tease, aren't you? I hope whatever you do, you're gentle. I'm getting on in years and I don't have a lot of stamina."

Bailey sputtered, horrified. "I think Uncle Rex might have something to say about you flirting with another man," she said. Though she was pretty sure Carter couldn't possibly think her aunt was serious.

He didn't. His upper lip was quivering and he was doing his best not to laugh. Bailey didn't think any of this was funny. Well, maybe a little.

Carter did a quarter turn and stared at the plain gray wall for a minute before blowing out a long, slow breath. Then, composed, he got back to business. "Tell me you don't have any more guns, and I'll let you go," he told Aunt Fiona. Then he looked at Bailey. "You. Stay."

"You can frisk me if you like, but I'm clean," Aunt Fiona said.

Carter opened the door for her and she was gone.

Bailey was nonplussed. So much for the Ventura women always sticking together. "Now what?" she asked.

"Now, we get something straight," Carter said. "I won't even pretend to know what's going on inside your aunt's head, but this thing with the guns has to stop. No more. Period. Is that clear?"

"Those are my feelings exactly. But how can I promise

such a thing? My aunt has a mind of her own."

Carter wasn't buying it. He crossed his arms over his chest, staring her down.

"Fine. I'll talk to her," Bailey said. "Plus, I'll check her bag to make sure she doesn't have any more guns. I'll also check her purse whenever she leaves the hotel room. That's about all I can do." She paused. "This gun business is all your fault, you know. My aunt never even used to like guns. I would think you'd be obliged to take part of the blame for her having such a fetish. You're a bad influence. You introduced her—*all* of Coupeville—to big city crime."

Bailey tossed her hands in the air and continued, "Mobsters... guns... stolen diamonds. It's beyond comprehension."

Carter just stared at her.

She pouted. "Okay, so maybe my aunt shouldn't be waving guns around, scaring people. But she's not dangerous. If she really wanted to shoot somebody, she'd use a *real* gun." She shuddered. The idea of her auntie with a real gun was *more* than beyond comprehension.

"Maybe you shouldn't have brought her here to Las Vegas with you," Carter said. "Obviously, she needs looking after."

"My auntie is just fine. She's old, that's all."

"Maybe you should take her home," Carter suggested.

Probably she should. But she wasn't about to let him think *he* was making her leave. "If we're finished here, I'd like to go find her."

"One more thing," Carter said. "You need to stop following me."

"What!" Bailey hitched her chin. "I am *not* following you."

"One could argue that point."

"How?" She hitched her chin even higher. "Just because I came to see you perform doesn't mean I'm following you. Maybe I happen to enjoy hearing you sing."

Carter arched an eyebrow. "I've had a lot of women follow me, using that as an excuse."

Bailey had nothing more to say, she was so furious. The

only response she had was to turn and stomp out of the room. She was going to find her auntie and they were going to... to... aargh! She had no idea what they were going to do.

Chapter Eleven

Carter made his way to the elevator that would take him up to the control room. His body ached, not only from performing, but also from dealing with Bailey Ventura and her aunt and whoever that crazy lady was who'd joined him on stage. It was a fiasco in the first degree and he just wanted to forget about it. And speaking of crazy ladies, he hoped he'd gotten his message through to Ms. Ventura, that her aunt couldn't expect to get away with running around waving guns at people.

He grumbled to himself, pushing the UP button. And what about Bailey? He'd given her a lot of thought. She was much more than just a fan. She was honestly in love with him, and that was bothersome. In fact, everything about her bothered him. Her small-town innocence, the way her freckles fanned across her cheeks, the way she bit into her bottom lip when she smiled, but really wanted to cry. Dammit, just being in her presence bothered him. She filled him with all kinds of strange thoughts and feelings that made no sense whatsoever.

He blew out a heavy breath, relieved when the elevator finally arrived. He had a job to do and work was just what he needed to keep his sanity.

It was a quick ride, no stops along the way, and when he entered the control room, his security team cheered for him, welcoming him back to work. Most of them had already gotten off work by the time he'd checked in the night before.

He gave everyone a scant nod and continued on his way, over to his office door. He whooshed it open and, at last, he was back to the familiar. He stood at his desk and did a quick scan through all the messages that had been left for his attention and found nothing important. Only then did he realize how tired he was. He moved around his desk, to his big leather chair, eager to take a minute to himself. But when he closed his eyes, his timeout was interrupted by a soft laugh. His hand went reactively to his chest, where he typically kept his gun. It wasn't there. He'd been in such a hurry this morning, he must have left it on his kitchen table.

It didn't matter. He knew the laugh.

"Maria," he said, turning. "I thought you were a dream." He vaguely remembered her being in his room while he was recovering from his adventure out in the desert.

"*Hola, Guapo*," Maria said. "No dream. Perhaps you are delirious being out of bed and back to work so soon."

"Don't worry about me. What are you doing here?"

"Ah, you don't remember that it was I who found you out there in that heat, all by your lonesome." She tilted her head, letting her shiny black hair drape to one side of her face. "Are you at least happy to see me?"

Carter studied the curves of her face, the swell of her cheeks. She was just as beautiful as ever. But she was smart, too, and in his opinion beauty and smarts usually added up to trouble. "Depends. What do you want?"

Maria laughed. "I want nothing, *mijo*. I'm only here because your sister called and said you needed rescuing."

"And that was your boot kicking me in the ribs when I was face down in the dirt?"

"I needed to turn you over to see if you were still alive."

"What about checking for a pulse? You are still a doctor,

aren't you?" Or more precisely, a surgeon… and a fine one at that. He remembered once when he and Maria were out having dinner and a man at another table began choking on a piece of steak. Another guest at the man's table tried to Heimlich him, but it wasn't working and time was running out. Lucky for him, Maria was available. She stepped in and performed an emergency tracheotomy right there in the restaurant, in front of everybody. As gory as it was, it was also damned impressive. And that was as easy as it had ever been between them.

Maria was a Southern gal, born in South Carolina to Cuban immigrant parents, which gave her a uniqueness he'd never found in another woman. The problem was she wasn't about to move away from her home to be closer to him, and vice versa. Eventually, the miles ended their relationship.

"I am. So you do remember some things."

"Some. Don't you have patients to tend to?"

"My patients can do without me for a day or two. Oh, *mijo*, let's not talk about patients or the past. Tell me what happened to you out there in the desert. Was it your old friend Frank Zoopa who did this to you?"

"Times are tough. Could be a guest who lost a house payment or two," he told her. Though Zoopa was as good a guess as any.

She seemed to consider his answer. "I think it *was* Zoopa. And I think you need to end this war with him."

He laughed. "Now you sound like someone else I know, and I'll tell you the same thing I told her… it's none of your business what goes on between me and Zoopa. Keep your nose out of it. The Gaming Commission and Metro will take care of him."

"Ha! I know you, Carter Davis. You are not about to let *la policia* take care of anything." She looked at him, assessing. "Then again, maybe you have gone soft." She rubbed a hand lightly over his arm. "Careful, *mijo*. Soft can get you killed."

"Let me worry about that," Carter told her.

She pretended to pout. "Okay, if I leave it alone, will you

tell me about your new love, Bailey? I did not know you liked freckles."

"I don't," Carter said.

Maria smiled, her ruby red lips turning upward to reveal a tiny chip in one of her otherwise perfect, top front teeth. "Then you are marrying the wrong girl."

"And who is the right girl? You?"

Maria shrugged. "Maybe there is no right girl for you. From what Twinkie has told me, your Bailey lives far away from here. I wonder… if the miles were a problem before, how will you make it work this time?"

Carter frowned. "I'm not discussing Bailey with you."

"Why not?"

"I can't discuss what I don't know."

"Ah," Maria said, nodding.

"Ah, nothing. Don't read anything into my lapse of memory."

Maria leaned in close. "But, for now, you don't remember your girl. So perhaps you are free for dinner?"

Carter breathed her in. She smelled of flowers. It brought back memories that were almost too much to bear. He gently nudged her back. "I just got out of bed. My bruises are still fresh."

"I do know how to be gentle."

"What would your parents think, you getting tangled up with me again?" It was a random question. He could barely remember them and didn't know what they would or wouldn't approve of.

"I don't want to talk about my parents."

"Okay. What would the pope think?"

Maria pushed her lips together, contemplating. "I doubt you even know who the pope is."

"John Paul George?"

She laughed, charging the air with electricity. "You just named three of The Beatles."

He shrugged. "I tried."

"You don't have to worry about my parents, Carter. They always liked you. It's my *abuela* you should be concerned with. She's constantly asking about you. Where is he? When is he coming back to visit? Why aren't the two of you married already?" She paused, pressing her lips tight again. "Honestly, what's to think about? You either want to have dinner with me or you don't."

Carter's eyes lit up. "Wait a minute. Your *abuela*? I remember her. Tiny, five-foot nothing, right? And fiery..." Just like Maria. He paused. "But she's ill, isn't she? Something to do with her kidneys?" Everything was coming back now.

Maria smiled weakly. "That's right. We're hoping any day now, God will hear our prayers and find her a donor."

"Anything I can do?" Carter asked with genuine intentions.

"You could pay her a visit. She adores you."

"She adores Elvis, the same as every other woman out there," he pointed out.

"Perhaps, and what about Miss Bailey?" Maria asked. "Who does she love? You... or the man you pretend to be?"

He spread his hands. "I wouldn't know."

Maria smiled. "Fair enough." She tugged off her boots, and then tucked her feet into Carter's lap. "Rub them, *mijo. Por favor.*"

Now, there was something he remembered. Maria Cruz never could resist a good foot massage. Well, far be it for him to deny her one of her biggest pleasures.

He took her foot into his hands and kneaded it tenderly, until her face softened and she closed her eyes. She was practically purring.

His eye caught a movement in the control room and when he looked, he saw a couple of his men turn their heads. They were pretending to be busy watching some man who was on a winning streak at a blackjack table. But it was too late. They were busted, and he made a mental note to chew their asses out as soon as Maria was gone. He wasn't paying them to spy on him. And to let them know they'd been caught, he reached into the center drawer of his desk and felt for two small nubs. The one on the left disconnected the ever-watchful cameras, and the one on the right lowered bullet-proof panels over the panes of glass that made up his office walls. He pushed them both.

There. No more prying eyes.

The distraction was enough to bring Maria out of her pleasure cloud. "Forget about who's watching us, Carter," she said. "We still have our clothes on."

"I pay my men to keep an eye on the casino floor. It's none of their business what I do in here with my guests," he told her.

A smile played on her lips. "You've changed. The Carter Davis I once knew didn't give a damn about privacy. He was so much bolder, so much braver." She ran her tongue over the edge of her teeth. "So much better."

Carter inhaled the sweet scent of jasmine rising from her chest. It brought back another wave of memories, many of which were created right there in his office. But that was before and this was now and nothing more was going to happen between them. "Don't worry about me, honey. I'm as bold as I need to be. And if I wasn't brave, you wouldn't be here."

Her eyes sparked, as though they were lit with fire. "What about better?"

He chuckled. "That's something you'll just have to wonder about." He curled his fingers around her slender foot, applying just the right amount of pressure to make her close her eyes again. Minutes passed. He massaged, she moaned. It was all cozy and innocent. He had no desires for her... other than friendship. God only knew what she had on her mind.

Chapter Twelve

First thing, when Bailey and her aunt got back to their room, Bailey checked for flights out of Las Vegas that were headed for Seattle. AlaskaAir had plenty of seats available, but Bailey was far from ready to give up on Carter. So why was she even checking for flights? This was ridiculous. She and Carter could work things out... if only they had a few quiet minutes together—without a bed in the room—so they could talk. At the very least, maybe he'd see she really was a well-adjusted, normal woman, whose only fault was being head over heels in love with him. She would never do anything that would make her a news headliner.

Thank goodness for Liza. She'd agreed to aunt-sit and had assured Bailey that the hotel would not be under lock-down at the end of the evening. Liza planned to take Aunt Fiona out to play slots, have dinner, and maybe even go to the wax museum over at the Venetian. Aunt Fiona had been saying how she wanted to get a good look at John Wayne. But Bailey wasn't so sure that was a good idea. She didn't put it past her aunt to try something, like make off with one of John Wayne's guns.

"Make sure you check her bag before you leave the museum," Bailey told Liza.

"Don't worry. I have things well under control," Liza said. "The twins are even gone for the evening. They said something about wanting to take in every show up and down the Strip that includes at least one naked woman."

"That's a lot of shows," Bailey said.

"Exactly, so they won't be around to distract me from keeping a close eye on your auntie."

It all sounded good, but Bailey was still uneasy. To be safe, and also because she'd promised Carter there would be no more gun incidents, she decided to give the room a thorough weapons search before heading out. She checked every conceivable hiding place—her aunt's purse, the closet, under the bed, inside the tissue dispenser—because one should never underestimate the wiliness of a senior citizen. When she was fairly certain the room was gun-free, she tossed a prayer in the direction of the ceiling. "She's an old lady. Have mercy."

She rode the public elevator down to the lobby, and then made her way over to the security elevator—which the public was not allowed to use without permission—and had to wait for only a minute before the doors opened. One of Carter's men stepped out and held the door for her.

"Our secret," he said.

"Thank you," she said. She appreciated the kindness. At least not everyone had forgotten who she was. She stepped inside, pushed the UP button, and was on her way. She stared at herself in the floor-to-ceiling mirror as the elevator ascended, taking a few deep breaths to prepare herself mentally. Of course, a shot of tequila would probably do the trick, too, but that might muddy things up. Alcohol had a way of going straight to her girl bits and at the moment that would be an unnecessary distraction.

Halfway to the control room floor, the elevator stopped and the doors opened. A long, gangly man with dark, slicked-back hair stepped inside. Bailey moved over, putting as much space between them as possible. Even so, she could feel his gaze roaming the length of her body and it gave her the oolie goolies.

As the elevator hummed upward, the man continued watching her. She was tempted to give him a good look back, just for future reference, but then she remembered a piece of advice her aunt had once given her. "Don't ever look a crazy person in the eye, and don't ever talk to them, because then you've entered their world... and no telling where that might be." Bailey thought that was great advice.

With wont for something to do, she busied herself with a loose thread on the hem of her blouse. She was tempted to pull it, but then the entire hem might unravel and that would never do. For one thing, she hadn't brought along a sewing kit for mending, and for another thing, she wasn't fond of sewing. That was something her mother's generation did to pass the time.

The elevator had just about arrived at its destination when the man reached in front of her to push the STOP button. She got a whiff of the tar and toxins that were emanating from his clothes. He was a serious smoker.

"Bailey Ventura?" he said.

The muscles in her back pulled tight and her heart began drumming hard and fast in her chest. Adrenaline pumped at warp speed through her blood vessels. She was ready for fight or flight, only she didn't see either of those being a good option. She considered screaming, but didn't want to over-react. She'd been accused in the past of having an over-active imagination.

She needed a plan. Was there a hatch on the ceiling? Perhaps, but she didn't want to be so obvious as to look.

She needed another plan. It was another what-would-Carter-do-in-a-situation-like-this moment. The answer was easy. Odds were he'd already have the man's face pushed to the mirror with a gun to his head. But being that she had no gun, nor the muscle power to push the man's face into the mirror, she had to settle for a shy smile.

"Yes, I'm Bailey," she said. She took the man's face into her memory... every line, every pore, plus the fact that his skin had an oily shimmer. Everything about him spelled lizard, as in Z-O-O-P-A.

"I have a message for you," the man said.

She swallowed, not at all sure she wanted to hear what he had to say.

"Tell your boyfriend he's not fooling anyone with his bogus amnesia act."

Bailey's mouth mentally dropped open. *So*, she wasn't the *only* one who thought Carter might be faking his amnesia. Still, she had no intention of discussing the issue with one of Zoopa's henchmen.

"I don't have a boyfriend," she said. *Admit nothing.* That was something she'd once heard someone say and, right now, it seemed like really good advice.

The man moved over in front of her and placed a hand on the gold rail behind her, one on her left and one on her right. The stench of his breath came at her in a cloud of stale nicotine. It was all she could do to keep from gagging. His gaze roamed over her, and he brought one hand to her face, dragging a greasy finger down her cheek. "You're a pretty thing," he said. "Davis is a lucky man."

"If you hurt me, he'll kill you," she told the man. But it was merely a faux brave front. Her knees were about to buckle. Thank God she had the rail to lean against.

The man grinned. "Yet, you say you have no boyfriend." He fingered a lock of her hair and pulled it to his nose, taking a whiff. Then his grin disappeared. Maybe he didn't care for the smell of Living Proof No Frizz Shampoo. Lucky her.

He pressed a finger to her chest. "Tell Davis we're watching him. Tell him we're watching you." Then elevator doors opened and he was gone.

Bailey whimpered and she thought she might crumple to the floor. But at least she was still breathing. When the elevator doors opened again, she took off in a run, feeling like she might fall down with every step.

She made it past an unmarked door, then a set of bathroom

doors, and then, at last, she came to the control room door. She pushed it open and several pairs of eyes shot in her direction, including those belonging to Mike Shur. Mike was Carter's right-hand man. He was big all over and he wore it well. Bailey knew she was safe whenever he was around.

"Is Carter here?" she asked. Her voice was tight and screechy, but she didn't care. The only thing that mattered was that she was alive. She made a move for Carter's door, but Mike stepped away from the wall of monitors and placed himself directly in front of her.

"I can't let you go in there," he said.

She frowned. She hadn't expected Mike to roadblock her. They were friends… sort of. "What do you mean?" she asked.

"Boss's orders," Mike said. He looked like he meant business, which was highly inconvenient, and didn't make one bit of sense. Sure, Mike was supposed to provide a barrier between Carter and the rest of the world, but *she* wasn't the rest of the world. The rules for the general public didn't apply to *her*.

"What do you mean?" she asked again.

"He's busy," Mike said, and he slid a hand inside his suit coat.

Bailey took a step back. She tensed, thinking the worst. And after her encounter with the man in the elevator, who could blame her? "You're not going to shoot me, are you?" she asked, a nervous laugh escaping from her mouth.

Mike gave her a puzzled look and drew his hand out of his coat. He was holding his cell phone. "I gotta take this," he said, and he turned his back to her.

Alrighty then, Bailey thought. Maybe she should take a chill pill.

She waited for Mike for as long as she could, until she heard him say something about a delivery. Then he went over to his desk and began pushing papers around. And that was her cue. She didn't need permission to see Carter. Nothing he could be doing would be off-limits to her. Sure, he'd probably ordered everyone to keep an eye out for her, but that was only because he thought she might be crazy. But she wasn't. And this was her opportunity to prove it. Besides, she had to tell him about the guy in the elevator.

She headed over to Carter's door, ignoring stares and even ignoring Mike when he shouted, "He's not alone."

Chapter Thirteen

As soon as Bailey opened Carter's door, she knew she'd made a mistake. She should have listened to Mike. Special Skills Maria had her feet in Carter's lap, and he was giving her a world class foot rub, looking like he was enjoying it just as much as Maria. Neither of them were aware they had company. Bailey took a step back. The floor creaked as she turned to leave and it was then that Carter and Maria looked and saw her.

"*Hola*, Bailey," Maria said.

"Can I help you?" Carter asked.

"Sorry. I shouldn't be here," Bailey said. She backed the rest of the way out the door and the next thing she knew, she was standing in the taxi line on the sidewalk outside the hotel. She had no idea where she was going, she was just going. Only thing was, she was fifth in line and, Lord help her, she just wanted to get out of there.

Her cell phone rang and she considered ignoring it, but then she saw it was her mom. Her mom was always good for a distraction.

"Hello?" she answered, blinking back tears.

"What do you know about bio-identical hormones?" her mom asked.

Bailey was caught off guard. She couldn't think straight, let alone answer one of her mom's out-there questions right now.

Her mom continued, "I was watching one of those talk shows, you know with doctors and people who have problems, and there was this woman on who was in her sixties, only she looked like she was forty."

Bailey rubbed her temple, trying to fathom what her mom was getting at. "Okay."

"I want to look forty, too," her mom said.

"You do," Bailey told her, hoping a little reassurance was all her mom needed at the moment.

"Well, I won't always. And you know I have reached 'that age.' The mood swings are scary. They might even be dangerous. Especially for your aunt."

Bailey pondered that thought, but seeing as her aunt was there in Las Vegas with her, it didn't seem like an immediate threat. "Can we talk about this when I get home?" she asked. "I was just on my way out into the desert to leave myself for dead."

"Lord," her mother said, sucking in air.

Bailey immediately regretted bringing her mom into her drama. That would do no one any good. Especially her. She laughed it off as best she could. "I'm just kidding. You know me, I'm such a kidder."

"Bailey Margaret Ventura, I do know you," her mother said. "Something is wrong. Is it Elvis? I told you it was bad luck for the groom to see the bride before the wedding."

Bailey heard her mother make a *tsk tsk* sound, because that's *exactly* what she needed to hear right now. She tightened her lips to keep from saying something to her mother that might hurt her feelings. "That only counts if the groom *knows* the bride," she explained.

"Well, for heaven's sake, what does that mean?"

Bailey caught her lip in her teeth. She hadn't wanted to

drop the information about Carter's memory loss in her mom's lap this way, but what choice did she have? It was looking more and more certain that the wedding was off... indefinitely. "I don't think there's going to be a wedding," she said. She could barely hold it together. Tears were all but gushing from her eyes. "I think it's over. I think it's really and truly over. Carter doesn't remember me."

"Don't be silly. It hasn't been that long since you've seen each other," her mom reasoned.

"I'm not being silly. Carter had an accident. He doesn't remember me." The flood gates were all the way open, and Bailey felt stares coming from all the people who were standing in line with her. "I need to go. I'll call you later," she said.

"What about the cake?" her mom asked.

"Cancel it."

"And the flowers?"

"Those too. Cancel everything."

Her mom gasped. "Are you sure? Maybe I should just put them on hold."

"I don't care. Do whatever you want," Bailey said. She disconnected and swallowed a lump in her throat the size of a poker chip. If she didn't get out of there right now, she was going to die!

As her eyes filled with tears again, a uniformed valet signaled the next cab in line and it rolled up to the curb. She got in and told the driver, "Anywhere." But before he had time to put his foot to the pedal, the back door opposite her opened and Mike Shur climbed in.

"Boss told me to come get you," he said.

Boy, if that didn't sound just like Carter, giving orders and making all the rules, while *he* got to break them. "Tell him I'm busy," she said.

"Doing what?"

"Getting some air."

Mike shook his head. "Can't let you do that."

She *hmmfed*. "You said I couldn't go in and see Carter, either, yet I did that!"

"And look where it got you."

Point taken. She slouched against the taxi door and wished she were back in Coupeville being hounded by Mark Jefferson. Only—aargh!—he was here getting his freak on with God knows how many showgirls.

The taxi driver frowned at them in the rear view mirror, and Mike waved him on. "Take me and the lady for a ride. Make it short."

The taxi motored down the Strip for a while, and then veered off in the direction of Nevada's brown hills. Bailey watched the scenery pass by. She didn't even look at Mike, but she could feel his eyes on her and it made her uncomfortable.

"What?" she said at last.

"I heard about the gun incident," Mike said. "That was damn funny, if you ask me."

"Which one?"

"There was more than one?"

"Don't ask." Bailey continued staring out the window, at a blur of Joshua trees and dirt and lifelessness in the form of mounds of dirt. She wondered how many bodies were buried under those mounds. Probably hundreds. Thousands even.

Such thoughts made her shudder. She looked over at Mike for a distraction. He had muscles that reminded her of river rock, and dark features that suggested Mediterranean ancestry. And if she hadn't already been in love with Carter, Mike would be worth a second, maybe even a third, look. But she *was* in love with Carter. Only at the moment, he didn't love her back.

Tears filled her eyes again, and she snagged a tissue from her pocket, silently dabbing them away. She saw no reason to share her pain.

"Sorry about what's going on between you and Boss," Mike said. "I know it's gotta be rough having him not remember you."

"Life is rough," she responded.

"Anything I can do to help?"

Bailey laughed, short and sardonic. "Are you willing to give Carter another knock on the head to make him remember me?"

Mike grinned. "Maybe."

Bailey smiled and it was genuine, the first real smile she'd had since she arrived in Vegas. Her spirits immediately lifted. "Thanks. Your offer is tempting, but I don't think I could bear the idea of Carter being hurt again. And, anyway, I need to deal with this in my own way." Only thing was she was tired of having to deal with all the issues surrounding Carter and Frank Zoopa. Even if Carter regained his memory, what about the next time... and the next? If he could never let what happened to his parents rest, they might never have their happily ever after.

And, too, what if he never regained his memory? Would he and Special Skills Maria pick up where they'd left off? From what she'd seen going on between them in his office, it seemed they might already be picking up.

She sobbed into her tissue, turning her head away from Mike.

"That bad, huh?" Mike said.

She nodded. "It's as bad as it could possibly get. Carter doesn't love me anymore. He loves someone else."

Mike frowned. "If you mean Nikki, you got that all wrong. Nikki and Carter work together. She's a casino host, that's all. Damned attractive, but Carter's not interested in her."

Bailey waved his comment away. "Not Nikki. The other attractive one."

Mike thought for a moment. "Maria?"

Bailey nodded.

He chuckled. "Carter's not interested in her, either. She's not his type."

"She looks like his type," Bailey said, sniffing. "In fact, they look perfect together."

Mike bobbed his head, like he understood exactly what she was talking about. "It's all that black. Black hair, black clothes, black everything... like they share some dark secret."

"Do they?" she asked.

"Used to, I guess."

"What happened?"

"Too much blacktop came between them."

Oh. She let out a loud sob. "I don't exactly live next door."

"Hey, now, don't listen to me," Mike said. "I'm always saying the wrong thing." He tossed an arm around her shoulders and pulled her in tight, and she snuggled up to him, allowing his comfort. And then he kissed her. And she kissed him back. And then she gasped and pulled her lips from his, and he did the same.

"Oh, no. I didn't mean for that to happen," Bailey said. She felt rotten, through and through.

"Boss is gonna kill me," Mike said. His eyes were big, and big drops of sweat beaded on his forehead. "He's gonna have the boys take me out into the desert and put a shot square between my eyes." He wiped the sweat from his forehead, and instructed the taxi driver to turn around and take them back to the casino—pronto!

"I am *so* sorry," Bailey told him.

"Me, too," Mike said. He continued sweating.

Neither of them spoke another word until they got back to The Oasis. As soon as the driver put the taxi in park, Mike had a piece of advice for him. "You utter one word of what happened out there between me and Ms. Ventura and I'll rip that meter off your dash and shove it down your throat."

The taxi driver nodded, and Mike and Bailey got out and the taxi sped away without payment. Bailey didn't blame him.

"Well," Mike said. He shifted uncomfortably from one foot to the other.

"Yeah," Bailey returned, not knowing what else to say.

"Guess I'll go tell Boss I couldn't find you," Mike said. He pointed to one of her eyes. "You got some mascara..."

Bailey wiped under both eyes, and Mike gave his approval.

"Okay, then," he said. "Guess I'll see you later."

"Yeah, later," Bailey repeated. She watched him walk into the casino and then she cringed. Good God, what had she just done?

She felt a pair of eyes on her and she looked and saw an elderly woman giving her the pity smile, like maybe she thought she'd just witnessed the tail end of a lover's quarrel.

"It's complicated," Bailey told the woman, and she turned away and smoothed her hair and wiped her eyes once more. But without a mirror, there was only so much she could do. Just as she was about to go back into the casino, another taxi pulled up to the curb. Bailey couldn't help but notice when a pair of toned, slender legs got out. The legs were followed by an equally slender body. It was Twinkie's.

Crap.

Bailey made a move to escape, but it was too late.

"Bailey? Is that you?"

Bailey turned and faced Twinkie, giving her a weak wave. "It's me."

Twinkie gave Bailey the once-over, and then frowned. "You look like shit. Is this Carter's doing?"

Why deny the obvious? Bailey nodded.

"Nikki?" Twinkie asked.

Bailey shook her head.

"Maria?"

Bailey nodded.

Twinkie frowned. "We'll see about that. I know people who'll bury her out there." She gestured in the direction of the brown hills where Bailey and Mike had just shared an illicit moment. "Just say the word, and I'll make her disappear."

Bailey's eyes opened wide. She didn't know if Twinkie was being serious or just talking, but she wasn't going to chance it. She wanted no part in adding another mound to the Las Vegas desert. "That's okay. I can handle Maria. But thanks for the offer," she told Twinkie.

Twinkie grabbed her by the hand. "Fine. But we're getting this amnesia business straightened out right now."

Bailey pulled her hand away from Twinkie. "I don't think that's a good idea. Carter and I had an argument, and I'm not ready to face him." Besides, she'd just kissed Mike, so who was she to judge Carter when it came to Maria?

"You sure? Cause I know some people," Twinkie said.

"I'm sure you do. But I have a better idea. How about we go nightclubbing?" Bailey suggested. She knew Twinkie couldn't resist a night out partying.

"You got it, sister. I'll take you to a place where we can get our groove on, and you can forget all about Carter and Miss *Thang*." She did a little shimmy, and she and Bailey bumped hips and Bailey knew she was probably in for a late night. Which was just as well. Maybe it would help her forget the kiss she'd just shared with Mike.

Chapter Fourteen

Five hours later, Twinkie dropped Bailey off at her door. Bailey didn't know how Twinkie could still be walking. She'd had three or five Purple Hooter Shooters and Bailey'd had only one. One was enough. She was shit-faced.

"Don't give up on my brother. He'll come around," Twinkie said.

Bailey felt her head nodding, but she couldn't feel her body. It was best that she get into bed.

Two hours later, her body was still numb, but she was awake. She couldn't stop thinking about Carter. She rolled over and rubbed a hand over the empty bed space where Carter would be... if only he were there next to her. "I don't understand," she whispered out loud. "I thought you loved me. I thought you were the love of my life. I wouldn't have slept with you had I known you were just going to become some man I slept with." She thought about that for a minute. "Well, I *might've* slept with you. You *are* hot." She sighed. "And persuasive."

"I know all about persuasiveness," a voice came from the other bed. "God knows, when your uncle wants something, he gets it."

Bailey sucked in air. "Auntie?"

"Yep. It's me. Liza's got a man over there, so I thought it best to make myself scarce."

"What man?"

"I didn't check his I.D."

Bailey heard the sheets in the other bed rustle and a few seconds later her aunt slid under the covers with her.

"Isn't this fun?" Aunt Fiona said. "It's like we're having a slumber party. Maybe we should order room service. Apple pie and ice cream sound good to you?" She reached for the phone.

Bailey was still stuck on the fact that Liza had company, a strange man in her room. "Forget room service, Auntie. Liza kicked you out, so that she could have a sleep-over?"

"I offered to leave. I don't go for that kinky voyeurism stuff. And, anyway, he's not as hunky as your guy, seeing as he hasn't got as much hair. But he's probably good for a couple of songs." Her aunt paused for a thought. "Me and Liza had a girl talk. She told me the temptation down here is fierce, hundreds of half-naked women walking around, plain as day, willing to give their all to the right man. Elvis is probably the right man for a lot of women. He can't be expected to hold out forever." She squeezed Bailey's hand. "I don't have as much experience with men as Liza, but she says your guy probably needs sex every day."

Bailey lay there, wondering what it would be like to be on a deserted island with nothing to do all day but count grains of sand. Heavenly, no doubt. She didn't have as much experience with men as Liza, either, but she didn't need anyone to tell her that Carter was a sexual being who would probably have sex *three* times a day if it was offered to him. And chances were, it was being offered to him this very minute.

"Your uncle Rex and I used to have sex every day," her aunt continued. "That is, until he started driving Lea Thompson around town in his Viper." She clucked her tongue against the roof of her mouth and it made a sound that told Bailey her aunt's uppers were in a glass somewhere taking a rest. "I'll show her," Aunt Fiona said. "That cougar will rue the day she ever messed with my man."

Bailey didn't know how old Lea was, but she was pretty sure Lea was well past cougar age. Even so, her aunt was wrong. Lea wasn't on the prowl, and her Uncle Rex wasn't cheating on his beloved Fiona.

"Don't worry, Auntie. Lea's got nothing on you," Bailey said, meaning it. After a few minutes of quiet, blackness began to close in on her mind. Sleep was but a moment away.

And then the phone rang. Bailey answered it, reluctantly. No telling who might be calling with bad news at this hour.

"Do you think a woman my age needs birth control?" her mom asked, foregoing all opening pleasantries.

Bailey blinked hard and stared into the dark. "Mom, do you know it's the middle of the night?"

"It's morning for me. I don't get much sleep these days," Bailey's mother said. "About that birth control."

Bailey did a mental groan. "Why would you need birth control? I thought you were on the cusp of menopause."

"Tell Olivia to read that book by Suzanne Somers," Aunt Fiona piped in. "She knows all about menopause. And sex, too, I'll bet. Plus, she survived breast cancer. I expect she has something she could tell all of us."

Bailey felt a pressure building inside her brain. It was so intense, like a ginormous pimple that needed squeezing. In her imagination, that's what she did. She squeezed and squeezed and squeezed, until finally she imagined her brains popping out. It was such sweet relief that she groaned.

"Are you okay?" her mom asked. "What's going on there? For the love of God, tell me you're not having sex right there in front of your aunt!"

Bailey snapped back to the here and now. "Of course, I'm not having sex in front of Auntie. Jeez. Could we talk about sex and birth control when I get home?"

"When will that be?"

"Soon."

"How soon?"

"I don't know how soon, Mom. Just soon," Bailey said.

"Let me talk to her," Aunt Fiona said. "I'll set her straight." She grabbed the phone from Bailey. "Here's the deal, Olivia. Elvis has jumped ship. Skipped town. Said adios, señorita. He got himself a case of swivel-butt and decided to swivel his butt right outta getting married."

Great. Bailey listened to her auntie setting her mother straight. Her auntie meant well, but she wasn't helping. She took back the phone. "Mom?"

"Yes, sweetie... I was thinking, if Elvis doesn't remember you and you take up with that Jefferson boy again, you might as well kill me. Better yet, I'll move to Kalamazoo."

And there it was. The Kalamazoo threat. Not that Bailey for one minute believed her mom would ever really move there. But what if she did? What if she truly believed that old guy she'd been trading text messages with was the real deal, and what if they were planning on running away together?

Bailey felt a moment of cold panic. She had to do something. No way in hell was she about to let her mom hook up with that geriatric Elvis wannabe.

"Mom?"

"Yes, dear?"

"You're not actually planning on sleeping with that old Elvis guy, are you? I mean, what do you even know about him?" Not that it was an immediate concern, considering she'd, just yesterday, seen him down in the casino.

"Well! What *don't* I know?" her mom asked with that impatient tone people get whenever they're talking about something that should be crystal clear. "Everything about him is readily available on the Internet. And, of course, there have been dozens of books written over the years. The poor man has no privacy." Then she lowered her voice to a whisper. "Course, he's managed to keep some things private."

"And some things are better kept private," Bailey said. "I'm hanging up now. We'll discuss this when I get home." She clicked off and Aunt Fiona jerked her head up.

"I think if Olivia and Elvis do the deed, he should wear a condom," she said. "I read something recently about one out of every two people having the HPV virus."

"I'm going to sleep now," Bailey said, and she turned over. And for the next two hours, she stared into the dark. No way was she going to get any sleep after a conversation like she'd just had with her mom.

But she did, and then at seven a.m., she sat straight up and looked over at her auntie's bed. It was empty. She listened for any sounds to indicate she needn't wonder what kind of trouble her auntie might have already found. She heard the shower running in the bathroom and her mind was set at ease.

After chugging a glass of water, Bailey went to the mini-bar to look for something to snack on. The only thing available was a half dozen miniature bottles of alcohol. They'd been cleaned out. Bailey suspected it was an inside job. Hungry for something other than a vodka miniature, she ordered room service—two bowls of fresh berries topped with whipped cream and a drizzle of chocolate. Breakfast perfection!

Aunt Fiona finished doing whatever it was she did for her morning bathroom routine, and then she came out and sat over by the window in the sun, letting it heat her old bones. She had a white towel wrapped turban-style around her head and another towel wrapped around her age-ravaged body. Bailey had never given it much thought, but now, seeing her aunt sitting there, all loose skin and bones, she considered how cool it would be if scientists found a cure for old age by the time she got to be all loose skin and bones.

Breakfast arrived and it was all that Bailey needed to start her day. She and her aunt shared quiet small talk, and then Bailey left her aunt unguarded while she went to the bathroom to perform her own morning routine. It was a risk, but she knew if she had a shower and clean hair, she'd feel a lot better physically, as well as mentally. She needed to clear her head and gain a new perspective on the situation with Carter. She couldn't let herself get caught up worrying about maybes that might not be anything at all. So what if she'd caught Carter with another woman's foot in his lap? That didn't mean a thing. According to Twinkie, he and Maria were just friends. Period.

Now, if only she could make herself believe that.

Full belly and clean all over, it was time to check in next door. Bailey couldn't believe Liza would risk having a strange man sleep over. Talk about poor judgment.

She knocked and listened at the adjoining door. She heard nothing and it made the hair on the back of her neck stand on end. What if Liza was in her room all tied up... and not in a good way?

Bailey considered just opening the door—she doubted it was locked. Then again, what if Liza still had company? That would be plain embarrassing.

She knocked again and waited another half a minute. Then she couldn't wait any longer. Liza might need her help.

Bailey's hand was on the doorknob. She was ready to turn it. But then the door swung open.

"Hey, Bailey, what's up? I was just coming to see what you and your auntie had planned for the day." Liza stood there in a cloud of pink and dazzling white. Every shiny blond hair on her head was in place and her morning smile was so bright, Bailey completely forget all the gruesome images that had been filling her head. So much for worrying. But now that she knew Liza hadn't been murdered in her sleep, she had something she needed to say.

"Auntie said you had a man spend the night with you," she began their conversation.

Liza smiled, unashamed. "He's long gone." She went over to a small dining table and poured herself a glass of orange juice.

Bailey followed her into her room. "I can see that." She

hated that Liza wasn't taking this seriously. She wished Liza would understand, and believe, that sometimes bad things happened to good people. "I was worried about you," she told Liza.

"Worried?" Liza set her juice on the table and moved over to the bed. She sat on the edge and went to work smearing Aveeno peach-scented body lotion over her legs.

"You know, I try to keep my opinion to myself when it comes to your personal life," Bailey said.

"Rarely, but go ahead."

"You take too many risks. This isn't Coupeville."

Liza gave a little laugh. "I know, this is Sin City, land of evil doers and ne'er do wells."

Bailey frowned, frustrated at Liza's flippancy. "I don't know why I bother. You're one of those people who refuse to listen until the worst happens."

Liza stopped smearing on lotion and regarded Bailey seriously. "Okay, Miss Sunshine. If you must know, Peter and I *didn't* sleep together. Not even close. I invited him up here so we could talk. I was sick of inhaling second-hand cigarette smoke and hearing the ding, ding, ding of slot machines."

"I find that hard to believe," Bailey said.

"Well, it's true. Even I have my limits."

"Okay, so I'm glad you didn't do *that*," Bailey said. She looked at the bed. "And I'm sorry for thinking the worst. Still, he could have been a weirdo."

"Probably was, but I'd spent the entire evening with him and he hadn't let his fangs show, so I thought I'd take the chance. I told him I was exploring career opportunities here."

Bailey raised an eyebrow. The only kind of career opportunities she could see for Liza in Las Vegas were either working as a showgirl or for an escort service. "What kind of opportunities? And why? Are you planning to move here?"

"Not unless my best friend does," Liza said. "Peter's in real estate. In case you haven't heard, the market is picking up and I told him I might be interested in selling homes. I also wanted to get some information out of him." She grinned wickedly. "You know that house you and Carter were looking at a couple months ago?"

Bailey nodded. "I'm in love with that house."

"Sadly, it sold."

Bailey let out a small gasp. "Correction. I loved that house."

Liza smiled. "Don't worry. You can still love that house. Carter was the buyer."

Bailey's heart skipped a beat. If that was true, it could only mean one thing. That Carter had really intended on going through with their wedding.

"And you know what else I found out?" Liza asked.

"What?"

"Carter will be there today. He's supposed to be looking everything over, making up a list of repairs that are needed."

Bailey put a hand to her mouth. She wanted to squeal she was so happy.

"The way I see it, there's no reason you couldn't go there and have some quality, alone time with him—no interruptions."

"In other words, you and Elvis could have sex without maid service busting in on you," Aunt Fiona chimed in from the adjoining doorway.

Chapter Fifteen

Sex with Carter. It wasn't that Bailey hadn't been thinking about it for the past twenty-four hours. But she and Carter had made absolutely no progress in regards to getting his memory back. Still, she wasn't one to let an opportunity pass her by when it was tossed in her lap.

Feeling downright giddy, Bailey made her way to the parking garage. Liza had agreed to aunt-sit again, so no worries there, and Mike Shur from Control had lent her his car. He'd met her on the gaming floor to hand off his keys and neither of them mentioned their kissing indiscretion, which seemed best. Better to forget the kiss had ever happened.

Mike's car was a late model Camaro, and Bailey had no trouble finding it. With all the chrome and a bright, shiny new paint job, it stood out like a beacon for the lost. Mike had done a first-rate job fixing up his old car.

Bailey got in, fired up the engine, and off she rumbled. The car garnered admiring looks all the way down the Strip, mostly from younger guys who were interested in seeing who had the "badder" vehicle. They revved their engines and made a lot of noise, trying to entice Bailey, but she wasn't interested. She

kept her eyes focused straight ahead. She was on a mission—
to get to Carter.

Once free of the traffic congestion, she relaxed and
loosened her grip on the steering wheel. She glanced briefly at
the dash and found all kinds of buttons to push and knobs to
turn. She didn't dare touch any of them. Mike had given her
stern warning, "Unless you want to turn the car into a rocket,
and launch yourself down the road at warp speed, keep your
mitts off."

It was a no-brainer. She didn't intend to put her mitts
anywhere near those shiny buttons. All she cared about was
that the car had four wheels and a full tank of gas. Air-
conditioning was optional. She had a nice breeze going simply
by opening a window. In fact, she was happy to have some
real heat. Coming from the Pacific Northwest, heat was
something of a rarity at this time of year.

Five minutes out of town and the *real* heat got *real* hot. The
landscape had changed drastically, from neon lights and
people o'plenty to an occasional sighting of a Joshua tree and
mile after mile of dry, cracked earth. She reconsidered the
need for air-conditioning. Or maybe just an oxygen mask.
She'd forgotten how physical the desert heat could be, almost
claustrophobic, and she was already feeling boxed in.

She looked down at the speedometer. It said she was going
sixty-five. But how about eighty-five? The road was clear and
dry, the sun was out, probably no highway patrol anywhere in
the vicinity. She pressed down on the gas pedal, and the
Camaro eased forward, taking only a couple of seconds to
reach the desired goal.

The boost in speed gave Bailey a sense of freedom, like
nothing could touch her. Hot air still surrounded her, but it was a
windy hot. If eighty-five felt this good, how about ninety-five?
She pushed down on the gas pedal and before she could blink, the
indicator fluttered at ninety. That was fast enough. She was at the
point now where any wrong move could be her last. She smiled at
the fun of how going so fast made her heart race.

"*Whee!*" said a voice from the backseat. "This is better than the roller coaster ride at New York, New York!"

Bailey jumped, nearly hitting her head on the roof of the car. She immediately lifted her foot from the gas pedal, slowing the Camaro to a mere sixty, just for safety's sake. She peered into the rear view mirror and was dumbfounded to see her aunt staring back at her. "Auntie? What are you doing back there?"

"I'm riding shotgun," Aunt Fiona said.

Bailey cut a look to the back seat, half expecting to actually see a shotgun lying next to her aunt. The seat was empty, but that didn't make her feel any better. Her aunt could have a shotgun hidden in her bag. It was one of those oversized jobs that could carry anything and everything, including the kitchen sink.

"What are you looking for?" Aunt Fiona asked.

"A shotgun."

"I was exaggerating," Aunt Fiona said. "But I do have an old pistol." She pulled a gun with an extra long barrel from her purse and took aim out the window at a passing cactus. She made *bang, bang* sounds, then drew the gun back inside and blew on the end of it.

Bailey nearly drove off the road. "Please tell me that thing is not real!"

"Sorry, sunshine. It's as real as it gets." Aunt Fiona held the long-barrel up so Bailey could get a good look. "It's a beaut, ain't it? I found it at an old west display in Sam's Town. Cowboys back then were real bad dudes. Not like the cowboys today, who ride those fake bulls and fall off onto foam pads, so they don't get bruised."

Bailey searched her memory. She couldn't think of a time her aunt had ever gone to Sam's Town. But maybe she'd gone with Liza. "Carter said no more guns," she reminded her aunt.

"No more *wooden* guns," Aunt Fiona clarified.

"I don't think so," Bailey said. "And now we've got to get that thing back to its owner."

"I don't think its owner cares one hoot. He's long dead."

Bailey frowned at her aunt in the rear view mirror. "Where's Liza? She was supposed to be keeping an eye on you. And I thought you wanted to give me some alone-time with Carter."

"I gave Liza the slip. I decided you might need some assistance with Elvis."

Lord. That's all she needed. Bad enough that her auntie was probably going to be arrested for stealing a museum artifact, but if Carter saw her with another gun, that was going to be it. He'd never even give either of them a chance to explain. "Tell you what, Auntie, you give me the gun, and I'll keep it up here with me for safekeeping." She was hoping for an easy bargain.

Just like that, her aunt handed her the gun.

Bailey narrowed her eyes. That was too easy. "What gives?"

"I'm thinking you need that gun worse than I do," Aunt Fiona said. "That Elvis of yours has turned out to be a real scoundrel. It's a shame. Me and your mom were looking forward to welcoming him into the family." She sniffed and set her uppers on the edge of her gums.

"Oh, Auntie, you don't have to worry about Carter. He's just having a little problem with his memory... the way you do sometimes."

Aunt Fiona let her teeth settle back into place. "Just make sure you keep that gun where you can grab it quick. No sense in having a weapon if it ain't handy."

Bailey shoved the gun under her seat... far, far out of her aunt's reach.

A couple more miles down the road and she took the Calico Ridge exit off I-215. She entered a quiet development that had winding streets and large stucco homes that were all of similar architectural design. They all had similar vegetation, too, which made it hard for Bailey to remember which house was the one she'd looked at with Carter. But then she remembered the one thing that had made it stick out from all the others. It was a magenta-colored bougainvillea that grew up one corner of the house and across the front of an iron balcony, off the master suite. She'd thought it a super romantic setting to be able to see the brightly-colored flowers through the French doors.

She drove slowly, negotiating the Camaro through the neighborhood. It was eerily quiet, pretty much deserted. No kids, no animals. No nothing. Not a surprise, considering the heat. It was a deterrent for most outdoor activity.

Eventually, she saw it—the bougainvillea. And its color was even more vibrant than before, like the hues you might see in a waning summer sky.

She smiled and pulled over to the curb and just sat there a moment, looking and daydreaming about the day she and Carter would be husband and wife living there in their mauve-colored palace. It wasn't really a palace, but Carter had always made her feel like she was his queen. And he was certainly her king.

"Would you look at that?" Aunt Fiona said. "Elvis must have a visitor. With those white stripes, that car almost looks like Rex's Viper."

Bailey had been so caught up in her daydream, she hadn't even noticed the strange car. It was sitting alongside Carter's silver Porsche. And it wasn't a Viper. It was a Mustang. Bright blue, with big white letters that spelled MUSTANG all the way down the side.

This was unexpected. Bailey made no move to get out of the Camaro. She sat and stared and wondered what to do… leave, or be a big girl and go see who Carter had for company. Her heart sank a little, thinking the worst, that he might be inside with Special Skills Maria. Probably giving her another foot rub.

She did a little deep breathing to try and snap herself out of her foolishness. She didn't want to be one of those women, though it seemed she already was.

Frustrated with herself, she finally opened the door of the

Camaro. "Do you want to come in with me?" she asked her aunt.

"It's always best to stay out of domestic squabbles," Aunt Fiona said. She nodded in the direction of a large palm in the front yard. "I'll be over there, in the shade. Take your time."

"There isn't going to be a squabble," Bailey assured her. "Carter and I need to talk, but if he has company, I'll just fill up my water bottle, and we'll be on our way." She grabbed her half empty bottle from the passenger seat. "If you get too warm, please come inside."

"I wouldn't dream of interrupting. I'll take a little nap while I wait for you and Elvis to take care of business," Aunt Fiona said. She waggled her eyebrows.

Bailey ignored the waggle. It was pointless to try and explain to her aunt that she and Carter wouldn't be engaging in *that* kind of business. They both got out of the Camaro, and Aunt Fiona hustled into the shade of the tree, while Bailey made a beeline for the porch. Pausing in the glaring sun was not an option. The result could be heat stroke or worse.

Bailey paused at the front door and wondered if she should knock. She had every right to be there. This was going to be her house, too.

So why did she feel like an intruder?

She glanced over her shoulder at her aunt. Instead of taking a nap, she was busy with *Taber's Medical Dictionary*. The idea that her auntie wanted to become a healer made her smile. But it was also scary, and Bailey understood completely why her mother was concerned.

Bailey turned back to the door, ready for whatever she might find inside. If Carter had a visitor, she'd just slip in, fill her bottle, and then slip right back out. No awkward moments. Probably he'd never even know she was there. And, certainly, he wouldn't expect her to take her auntie back out into the desert without sufficient water.

She wiped the back of her neck and her forehead. She wasn't sure if it was the heat or the idea of seeing Carter that had her in such a state, but it didn't matter. Ready or not, she was going in.

She tried the door and found it unlocked. She nudged it open on a prayer—*Please, don't let me hear voices. But if I do, please don't let them be of the moaning and groaning variety.*

She tiptoed in and heard nothing but quiet. Other than the quiet, the first thing she noticed was the smell of fresh paint, which brought her a measure of comfort. Carter must have been in the process of getting the house ready for her. They'd talked about painting. She only hoped he remembered the colors she'd pointed out when they'd gone to the hardware store.

She took a few steps down the hallway and poked her head into the living room. She smiled, seeing that Carter *had* remembered. The walls, once drab off-white, were now a cool mint green. It was refreshing and brought a clean calmness to the room.

Bailey felt silly all over again for having ever thought Carter would do something as sinister as faking his amnesia. She vowed to never again think such thoughts.

Her gaze strayed across the room to the wine bar, where two empty wine glasses sat. She crossed over to the bar and saw a film of coral-colored lipstick smudged along the rim of one glass. She tried not to let her imagination run wild. Carter was a grown man. He could have a friend over for a glass of wine. Even if that friend was a woman.

She made her way back down the hallway, doing a reasonably good job of keeping her thoughts positive. Until she heard noises coming from the kitchen. Then her imagination revved back into high gear. The kitchen had an unusually large center island. She had to take a look. She tiptoed over and peered around the wall and yikes! Carter and Nikki Amsterdam were going at it, kissing!

Stumbling back into the hallway, Bailey had only one thought on her mind. She had to get out of there, pronto! To hell with filling her water bottle. If she and her auntie needed something to drink, she'd stop and stab a cactus for its nectar.

She dropped the bottle and made her way to the door. Her fingers were so sweaty she couldn't get a grip on the handle. While she fumbled, she heard footsteps coming up behind her. She knew it was Carter. He grabbed her just as she got the door open.

"What are you doing here?" he asked, swinging her around. "I thought we talked and agreed you wouldn't follow me anymore."

Bailey had no idea what to say. It certainly could appear that she was following him. She felt her eyes fill with tears. She tried yanking her arm from his grip, but he held tight. "Let me go. I have a plane to catch," she said. She was frantic to get out of there. More than anything, she did not want Carter to see her cry.

"We need to talk," he said, ignoring her plea.

"Let me go!" she said again, and with a fierce tug, pulled her arm free. She practically sprinted to Mike's Camaro, calling over her shoulder to her aunt on the way, "C'mon, Auntie. It's time to go."

At the car door, she stuffed her hand into her pocket for the key. It wasn't there. *Crap!* She must have dropped it when she dropped the water bottle.

Chapter Sixteen

Bailey thumped her head on the car door. What had she ever done to deserve this? She was a good person and a good daughter—mostly—except when she pooh-poohed her mom's Elvis disappearance theory. She was a good friend, too. After all, how many friends did Liza have who were secure enough in their shortcomings that they would accompany her to a swimming pool?

She looked back at the house. Carter was standing on the front porch, arms crossed over his chest. His eyes were like steel and he was wearing his mad face. He also had a key dangling from one finger.

"You won't get far without this," he said. He came down off the porch toward her.

Bailey looked over at her aunt, who was still under the tree, perusing *Taber's*. She was oblivious. Either that or she was sticking by her rule of not getting involved in a domestic squabble.

As Carter approached, Bailey backed up against the Camaro. "I'm not in the mood to talk. Just give me the key," she told him.

"You were in the mood to talk yesterday. And I doubt you came all this way just to say 'hi'."

Bailey frowned. "I've changed my mind. I don't think I ever want to talk to you again."

"Because you saw me kissing Nikki?" Carter asked. "If you'd listened to me and gone home when I told you to, none of this would be happening."

"Are you saying it's *my* fault you were in there kissing that woman?"

"Not at all," Carter said. He cut a look in Aunt Fiona's direction. "Let's go inside, where we can talk in private."

Bailey hefted her chin. "I'm fine right where I am. Besides, how much privacy will we have in there, where your girlfriend is?"

"Doesn't matter. It's hotter than Hades, and I'm not going to stand out here and cook." Carter grabbed her by the hand, and half-led, half-dragged her back into the house. They bypassed the kitchen and the living room and went farther down the hall to a large room they'd once talked about using for entertaining guests. Bailey had envisioned gala events with live music and dancing all night long, until they retired to their bedroom for a long night of romance. Now all she envisioned was the man she loved kissing another woman.

So much for romance.

Car tires squealed out front and she didn't need to look to know that it was Nikki, taking off in the Mustang. Carter didn't flinch.

She looked up at him through a haze of tears. "Why would you kiss another woman in our house?"

Carter looked pained, like he truly regretted hurting her. Or maybe it was that he regretted getting caught. She didn't know which, but now she had that image of Carter and Nikki kissing in her head and she just wanted to get away from there.

"I don't know what you want to hear," he said. "I don't remember this being our house. I just know I bought it and I've been spending time here fixing it up." He thumbed a tear from under one of her eyes and pulled her close. His breath was warm on her cheek and she found comfort in his arms.

"I want to hear that you love me. And that you remember me." Fat tears spilled from her eyes. "Don't you? Don't you remember anything about me? Coupeville... my dogs, Tucker and Maggie May? And what about my mom? She adores you. *I* adore you. How could you forget us, like we meant nothing to you?"

Carter gazed at her, his blue eyes unwavering. Then he kissed her, full mouth, with plenty of body contact. And Bailey wanted nothing more than to give in and kiss him back... but not until he explained why he'd kissed Miss Perfect Eyelashes.

She pulled her lips from his. "Let go of me."

He tightened his grip. "This is what you wanted, right? For us to do something that might spark my memory?"

"I'll scream. Your neighbors will think you're an axe murderer."

He chuckled. "Have at it. They'll just think I've got some Elvis groupie over here who's gettin' her freak on."

Anger flashed through her. "Is that what you've been doing while I've been away, entertaining groupies?"

He gave her a *c'mon* look. "What do you think?"

"I don't know what to think. I'm not even sure I ever knew you."

They stood there, neither one of them giving up. Carter's grip was firm and Bailey hated that she was enjoying every minute of him having his hands on her. Hot air rushed through the house, through the open front door, blowing loose strands of hair across her face. One of them stuck to her bottom lip and Carter brushed it away. And then he snapped her hair band, releasing her ponytail so that her hair fell freely about her shoulders. The action stirred Bailey's emotions. That was exactly the kind of move *her* Carter would have made, not this strange man who'd just kissed her.

A cell phone buzzed in Carter's pocket and he pulled it out and checked caller I.D., then he disappeared into another room to take the call.

Bailey wanted to scream. She was more confused than ever. Every time she thought she knew what was what, Carter did something to make her wonder if he was faking his memory loss.

Carter answered his cell phone with an annoyed "hello." It was Twinkie calling and he wasn't in any mood to deal with any issues she had right now. Not when he had Bailey and *her* issues waiting in the other room.

"What have you done?" Twinkie began their conversation.

"Can you be more specific? I don't know what you're talking about," Carter said.

"Right. And it's not a hundred freaking degrees out, either," Twinkie raged.

"A hundred and ten, but who's counting?"

"So freaking what! I'm not calling about the weather. I'm calling to tell you you've gone too far."

Carter saw Bailey glance in his direction and he edged farther into the kitchen. "What happened, did you get your curling iron stuck in your hair?" he asked Twinkie.

"Very funny. Are you going to take this seriously, or not?"

"Get to the point and maybe I will."

Twinkie let out a heavy breath. "Someone carved a kidney out of a guest over at the Phoenix. Jesus, Carter, have you got a death wish? Frank will have us all killed."

Carter rubbed a hand over his face. "Christ." Just what he needed right now, Zoopa on the warpath.

"Yeah, Christ. You're just lucky that guest will survive. Whoever cut into her was kind enough to leave her in a tub of ice. But sure as shit, she's gonna sue, and who do you think Frank's gonna blame for this? Goddamn it, Carter, you've really done it this time."

"Calm down. I've done nothing. Did you ever think maybe Zoopa has other enemies besides me?"

"Yeah, but you're the only one with balls enough to do

something this crazy."

"Honey, I have many talents, but performing surgical procedures isn't one of them."

Twinkie scoffed. "Like you'd let that stop you. God, Carter, I'm afraid to even leave my room."

"Then don't. Stay put while I sort this out." He disconnected and muttered a curse meant for just one person—Doctor Maria Cruz. Figuring out her involvement in this couldn't be any easier. Her *abuela* needed a kidney, and who better to perform surgery in a hotel room without the usual hospital amenities than a woman so highly adept with a knife?

The back of Carter's neck bristled. Twinkie was right. Zoopa wasn't about to let whoever did this get away with it. A shit storm was about to rain down on Vegas. And that meant Bailey had to leave town immediately. He wouldn't be able to relax until she was back home, safe and sound, in quiet little Coupeville. He glanced back over to where she'd been standing and saw her backside as she went out the door. Great—if she was going to the airport. If not, he had a mind to put her on a plane himself and handcuff her to a first-class seat. The last thing he needed right now was for her to get caught up in the middle of this business with Zoopa.

He headed for the front door and caught a whiff of Bailey's perfume—Giorgio. Of course he remembered that scent. He also remembered the taste of Bailey's lips, the feel of her hair, and the way she fit just so in his arms. He hadn't gotten everything back—a lot of his memories surrounding her were still fuzzy around the edges—but the pieces were slowly coming together. So when Peter Nichols, from Las Vegas Realty, called and told him that a woman named Liza Blair had been asking about the house, he knew the odds were better than fifty-fifty that Bailey would show up there today, hoping they could talk. But he didn't want to talk. He wanted her to go home, which is why he'd staged that kiss with Nikki. He only hoped it was enough to drive Bailey back to Seattle. Only now, he felt like a shit for hurting her so.

Bailey was tired of waiting for Carter. She stepped back outside to check on her aunt and saw her splayed out on the grass, mouth open, with no perceptible rise and fall of her chest. Bailey was beyond alarmed. For one terrifying second, she was afraid her aunt might've suffered heat stroke. She rushed over and grabbed her aunt's wrist to feel for a pulse. It was there, steady as ever. "Auntie! Are you all right?" she called out. She'd never forgive herself if something had happened to her auntie while she was inside with Carter.

Her aunt stirred and pulled her arm away. "I had a dream," she said. "That Zoopa fella was in it, and he was causing you all kinds of problems." She narrowed her eyes and looked thoughtful. "He's a rat fink. Someone needs to teach him a lesson."

"Maybe so," Bailey said. "But it's not going to be you. Besides, we don't have to worry about that man anymore. We're going home." She helped her aunt to her feet, and they were making quick pace to the Camaro when the front door of the house swung open.

Carter stepped outside and saw them and his face took on a dark cast. "I'm taking you back to the casino," he said. "You're getting on a plane back to Seattle. Don't argue with me."

"I'm not going anywhere with you," Bailey told him. She swept her hand in the direction of Mike's Camaro. "As you can see, I have my own transportation."

Carter gave Mike's car a scant glance. He came down off the porch and steered her over to the car door and practically shoved her inside. "Buckle up," he said. And then he looked over at Bailey's aunt, but she was already buckled in. "Don't make me regret not taking you to the airport myself," he told Bailey, and then he turned and went back into the house.

Bailey fumed. She could practically feel steam coming out her ears. The *nerve*. Did he really think she was going to let him order her around after she'd just caught him kissing another woman? She reached inside her purse for the car key, but Carter hadn't given it back to her!

"Damn it!" she said. She groaned and felt a tear—or maybe it was a drop of sweat—roll down her cheek. "Auntie, I have to go back inside the house for a minute."

"Okay, cupcake. I'll be right over there, under that tree again." Her aunt climbed out of the car once more and headed back across the yard.

Bailey hurried to the porch and pushed through the door. She looked in the kitchen for Carter, but he was nowhere in sight. She listened and could hear him talking on his cell phone, down the hall in another room. He didn't sound happy.

She tiptoed into the kitchen, hoping for a miracle. Luck was on her side. Carter had left the key on the counter. She grabbed it, and was just going for the door when Carter's voice boomed like thunder down the hallway. She let out a little shriek and watched as an object flew past and crashed against the wall. The object broke into a hundred tiny pieces, and looked like it might have been Carter's cell phone.

Carter appeared two seconds later. They stared at each other for a moment, and then the front door crashed open. It was Aunt Fiona, and she was positioned in the doorway with both hands wrapped around the hand piece of the long-barrel she'd "picked up" in Sam's Town.

Bailey screamed, and Carter held his hands up, shouting, "Whoa, whoa, whoa!" He dodged to one side, grabbed Bailey and pushed her down to the floor, then covered her with his own body.

Carter was heavy. He'd definitely put on a couple of pounds. Bailey felt like the breath was being squeezed out of her. Her cheek was pressed to the floor and she could feel Carter's heart beating against her back. Then, as quickly as it began, it was over. Aunt Fiona had gotten startled when Carter knocked Bailey to the floor. She'd dropped the gun and Carter quickly grabbed it. He helped Bailey to her feet, and then he stepped back, putting some distance between himself and Bailey and her aunt. Bailey could hardly blame him. She wanted to put some distance between herself and this entire day.

She watched in silence as Carter paced. She knew he was trying to regain some sense of control, but his face was the color of the bougainvillea out front and she was afraid he might stroke out. After a minute, he seemed to stabilize and he just stood there staring at the gun, turning it over and over in his hand. He finally gave a low whistle.

"This is real," he said. "And old. Mid-1800's, I'd say. Double-action, full-fluted cylinder. Clean, too." He looked over at Aunt Fiona. "Where did you get this?"

"She found it," Bailey said, ready to defend her aunt.

"Not out in the desert," Carter countered.

"How do you know?" Bailey asked.

"Like I said, it's clean. Too clean. This gun hasn't been lying out in the sand for the last hundred and fifty years, waiting to be found. My guess is this gun belonged to an outlaw at one time. Now it belongs in a museum." He cocked an eyebrow at Bailey. "Care to explain?"

Of course. It's what she lived for. Only she had nothing for him, the Fifth and all, so she pressed her lips together and kept quiet.

But Carter wasn't going for the silent bit. He turned to her auntie. "What is it with you and guns?" he asked. "And what were you thinking, busting in here like that?"

Aunt Fiona's eyes narrowed into little slits. "I was thinking my niece needed protection. God knows I don't want to go down in history as being the person who shot Elvis, but I'd do it if I had to."

Carter was quiet for a long few seconds, looking like he couldn't decide whether to laugh or cuss. Eventually, he got it together. "Why would you think Bailey needed protection?"

"She screamed. She doesn't scream for much, not even when she gets a flu shot—though I did hear about how she let loose one night when she was out with that Mark Jefferson..."

"Okay," Bailey said, holding up a hand. "That's enough.

Carter doesn't want to hear all that." Besides, no telling how much the story had changed over the course of time.

"I told you no more guns," Carter said to Bailey's aunt.

"You said no more *wooden* guns," Aunt Fiona corrected him.

"I said no more *guns. Period.* Plastic, rubber, wooden, *real. None.*"

Bailey moved closer to her aunt. "There's no need to be so harsh with her. She didn't mean any harm."

"She was going to *shoot* me. You think that wouldn't cause me any *harm*?"

"But she didn't," Bailey reasoned. Carter stared at her for a long minute, probably trying to assess who might be crazier, she or her aunt. She knew his plight and felt bad that he was having to deal with all this, but her auntie was old and, well... her auntie. Which meant that no one, not even the love of her life, was going to be mean to her.

Carter's forehead finally relaxed, and the grim lines around his mouth softened. "All right," he said. "Will you at least tell me where this gun came from?"

Bailey looked at her aunt. Her aunt's mouth was pinched closed. "Go ahead, Auntie. Tell Carter where you got the gun."

Aunt Fiona grinned. "I lifted it off an old West display in Sam's Town. I saw an opportunity and I took it. I guess that makes me a thief. Are you going to cuff me?" She held out her hands in front of her.

Carter's mouth twitched, like he was amused, though Bailey thought he was doing a pretty good job of hiding it. "No," he said, "I'm not going to cuff you, or have you arrested. But I want you to be on a plane out of here tonight. *All* of you."

"What do you mean, *all* of us?" Bailey asked.

"You, your aunt, *and* your friends." He looked at his watch. "I need to get back to town, so I need for you and your aunt to get out of here. Now. Get packed, and be at the airport in two hours."

"My friends don't have anything to do with this," Bailey protested. "And none of us have tickets."

"You all purchased one-way tickets when you came down from Seattle?"

Bailey shrugged. "I didn't know how long I'd be staying. And I have supportive friends." She could tell she was testing Carter's patience. His face had taken on a stony glare.

"Fine. Don't worry about tickets. Just get yourself, your aunt, *and* your friends to the airport," he reiterated. "I'll take care of the rest. I don't want to see you again. I mean it." He paused and softened his tone. "I'm sorry this hasn't turned out the way you'd hoped. But I don't remember you, and you have to listen to me. Go home. If by chance anything changes, I'll be in touch."

Bailey couldn't believe it. Just like that, he was saying good-bye? A sob filled her throat. "Are you sure?"

"Positive," Carter said.

Aunt Fiona leaned and whispered in Bailey's ear. "I always knew he was a punk, wearing black all the time and talking all smooth like he has the answer to every woman's question."

Bailey had no idea know what question her aunt was referring to, but at the moment, she wasn't in any mood to argue the point. She wanted to get as far away from Carter as possible. Home sounded real good right now. She grabbed her aunt's hand and pulled her along behind her out to the car.

Chapter Seventeen

Carter pushed his Porsche to the limit and rolled onto the Strip in record time. He forged his way through the throngs of guests and made it to the elevator without incident. Either no one was out gunning for him yet, or Frank Zoopa was still undecided about how he wanted to deal with one of his guests losing a kidney.

Carter took the elevator up to the eleventh floor and knocked on Maria's door. He didn't wait for her to answer. His knock was merely a formality to alert her of his arrival.

She was standing with her back to him, staring out the window, arms folded across her chest. He spun her around and, for a brief second, thought he saw fear. But that was impossible. Maria Cruz wasn't afraid of anything. He brushed off the look on her face as regret for having done something that might have serious repercussions for all of them.

"Why'd you do it?" he asked.

"I would love a martini. How about you?" Maria moved over to a wet bar and began mixing herself a drink.

"I think you've had enough to drink. Or maybe you're high on something." He stepped over next to her. "What the hell have you done, Maria?"

She shrugged. "My *abuela* needed a kidney. I found one."

"Jesus, you're not even going to deny it. Just like that, you cut open a body and carve out a piece to take home to Grandma?"

Maria's mouth curved into a tight smile. "Something like that."

"That's a little extreme, even for you, isn't it?"

She sipped her drink, saying nothing.

Carter paused, thinking. "I may not be a doctor, but I do know that kidneys aren't one size fits all. How did you know that woman's kidney would work for your grandmother?"

"It just so happens, I *am* a doctor. And that gives me special powers." She chewed and swallowed an olive garnish. "And, anyway, I thought you liked my *abuela*. You should be happy. She will live, and Frank Zoopa will be ruined."

"Don't kid yourself. He won't be ruined. Not by any means. He might be wounded, but he'll bounce back and he'll be out to even the score. If I know him, he's already putting together a plan to take care of everyone he thinks might be involved."

"You exaggerate, *mijo*."

"You don't know the man."

"No. Not like you. But I am not afraid of him."

"You should be."

Maria's brown eyes were unwavering. Her lips twisted. "What would you have me do, wait until it is too late to help my *abuela*? The list is long. This way, we can all stand back and watch Zoopa's empire crumble."

"I'd rather see him lying face down in the desert, like he left me."

Her eyes sparked. "So, you remember. It *was* Zoopa."

"Never mind that," Carter said. He wasn't in any mood to get into his episode in the desert with her. "What about the woman? No apologies for what you did to her?"

"She will be paid."

Carter bristled. He uttered a curse and moved across the living room over to the window. He looked out at the sun, high in the sky, so blue it was purple. Down below on the sidewalk, people moved along at a brisk pace, busy having a good time. Busy living, the same as what Maria's grandmother could now do. He couldn't blame Maria for wanting to help her, but doing something this drastic made no sense.

He turned back to her. "This thing you did... it doesn't fit you. It's not your style."

"How would you know what my style is? You and I, we were finished almost before we got started. And it's been a long time since we shared... styles." Her bottom lip began to tremble, but she caught herself and made it stop.

He couldn't believe Maria's feelings for him had ever been that strong. She'd been so adamant about going back to South Carolina, back to her family and her job. He tipped her chin up. "It was you who chose to say good-bye. Too many miles between us, remember?"

Maria threw her hands up. "I know, I know!" She turned away. "That doesn't mean it didn't hurt. It doesn't mean I stopped caring. And, damn you! It wasn't the miles!" Her voice was fierce and hot. "It was because you had to keep an eye on Zoopa! How could we work anything out when you were so caught up in wanting to destroy him?"

"What are you saying? That you're still in love with me?" He moved around so he was facing her. Her eyes were liquid, and it surprised him. She tried to turn away again, but he held her and forced her to look at him.

"You knew I was in love with you," she said.

"That's right. Was. What about now?"

"There is no now for us, *mijo*. I know that. You belong to Bailey." She smiled a small smile. "Don't bother denying it. You may have everyone else believing you have lost your memories of her, but I can tell you remember by the way your eyes light when the two of you are in the same room."

They were both quiet for a minute. Carter didn't know what

to say. She was right, though, when they'd been together, he'd been so hell bent on getting revenge for what Zoopa did to his parents, that he wasn't paying attention to what anyone else wanted or needed.

Things were different now. These last few days, he'd gotten a glimpse of life without Bailey and he didn't like it one bit. But until he straightened things out with Zoopa, they couldn't be together. She would always be a target. He had no other choice but to call a truce with Zoopa. And he'd been ready to do that, until the incident with the kidney... which he was still having a hard time with. It really wasn't like Maria to do something so out there. It had him wondering.

"Did you think if you did something to destroy Zoopa that you and I would have another chance? That I would leave here and go back to South Carolina with you?" he asked.

Maria's lips twisted. "Wasn't that foolish of me to presume such a thing?"

"I don't know about foolish. Risky maybe. But I know that you enjoy a good risk every now and then."

She laughed lightly. "True. What I don't enjoy are puzzles."

"Meaning?"

"If you remember Bailey, why do you pretend otherwise? Why not tell her, so that you and she can be together?"

"I need to finish things with Zoopa."

"Again with Zoopa," Maria said, frustrated. "When will you leave the man alone so that you can have a life?"

"It's not like that. I've no more interest in him, and I'd already planned to make it clear that I'd agree to stay out of his business if he'd agree to stay out of mine."

"You really are in love with Bailey."

Carter nodded.

"And I have ruined it, by taking that woman's kidney."

"You didn't help matters any. But handling Zoopa and getting him to agree to co-exist here on friendly terms wasn't going to be a walk in the park, anyway. No telling how things would have ended up." He wasn't going to put the entire blame on Maria's shoulders. "In the meantime, I'm sending Bailey home."

"You are going to let her leave without knowing your memory has returned?"

"That's the plan."

"Not a very good one." She placed a hand on his cheek. "Don't be surprised if she does not take you back. Then there will be nothing to keep you here. Zoopa will be done. You will have no reason to stay and make his life miserable."

Carter's mouth was set in a grim line. "I know you think me choosing to stay here in Vegas is all about Zoopa. But this is my home. What would I do in South Carolina?"

Maria slapped her hands to her sides. "I don't know. *Sing*. Be Elvis. Anything. Hell, Carter, I make enough money, you wouldn't have to *do* anything."

"I need to make my own way."

"It's not like you don't already have plenty of your own to live on… probably for the rest of your life," she pointed out.

"I can't sit around all day watching reality TV. Or dine at the Charleston Grill until I'm so big you can't stand to look at me. You know what would happen then. You'd find someone new, and I'd get jealous and do something crazy. Have you forgotten how jealous I can be?"

"There is more to Charleston than dining, *mijo*. You could become a member of Briar's Creek. Spend your days golfing. That would keep you in shape."

He did enjoy a good game of golf. But golf wasn't how he wanted to spend his time. Besides, he didn't plan on letting Bailey go. If she refused to take him back, he'd work on her until she did. He shook his head. "I'm not leaving Las Vegas. You and I tried. It didn't work. Bailey is my life now." He touched a finger to her chin. "Go back to Charleston. There's someone there for you. You just need to find him."

She gazed up at him with genuine tenderness. "So, this is good-bye?" The fire in her voice was gone, replaced with a gentler tone he'd seldom heard come from her.

He smiled. "If I know you, we'll see each other again one day."

"Out in the desert, perhaps?"

"Not if I can help it."

She pushed her lips into a pout. "Your Bailey, she is a lucky girl. I hope she treats you the way you deserve to be treated."

He grinned. "Something tells me you don't mean that in a good way."

Chapter Eighteen

Bailey and her aunt made it back to the hotel room with no more incidents—gun or otherwise—just as Carter ordered. And now it was time to inform Liza they were being booted out of Vegas.

She knocked on the adjoining room door, but Liza didn't answer. Not that she expected Liza to be there—not when there were ten thousand slot machines to be conquered—but she at least wanted to be able to say she'd made a real effort, should the subject ever come up between her and Carter at some point in the future.

Though if she were really making an effort, she'd go down and make one pass through the casino. Liza was probably down there on the gaming floor playing her favorite Little Green Martian machine.

She looked over at her aunt and calculated the odds she could leave her alone for even a few minutes and come back to peace and harmony. A trillion to one was a safe bet. And what were the odds Carter would find out she hadn't left Las Vegas? Even money. He had eyes everywhere.

But, of course, if he *did* find out she'd missed her plane, it could work in her favor. He might get so angry he'd personally escort her home. Then she'd have him right where she wanted him—all to herself, away from all the women here who kept getting in her way. And, too, he'd see her babies and her mom and everyone in Coupeville who adored him, and maybe that would be just enough to snap him out of his amnesia.

If only.

She sighed. Who was she kidding? If it came down to her needing an escort home, Carter would simply have one of his men do it. And that man, in all likelihood, would be Mike. Yikes. She stood better odds at avoiding trouble if she left her aunt alone for a few minutes to go look for her friends.

She took hold of her aunt's shoulders and looked her straight in the eye. "I need to go out for a minute, and I want you to promise me you'll behave yourself while I'm gone."

"I could come with you," Aunt Fiona offered. "If you're looking for someone, four eyes are better than two."

"Yes, but two eyes take up less space. And if I'm alone, and I see Carter, I might be able to slip behind a slot machine or a wall or something before *he* sees *me*."

"Okay, cupcake. I'll be here when you return."

"Promise?"

"Cross my heart." Aunt Fiona did the cross-her-heart thing over her chest, which only gave Bailey a slight boost of optimism. And to swing the odds even more in her favor, she decided it might be worth giving the room another look-see for weapons.

She went through her aunt's designated drawer, pushing things from side to side, sorting through cotton underwear, fuzzy socks in a variety of colors, and pajamas. God only knew why her aunt needed pajamas. The room was sweltering.

"If you wanna borrow some underwear, just ask," Aunt Fiona said.

"It's not underwear I'm looking for. It's lethal weapons."

Aunt Fiona folded her arms over her chest. "Well, I never."

"Yes, you would, and that's why I'm looking," Bailey said.

She continued plowing through her aunt's unmentionables. "You heard Carter. No more threatening anyone, or you'll be locked up. *We'll* be locked up. Then I'll never get him back."

"He'd never know," Aunt Fiona said.

Bailey shoved the drawer shut and turned around. "That's just it. He *would* know. He knows everything."

Aunt Fiona *hmmfed* and said, "He doesn't know *every*thing."

The hairs on Bailey's arms stood on end. "What's that supposed to mean? Are you saying you've got another gun stashed somewhere?"

Aunt Fiona compressed her lips and without the plumpness of youth, they all but disappeared. "I'll need to talk to my attorney before I can answer any more questions."

Bailey got right in her face. "Do you want us to spend the rest of our lives in jail?"

"Do you think they'd put the cuffs on me?" her aunt asked. Her eyes were gleaming with excitement. "Rex and me tried cuffs once. They were lined with fur. I don't think it was real, but it took the edge off." She winked at Bailey.

Bailey felt her cheeks flush. "I don't know, Auntie. They might cuff you. But I think police handcuffs are one hundred percent cold, hard steel. No fur, so probably they would hurt."

She certainly didn't have any personal experience, but she knew there were plenty of people who used handcuffs during sex play. In fact, Mr. Perkins, back in Coupeville, kept a healthy supply of the fur-lined variety behind a cloth curtain in his tanning bed, slash coffee shop, slash video game store. She'd seen them once when she'd stopped in for a mocha and had taken a peek in back where he kept the adult items.

"They might be wasting their time, too," her aunt said, and she held out her wrists. "You ever see wrists this skinny? I might be coming down with that anorexia disease. I better have Olivia take me in to Oak Harbor to see a doctor. I might need a good dose of antibiotics."

Antibiotics? For anorexia? Sheesh. After spending the last

couple of weeks poring over *Taber's*, you'd think her aunt would know antibiotics were definitely not the treatment of choice for anorexia. Even so, she decided it would be a waste of time trying to explain the intricacies of treating an eating disorder to her aunt. Still, to assuage any concern, she took her auntie's bony wrists in her hands and gave them a good once-over. Skin covered bone. No meat. No muscle. A million age spots. Everything seemed in order—and normal for a woman her aunt's age.

Next, she turned her attention to her aunt's face. Lines every which way, but not a lot of sagging. Her aunt had always managed to keep herself thin, so excess skin wasn't an issue. The plain truth, though, was that her aunt's clock was ticking toward an end that couldn't be derailed. Eventually, her aunt would have some serious health problem, and when it happened, Bailey only hoped she wouldn't regret dropping out of med school. Right now, though, anorexia didn't seem to be an issue.

"You look fine, Auntie, and I agree. Putting handcuffs on you would be a waste of time. Somehow, you've managed to keep your girlish figure and if anyone were to put cuffs on you, you'd slip right out of them. I think you might even slip through the bars, should the police be silly enough to put you in jail."

Her aunt's face beamed. "I could use a set of falsies, though, huh?" She reached down in the general area of her stomach and hefted her water-balloon shaped breasts up five or six inches. "These babies used to be perky. But lately, it's a chore just tuckin' 'em into a brassiere. And I think Rex might like something a bit perkier, too." She clamped down on her molars. "Lea Townsend has one of them 18-hour bras. I hear she even sleeps in it."

Bailey gave her aunt's breasts a quick glance. They'd been hanging low for a good twenty years. It'd look downright odd if they were suddenly back up in the middle of her chest. "I think Uncle Rex likes you just the way you are. *Au naturel*," she said, smiling gently.

Grinning wide, her aunt exposed her recently replaced dentures. Unless told, one might never suspect they weren't real teeth. Her dentist, Dr. Kibble, had done a good job, even giving them the right amount of age-related stain so they wouldn't stand out. For sure, getting old wasn't pretty. But when you had someone to grow old with, who cared?

She kissed her aunt's cheek and reiterated the no-gun rule for good measure, then made a promise. "If all is well when I return, the next time we're here, I'll take you to see Thunder From Down Under."

"Why wait? I hear there's an eleven-thirty showing over at Excalibur," Aunt Fiona said. "I hear those boys can make a woman's hair curl. I haven't been to the salon since we got here and I could use a tune-up."

"Next time," Bailey promised.

The door opened, and Liza and the twins poured themselves into the room. They smelled of fermenting alcohol and grilled food. Probably they'd been to Toby's. It was one of Liza's favorite places to eat. Liza tossed her purse on the bed and it landed with a thud.

"Good day on the slots?" Bailey asked, happy that at least one of them would be leaving Las Vegas a winner.

"Very good," Liza said. "And how about you? How did it go with Carter?"

"They sucked face, and then she screamed, and then I almost gave him a backside full of lead," Aunt Fiona told her.

Liza's eyes lit up. "You and Carter sucked face? Does that mean he remembers you? Does that mean you guys did it?"

Mark cozied up to Bailey and his eyes immediately focused on areas of her body that were none of his business. She felt an uncomfortable warmth below her waist, which was why she generally tried to stay away from him. And even though she was ninety-nine percent sure she no longer had any interest in doing anything sexual with him, he had a way of making women do things they wouldn't normally do. It was much the same power that Carter possessed over the opposite sex.

Scary.

She stepped away, putting some distance between herself and Mark. "What goes on between me and Carter is private," she said to everyone, but mostly to Mark.

"Oh," Liza said, sounding disappointed. "I guess that means you didn't let him get past first base."

"*We've* had private moments," Mark said, sidling back up to Bailey.

Liza shot Brian a look. "Maybe you and I should go down to the casino, so your brother and Bailey can share *more* private moments."

"Sweet," Mark said.

"No, not sweet," Bailey told him. "You and I aren't sharing anything." Once more she stepped away.

"Why not?" Liza asked. "It wouldn't hurt to have Carter see what he's missing, what other men will be enjoying, if he doesn't care to step up."

"Sweet," Mark said again, running his gaze from Bailey's feet all the way up to her chest. He reached for her, hooking the front of her tank top with one finger. He gave a tug and it was either go to him or risk losing her shirt right there in front of everybody.

"Let go of me," Bailey said. She and Mark were chests touching and she was afraid of what might happen next.

Mark's eyes were gleaming. "Peaches... you don't really want me to let go," he said. And then he planted his lips on hers.

Bailey hated herself for it, but it wasn't long before she was enjoying the sensation of having Mark's tongue inside her mouth—she was only human, after all. And as far as tongues went, Mark's was a like a gold medal gymnast. It had a routine that could make a good girl go bad. And, evidently, she was well on her way to going bad. First Mike, now Mark! Egads! She needed to pull herself together. But first she needed to pull herself away from Mark.

She did, and then she wiped her mouth, hoping it would be enough to erase the sensation of his lips being on hers. "Don't ever do that again," she told him.

"We need to practice," he said. "You want Sideburns to think our romance is the real deal, don't you?"

"You don't need any practice," she said, hating to admit it. It wasn't that Mark was all bad. In fact, he was a great friend and she could count on him to be there whenever she needed... anything. Problem was, Mark was a fixer-up and she didn't think she was up to the challenge. Not only that, but Mark was offering something she didn't need. Carter fulfilled *all* of those needs. Or did, until recently.

"Peaches," Mark said again, and he tried to pull her back. But this time she was prepared. She put an arm up to block him.

His eyes turned dark. "Playing hard to get. I like that," he said.

Where was a gun when a girl needed one? "Try *impossible* to get. And I don't care what you like. You and I, and that tongue business"—she waggled a hand—"is not ever happening again. Carter is the only man I want kissing me."

Aunt Fiona leaned in. "No need to feel guilty. Elvis doesn't know he's engaged to you. Technically, you're a free woman."

Bailey looked over at the large window that made up one side of her room and considered throwing herself out. But that was impossible. All the windows were sealed shut. Probably to prevent people who'd gambled away their houses and their savings accounts from jumping to their deaths. And since throwing herself to her death wasn't an option, she instead sat on the edge of the bed and dropped her head into her hands. "I think I might be losing my mind."

"Oh, sweetie." Liza sat next to her and rubbed her back. "I don't see what the big deal is. If Carter sees you with Mark, maybe his primal beast will surface and he'll do the man-thing and beat the crap out of Mark. At the very least, he'll see that another man is interested in you."

"Makes sense to me," Aunt Fiona said.

"I don't think I like the part where Sideburns beats the crap outta me," Mark piped in.

Bailey considered Liza's suggestion for a nanosecond. But only because she was so desperate. On the other hand, having Carter's primal beast rise to the surface could be risky. Not that she cared one iota about Mark getting pulverized—after all, he did deserve it for sticking his tongue in her mouth—but what if Carter killed Mark, and was subsequently sent to prison? For the rest of his life? Sure, it might be considered a crime of passion, but if Carter was behind bars for all eternity, she'd be no better off than she was right now. And obviously, she *was* losing her mind for even thinking of going along with a plan like that.

Bailey shook her head. "It's not a good idea. Anyway, we have to go home. All of us. Carter wants us out of Las Vegas tonight."

Liza stiffened. She held up a hand. "Whoa. What are you talking about? I'm on a winning streak. I think I might even have a chance at winning a progressive jackpot."

"Sorry," Bailey said. "We have to go. Carter's made arrangements for all of us to fly home." She looked at her watch. "In fact, if we want to make our flight, we have to leave in the next half hour."

Liza twirled a finger at the side of her head. "You've gone loco. Breathing all that second-hand smoke has affected your brain. I'm not even packed."

Bailey flapped her arms to her sides. "Carter wants us gone. What part of that don't you understand?"

Liza folded her arms across her chest and swiveled her head back and forth. "Sorry, girlfriend. *No comprendo su English.*"

Bailey gritted her teeth and thought about sending some harsh words Liza's way. Something like, *Got gambling addiction?* But, no, she wouldn't do that. Liza might be slightly obsessive when it came to playing the slots, but it'd never posed a problem. *Until now! Aargh!*

Bailey glanced at her watch again. Time was running out. If she didn't get Liza on that plane, Carter might never talk to her again. She thought fast and hard about what to do. It might be time to play hard ball... in the form of sending Liza on a guilt trip. A little guilt tripping never hurt anyone.

She made a mental list of Liza's loves, the things she considered most important in her life. It was pretty easy. The list was short—playing slots, friendship, family, hot men, and having white teeth and shiny hair. Not necessarily in that order. For sure, though, friendship was near the top of the list.

Bailey knew what to do. First came sniffling. That was the easy part. Then, she tried to muster a tear. Harder than sniffling, but doable. Maybe. After half a minute, she let out a frustrated groan.

Liza looked at the twins. "Give us a private minute, will you?"

Brian and Mark made themselves scarce, but Aunt Fiona stood firm. In fact, she'd gotten bored and was perusing the view out the window.

"Are you okay?" Liza asked. "You sounded like you were trying to have a bowel movement."

"I'm fine," Bailey said. Why was it so hard to produce one little tear? Actresses did it all the time. "It's just that I thought we were friends. I thought you liked Carter, and wanted us to be happy." Surprisingly, her eyes quickly filled with genuine tears. She snatched a tissue out of the box on the table and put it to her face. "I'm afraid if we don't do as Carter wants, I might lose him forever. Is that what you want?"

Liza pressed her lips tight. "You know I don't."

Bailey felt a glimmer of hope. "Does that mean you'll pack?"

Liza smiled big. "I have a better idea. Plan C."

Bailey tensed. Plans A and B had involved using the twins to make Carter jealous. Liza was going to have to do better if she expected Plan C to get any serious consideration. "I draw the line at doing anything physical with either of the twins," she told Liza.

Liza waved a dismissive hand. "Forget the twins. This involves only you and Carter. Now, tell me, is he or is he not a man?"

Bailey hesitated. She in no way wanted to take a chance she might be agreeing to one of Liza's outlandish plans. "Yes," she said, cautious.

"Great. Then it's easy. All you need to do is go after Carter. *Really* go after him. As far as I can see, you've been letting all those other women take advantage of the situation. *They* know he belongs to you, even if *he* doesn't. Am I right?"

"Right," Bailey said. Sort of. "But I don't know what you mean. I *have* been going after Carter. I went to his office and found him giving Special Skills Maria a foot rub. Then, I went out to the house and, well, that didn't exactly work in my favor."

"*Pfft,*" Liza said. "You've been going about this all wrong. Have you looked in the mirror lately? You're every bit as beautiful as those other women." She stepped back and gave Bailey a solid appraisal. "All you need is a little glamming up." She fluttered a hand at Bailey's clothes. "Honestly, honey, the way you're dressed now is fine for Coupeville, but why not give Carter something to think about?"

Bailey looked down at her skirt and blouse. They were kind of hometown. Certainly, not Vegas-style. "I didn't bring anything glamorous here with me." Plus, all she knew about being a seductress was zilch. She seduced Carter by baking him his favorite pies. He loved pie, especially marionberry.

"Hell, I can help with that." Liza took a wad of cash from her purse and peeled off several one hundred dollar bills. "Here," she said, handing the money to Bailey. "Take this and go down and buy yourself something sexy in one of the forum shops. And then take your butt over to The Oasis Spa. I saw a sign in the window offering a full glam treatment. Once you get yourself all dolled up, Carter won't even look twice at those other women." She sidled up to Bailey's Aunt Fiona and slung an arm over her shoulders. "I'll keep an eye on your auntie. We'll go have ourselves some good, old-fashioned fun, won't we, Fiona?"

"Can we go see the naked Aussies?" Aunt Fiona asked.

Liza gave her a wink. "You bet your sweet, wrinkled ass."

Chapter Nineteen

Bailey knew exactly where she wanted to spend Liza's winnings—Rizzo's, a glitzy shop that sold glitzy dresses to women who wanted to explore their wild side while "doing" Vegas. And speaking of glitzy, a dress with sequins the color of pink champagne was at that very minute hanging in Rizzo's front window. She pointed it out to the saleswoman, who also picked out a pair of sexy shoes and an equally sexy evening bag for Bailey.

Stunning! That's how Bailey felt when she came parading out of the dressing room and stood in front of a full-length mirror. She was every bit as glamorous as Special Skills Maria or Nikki Amsterdam. If this get-up didn't take Carter's mind off the fact that she hadn't yet left town, nothing would.

She changed back into her home-town clothes, then paid the saleswoman and then took off in the direction of the legendary Oasis Spa, which had a reputation for turning drab into *zow*! She so wanted to *zow*! Carter. She could hardly wait to get the full spa treatment that Liza had told her about.

When Bailey arrived, she stood outside the spa's opulent glass doors to take a lengthy peek inside. What she saw bordered on mystical. Beautiful People, clad in silky cream-colored sheets and looking like Greek gods and goddesses, were everywhere, gliding effortlessly over a rich-looking, gold-veined marble floor.

Bailey watched for several minutes as the Beautiful People tended to guests, women mostly, bringing them magazines to read, as well as small cups filled with some kind of liquid. Bailey surmised it might be the secret health potion she'd often heard tell about that contained a rare, youth-sustaining mineral. It was all the current rage. She definitely wanted a cup for herself.

She closed her eyes and envisioned one of the Beautiful People coming to collect her, where she'd be taken to a room for hours of pampering that included hot-stones, wrapping, rubbing, and polishing. And only when her transformation was complete would she be allowed to resurface, wearing her very own silky sheet and displaying a radiant, peaceful glow. She prayed Carter wouldn't be able to take his eyes off her.

She pushed on the floor-to-ceiling glass doors and followed a red strip of carpet over to the front desk, where two beauties stood smiling and posing in all their loveliness, waiting to take credit cards or cash from those wanting to be pampered. A sign, detailing the full spa deal Liza had told her about was posted at eye level behind one of the women. Bailey focused on the sign and was dismayed when she read the words Appointments Required.

Liza hadn't mentioned a thing about her needing an appointment. She'd just spent a small fortune on new clothes, and now she might not be able to finish her transformation?

That was unacceptable.

She swung her gaze over to the lobby area. A few women remained sitting, awaiting their turn, but, certainly, not enough that The Oasis Spa could claim they were fully booked. Plus, Beautiful People were wandering around everywhere, looking like they had nothing to do.

Hmm. Bailey suspected this was a situation of people being

turned away... just in case.

But wait. Wasn't she a just-in-case? After all, she was engaged to Carter Davis, head of security.

She decided to take a chance... if she could at least get hot-stoned. She moved over and stood facing the woman who had the appointment book spread open in front of her. "I'd like to take advantage of your full spa special," she told the woman, smiling pretty and folding her hands in front of her, being as pleasant as she could possibly be. It was the perfect time to test her aunt's theory that honey draws more bees than vinegar.

The Beautiful Woman looked her up and down and asked, "Do you have an appointment?"

"No," Bailey answered, still smiling.

The Beautiful Woman raised one Beautiful Eyebrow into a delicate arch. She looked over her appointment book and began to shake her head. "I'm truly sorry. I don't see..."

Bailey felt her plans begin to go belly up. She had to do something. She raised her wrist and looked at her watch. "Gosh, look at the time. Carter will be so upset if I'm late. We have a big night planned."

"Carter?" the woman asked.

"Mmm hmm," Bailey said. "You know, head of security? I'm his fiancée." And she wasn't afraid to use it to her advantage.

The woman arched her eyebrow again. "I'd heard a rumor that he was getting married. But that was before..."

"His accident?" Bailey finished for her.

"Yes, and... how is he?"

"He's doing well." Bailey looked at her watch again. "Gee, I hate to make him wait." She lowered her voice and leaned toward the woman. "You know how he can be. I could call him if there's a problem," she offered. Then she started digging in her purse, looking for her cell phone, which she'd never find because it was back in her room on the nightstand.

"That won't be necessary," the woman said. "I think we can fit you in. Facial, hot-stone massage, mani, pedi?"

Bailey smiled. "Yes, the works, please. I have new clothes, too." And she held up her bag as proof.

The woman smiled sweetly, completely uninterested in Bailey's new clothes. She reached under the counter and brought out a pair of way-too-big rubber sandals. She handed them to Bailey and instructed her to follow. She sashayed her Beautiful Ass through a door and into an area where she further instructed Bailey to change into a fluffy white robe and the over-sized sandals.

"Once you've changed, kindly make your way back out to the sitting area and someone will offer you something to drink and a magazine to read. Then, Thomas, our best hot-stone masseur will be with you shortly." Then she was gone, leaving Bailey to survey her surroundings.

The first thing Bailey noticed was the smell. It was like the Garden of Eden. An herbal-like essence infused the air, and she half expected to see butterflies flitting about from flower arrangement to flower arrangement. But butterflies must have been *non grata*, as there were none to be seen.

By the time Bailey changed into her robe and sandals, she could already feel her transformation process beginning. Her robe had yet to change into a cream-colored silk sheet, but she had no doubt that by the time she left the spa, true beauty would be hers.

Shiny and new. That's how Bailey felt after Thomas, Brianna, and Marissa had each had their way with her skin, nails, and hair. She'd officially attained goddess status. Or at least felt like she had. And it had only taken a scant four hours... plus a bundle of Liza's money.

She practically floated to the Security elevator, and didn't even need to wait for someone to come along and grant her entrance. The elevator doors just magically parted, and she was on her way to Carter's office.

She spent the ride up staring at herself in the elevator door mirror, admiring her new self, wondering where she'd been all her life. Maria Cruz, watch out. There was a new girl in town.

When she stepped off the elevator, she sashayed down the hall and into the control room. Everyone, including Mike, did a double take. Which only brought to mind the kiss they'd shared. Eventually, that indiscretion would need to be dealt with. But for now it was best tucked far, far into the back of her mind, where it couldn't hurt anyone.

She glanced at Mike, holding her head high. She had a new attitude. She was woman—W-O-M-A-N—and she needed no clearance from anyone to see her man.

But the nearer she got to Carter's door, the slower she sashayed. What if Carter had company again? What if he was in the middle of another foot rub? Or something else... unmentionable?

She broke pace, and felt everyone in the control room lock eyes on her.

What now? She stared at Carter's office door and took a couple deep breaths, wondering whether she should go in or run away. But she couldn't run away. Not with everyone watching. They'd think she was afraid. And maybe she was... of men like Zoopa and bears and Great White sharks. But that didn't make her a coward. That made her smart.

She glanced over her shoulder at Mike. "Is he alone?"

Several voices responded, "Yes," so she forged ahead, pushing open Carter's door. He was at his desk, pen in hand, head down. She cleared her throat, and he looked up. His eyes grew big, but at least he didn't curse, so she took that as promising. Even so, her back broke out in a cold sweat.

"I didn't expect to see you again," he said. He got up from his chair and came around to the front of his desk, settling against it. She was cautiously optimistic that he was going to let her stay. But then she got a whiff of his aftershave and, suddenly, she felt ill, like she might throw up.

Gah! This was no time to be sick. "Be right back," she told Carter, and she ran off and slipped into his private bathroom. She quickly positioned herself face-over-toilet and waited.

And waited. But nothing happened. It was puzzling, to be sure. She waited a few moments more, and then stood and looked at herself in the mirror, wondering what could have made her feel so poorly. Certainly not Carter's aftershave. She'd always loved its woodsy, earthy scent. If she could, she'd bottle it and spray it all over her body, every morning, noon, and night.

Oh, no! She put her hand to her mouth. There it was again, the feeling she might hurl.

Breathe, she told herself, and she promptly hung her head between her arms over the sink to let the moment pass. With head hanging, she recalled how her auntie had recently hinted that she might have a bun in the oven. Which was ridiculous. In the past few months, she and Carter had only been together for one brief romantic interlude... and, of course, they'd practiced safe sex. Or *had* they?

Egad! Might she actually be pregnant?

There was a rap on the door, followed by Carter's concerned voice. "You okay in there?"

Bailey braced herself on the sink. "I'll be right out," she said, not at all sure she was ever going to leave the bathroom. She turned on the cold water and dabbed some to the back of her neck and a little more to her chest, until the *eww* feeling subsided and she was ready to face Carter. She opened the bathroom door and found him standing right outside waiting for her.

"Problem?" he asked.

She shook her head. "No problem. I just needed a drink of water." No sense in dropping the possible pregnancy bomb on him until she knew for sure.

He looked at her chest. "Looks like you missed your mouth."

She waved his comment away, pushing past him. "I couldn't find a cup."

"An entire dispenser, filled with Dixie cups, is hanging on the wall right next to the sink," Carter said.

"Do tell. I didn't see them," Bailey said. No way did she

intend to go into all the gory details about how she'd just been bending over the toilet waiting for her stomach to erupt. According to her auntie, it was okay for a woman to let a man see her in her jammies, or without makeup. But she must never, under any circumstances, allow a man to see her make the barfy face. No woman, no matter how beautiful, can make the barfy face look good.

Carter looked at his watch, and gave her a peeved look, which was the exact opposite of what she'd hoped for, dressed as she was.

"You should be at the airport," he said. "You need a ride?"

She stared at him. Men. Here she was in a flashy new dress and shoes, and he hadn't even noticed. She dropped her flashy new bag on the chair at the front of his desk.

"About that," she said, realizing this might be her one and only chance to beat those other women at their own seduction game. Though God help her, she didn't want to make a fool of herself. "I'm not going anywhere... and you can't make me." She looked at him with big doe-eyes and blinked three times, hoping for the best. He cracked a grin, and she relaxed slightly. At least he wasn't cursing.

"Where's your aunt?" he asked. "She's not about to bust in here with a gun, is she?"

"That depends," Bailey said. "Will I need saving?" She stepped closer, hoping that he still wanted to practice his Elvis act on her. She saw his pupils dilate.

"I don't think you get the seriousness of the situation with your aunt," he said. "Guns, even toy ones, can be dangerous."

"Of course," Bailey said.

"People tend to shoot first."

"And ask questions later."

Carter's mouth hitched up at one corner. "So you understand my position?"

"Oh, yes," she said. "I understand perfectly."

A moment of silence ensued.

"Could be I've misjudged you, Ms. Ventura," Carter said at

last. "Maybe we should get to know each other better." He leaned in and caressed her ear with his lips.

Oh! She hadn't expected that. She cut a look over to the glass panels that made up Carter's front office wall and caught a couple of his men in the control room enjoying the view. "We have an audience," she whispered.

He shrugged and continued nuzzling her ear. "Ignore them."

She squirmed in his arms, wanting to give in, but she just couldn't. Not with others watching. This wasn't at all what she'd imagined. Some seductress she was. This was turning out to be a big mistake. She edged away from him. "I'm sorry. This is all wrong. What we do behind closed doors is private." Her heart hammered against her ribs. "I don't like to be ogled while I'm making love."

Carter grinned. "Ogled?"

"Yes, ogled. *Watched*. Don't be insensitive."

"Fair enough." Carter got up and went around behind his desk. He opened the top drawer and a few seconds later, three steel panels lowered down over the glass. "Happy?" he asked, joining her again.

Bailey nodded. But she wondered... had she just gotten what *she* wanted, or was she simply about to give him what *he* wanted?

Chapter Twenty

Bailey's emotions were all over the place. She and Carter had done *it*—right there in his office. What was she thinking? She wasn't... and that was the problem. Carter still didn't remember her. But the thing is, they hadn't just had sex. They'd made love. She sighed, reliving all his kisses.

"I know a man doesn't usually do this, but what are you thinking?" Carter asked.

"We just made love," Bailey said.

"Glad you noticed." He began plying her with more kisses, probably trying to wear her down so he could have his way with her again.

"How do you do that?" she asked.

His kisses stopped. "Do what?"

"Make love to me like you really love me, when you don't even know me." She couldn't imagine faking being totally involved with someone. Either Carter had a good deal of acting ability—he did pretend to be Elvis, after all—or his true feelings for her were showing. And there it was, that nagging suspicion that he could be lying to her.

She moved off the sofa and knelt before him, on the floor.

She wanted to face him square on, so she could look into his eyes. "I'm confused," she said.

"About what?" His eyes were open wide now, seeing her kneeling there between his legs.

"You. And get your mind out of the gutter," she told him. "I'm not about to give you a... a job... of any kind. I simply want to talk."

He laughed and put up his hands. "I didn't say a word."

"No, but you were thinking something, and that's just as bad. Honestly, how would you feel when you finally do remember me and you also remember I pulled out your ding dong and gave you the business without us even being a real couple?"

"According to you, we *are* a real couple."

"Yes, but *you* don't know that."

"No, but I'm beginning to think I might know how it would feel."

She pressed her lips tight, refusing to get into such a silly argument with him. "I'm trying to be serious."

"Okay, honey, let's get serious."

"Am I a stranger to you? Do you really not remember me, or are you just faking your memory loss so you don't have to marry me?"

He shook his head. "I was afraid of this."

"Afraid of what?"

"That you were the kind of gal who does something she regrets, and then goes all crazy on a man."

Bailey's frustration mounted. "I'm not being crazy at all. I just asked you a simple question."

"Honey, nothing about you is simple." He squeezed her shoulder. "You should probably get dressed now. You never know when someone might walk through the door."

Yikes! He was right. She stood, afraid at any moment, they might get busted. She gathered her clothes and fumbled to put her bra back on. She couldn't fasten it. He was on his feet now, already half dressed. She turned her back to him. "Hook my bra, please."

"Gladly." He fastened her bra, and then slapped her lightly on the butt. She jumped, but not because it hurt. It was unexpected. *Her* Carter had never slapped her like that.

She turned to him, searching his face, not quite sure what she was looking for. She didn't want to believe he would lie to her.

Carter reached a hand to her face. "Just so you know, I have no regrets about what we did."

"I don't, either," she said, her voice soft and quiet. She was feeling achy and vulnerable all over.

Carter picked her dress up off the sofa and handed it to her. He finished buttoning his shirt, and then tossed his tie around his neck and left it hanging loose. "To answer your question, as screwy as your family seems to be, I can't see any man not wanting to marry a gal like you. So, the answer is no. I'm not faking my memory loss to get out of marrying you."

Bailey slipped her dress over her head, and Carter moved around behind her to zip it up. That was something *her* Carter would do. She had no idea what to think anymore. "As crazy as it may be," she said, "I'm not the only one who thinks you could be faking it. Some man I saw in the elevator thinks you're faking it, too."

Carter turned her around. His brow arched. "What man?"

Bailey shrugged. "A man. Yesterday. I was on my way here to see you and he got into the elevator with me. He told me to tell you that your bogus amnesia act wasn't fooling anybody."

Carter cursed under his breath as he moved over to his desk. "Why didn't you tell me about this sooner?"

"I suppose I was in shock at seeing you with another woman's foot shoved into your crotch."

The door swung open, and Mike Shur stuck his head in. "Sorry for the interruption, Boss, but there's trouble on the floor, near the Shadow Bar. One of Zoopa's men is down there harassing the dancers. He was asked to vacate the premises, but he says he ain't leavin' 'til *you* ask him to leave."

"Give me a minute," Carter told Mike, and Mike clicked the door shut.

Carter got on his phone and repeated some numbers, writing them down on a pad of paper, and then he tore the paper from the pad and handed it to Bailey. "That's your new flight time and number. I've purchased enough seats to fly all of you home. This time, please be on it."

Bailey felt a chill in the room. "Wow. Please? You must really want me to leave Las Vegas."

"I do. Me saying 'please' is just my way of giving you one more chance. This time, I hope you don't disappoint me."

She swallowed, feeling the finality of his words. "So this is it? We're done?"

He nodded. "Sorry, honey."

A warm sensation grew behind her eyes. She wasn't going to beg or even try to reason with him. "I'll be gone in a minute," she said, and she moved toward the bathroom door. Once inside, she allowed herself to cry. But only for a moment. Then she pulled it together and did her best to make herself look presentable. She fluffed her hair, wiped smudged mascara from under her eyes, and took a few cleansing breaths. There. She was ready to go home.

When she left the bathroom, Carter was just getting off the phone. She stopped at the front of his desk.

"My aunt will miss you. Having you in the family gave her something to talk about with her friends at the hair salon. Then there's my mom, of course. She thinks you're the real deal. It's silly, I know, but you really are that good." She smiled. "I'll miss you, too."

"And who do *you* think I am?"

"We've had this discussion. You're big bad Security Guy Carter Davis, who just happens to have a voice that makes women swoon."

Carter laughed and moved in close. He slid a hand up her back and into her hair, and then he kissed her... just the way she liked. But that only made her feel worse.

"Stop kissing me," she said.

"*You* stop kissing *me*," he told her.

"I can't. You know I can't."

"You love me," he spoke softly, his words caressing her like a tender touch.

She nodded.

"What can I do to help?"

"Nothing." Everything. She looked up at him. "Come home with me. Let me show you my life. Maybe it'll jar something and you'll remember me." She hated herself for begging. She'd promised herself she wouldn't. But she was in love and women in love were known to do crazy things. Like drive cross-country wearing a diaper... like beg. "How about it? I'll even fix up the guest room, so you can sleep alone if you want. It's actually a dog room, but I'll change the sheets and pick up all their toys. It'll be like our first night together."

Carter grinned. "I'm sure it was magic. But I can't go home with you. I'll tell you this, though. If I ever do consider running off with some strange woman, that woman will be you, Bailey Ventura."

Bailey's shoulders sagged. She'd done everything she could, but it wasn't enough. And now she had to get out of there before she drowned them both with her tears.

Watching Bailey walk out of his office made Carter feel like he'd been stabbed in the heart. Pretending not to know her was killing him. When all this business with Zoopa was over, he had a lot of making up to do.

Mike Shur filled the doorway to his office. "Don't worry about the Shadow Bar. I sent Mitch down."

Carter nodded, but he had nothing to say. After telling Bailey good-bye, he'd completely forgotten about being needed downstairs.

"I saw Bailey when she left," Mike said. "She was upset."

"People don't always smile," Carter said. He stared at the bank of monitors along his wall. "She's supposed to be getting on a plane tonight. Make sure she does."

"Just like that, you're gonna let her go?"

"Mind your own business," Carter told him, speaking sharply. He was in no mood to discuss Bailey with anyone. When Mike didn't immediately remove himself from his office, Carter became even more agitated. "Is there something else?"

"Nah," Mike said. "Only thing is, sometimes you can be an asshole." He shut the door, and left Carter to his own misery.

Carter went back to staring at the monitors. Yep, he was an ass. Especially when it came to protecting those he loved.

Chapter Twenty-One

Bailey made it all the way to the elevator, and was half way down to the lobby when the elevator music switched to something snappy. It was an Elvis tune—"Rock-A-Hula Baby."

This time, she made no effort to stifle her tears. They slid from her eyes, big and fat and sloppy, making tracks all the way down her cheeks. She could see herself in the elevator mirror and didn't even care that she looked like a raccoon. So what! People who saw her would probably think she'd just lost her house payment on a slot machine.

She stepped out into the lobby and a cloud of cigarette smoke engulfed her, making things even worse. Her eyes burned, her throat burned, and she was on the verge of choking.

It was too much. She needed a time-out. She leaned against a wall to gather herself, and while she was leaning, she considered writing a letter to the president, demanding that he outlaw smoking in absolutely every public place in America. But probably that was too much to demand because he might be a smoker, too.

A hand touched her shoulder. "Jesus, honey, what happened to you?" a voice asked through the smoky haze. It was Twinkie.

Lord, Bailey thought. Could she catch just one freaking break? Everywhere she turned, it was Carter or something or some*one* who reminded her of him. Her aunt would call it a sign, but she called it torture and all she wanted right now was to go home, crawl into bed, and sleep off this nightmare.

She waved Twinkie off. "I can't talk right now." Then she rounded the corner of a Wild Cherry slot machine and kept her eyes focused straight ahead, praying that she wouldn't see anyone else who reminded her of Carter.

When she got back to her room, it was empty. Which she didn't mind at all. She could use a little alone time before her flight home. She looked at the slip of paper Carter had given her, and then she checked the time. She had three hours.

She sat heavily on the bed. It'd be late when they all got back to Seattle, and that might be a good thing. She'd be so tired, she'd fall into bed and maybe even get a little sleep. Then she could wake up to a new morning and stare out into another gray-sky day that was so typical for Seattle this time of year. Leaves would be somersaulting in the wind, coats would be tugged closed, and Penn Cove Bay would be as murky as her mood.

Talk about morose. About the only thing that might cheer her up was if it were snowing when she landed at Sea-Tac. She loved the snow. Unfortunately, it was too early in the season for that.

She kicked off her shoes and headed to the bathroom. Fifteen minutes later, she was showered and had her makeup restored to presentable. All that was left to do was pack. With her aunt and Liza off to places unknown, it would go quickly. She wouldn't even take the tiny bottles of shampoo and conditioner from the bathroom.

She opened her bag and filled it with everything from the closet and dresser drawers. Surprisingly, it all fit. Then she sank into a chair by the window, where the neon lights on the Strip blinked up at her in all the colors of the rainbow. It was all so beautiful and twinkly, just like Christmas tree lights, which only made her mood sink lower. In all likelihood, she and Carter would not be spending Christmas together this year. Maybe not any year.

Another ten minutes passed and she was growing impatient. Now that she'd made the decision to go home, she wanted to just go. She sat a few minutes more, staring out at the Strip. As she continued to watch tourists move along the sidewalk below, the faint *boom, boom* of music being played somewhere made its way to her ears. At first, she thought it might be coming from somewhere outside. But that was impossible. The rooms were soundproof. She listened closer, even got up to follow the sound. It led her over to the door that adjoined her room to Liza's. She tried the door, and it swung open.

She looked inside and thought *oh boy*, because Liza, Mark, and Brian were sitting on the bed amidst at least two dozen empty miniature liquor bottles. They were watching her Aunt Fiona as she stood in the middle of the room gyrating her hips to a song called "Buttons" by the Pussycat Dolls. Brian and Liza were all tangled up, and Mark was in a world of his own, looking half-slogged with a vodka miniature stuck to his bottom lip. Someone had to do something and Bailey figured that someone was her.

"Auntie, what are you doing?" she shrieked. She quickly positioned herself in front of her aunt and buttoned her aunt's blouse all the way to the top button.

"No need to get yourself into a tizzy," Aunt Fiona said. "I was just showing the twins and Liza some moves I learned from the boys at Thunder From Down Under."

Mark groaned. "Way to spoil a show, Peaches."

Brian untangled himself from Liza and grinned a sloppy grin. "Your aunt's a hoot. She's got some good moves for an old chick."

Bailey fisted her hands on her hips, giving her friends the sternest look she could muster. "You should all be ashamed of yourselves."

"We're too drunk to be ashamed," Mark said. He patted the empty bed space next to him. "There's room here, if you wanna sit and enjoy the show."

Bailey glared at him. "Show's over." She turned back to her aunt. "If Mom gets wind of this, you and I will both be grounded."

"Grounding is for kids. In case you haven't noticed, I'm long past puberty," Aunt Fiona said.

"Mom will not care. She'll lock us both in our rooms."

"I don't think I want to be locked up. I think I might want to become a showgirl," Aunt Fiona said. "I got me some tassels under this blouse. Wanna see?" And her hands went to the top button of her blouse.

Bailey stopped her. "No! I've seen enough!" She clenched her teeth and tightened her jaw to the breaking point. She began pacing. She walked three steps one way, then three back, over and over. How had things gotten so out of control?

Mark made a grab for her. "You sure you don't wanna come sit by me, Peaches? You look like you could use a rest."

Bailey gave him the death glare. "If you *ever* call me Peaches again, I. Will. Kill. You. Plus, if you ever tell anyone back home about this, I'll never *ever* drink peach schnapps with you again."

Mark gave her a smarmy smile. "Is that a date, Peaches?"

Bailey put a hand to her forehead. If she could only go into a coma right now, maybe everything would all be straightened out when she woke up.

The phone rang and Liza picked up. She uttered a few words, and then pushed the receiver at Bailey. "It's your mom."

Bailey waved her hands and did a frenzied head shake.

Liza put the phone back to her ear. "I'm sorry, but Bailey is in the middle of doing damage control. Can I have her call you back?"

Bailey grabbed the phone before Liza could say another word. "Hello?" she said.

"Was that Liza?" Bailey's mom asked. "Is she all right? And what's this about damage control? What kind of damage? Did you have a car accident?"

Bailey glared at Liza. Some friend. "No, Mom, I didn't have a car accident. And there is no damage. I'm fine. Auntie's fine. Liza's fine. We're *all* fine."

"Your aunt isn't causing you any trouble, is she?" her mom asked.

"Nope," Bailey said. "Auntie went to a show earlier with Liza, and now we're all getting ready to come home."

"So soon? Does that mean the wedding is back on? Should I call the caterer and Reverend Johnson?"

"That won't be necessary," Bailey said.

"Oh." And there was a stretch of silence.

Bailey grew concerned. "Mom? Are you all right?"

"Yes. Hurry home. Your Uncle Rex is having a time of it with these spoiled dogs of yours." Then she clicked off.

Bailey looked over at her aunt. "I think she might be crying."

"Don't you worry," Aunt Fiona said. "It's just the hormones. This phase will pass in ten or twelve years. That's how long it took me to get through the 'change.' Course if your mom was to take those bio-identicals, it might be easier on everybody."

Bailey's forehead knotted up. Ten or twelve *years*? She wouldn't last. For sure, as soon as she got back home, she was hooking her mom up with someone who could explain and maybe prescribe hormone therapy.

Right now, though, she needed to get everyone sobered up and to the airport. She got on the phone and ordered a large pot of coffee. Straight, no sugar, no cream. Then she told Liza to put the twins in the shower, clothes and all, and turn the cold water on full bore. That would sober them up, as well as teach them a lesson for watching her auntie do a semi-striptease.

Maybe a shower would do her aunt some good, too. A good dousing might snap her out of thinking she wanted to become a showgirl.

She left Liza in charge of the twins, and she and her aunt went back to their room. Into the bathroom they went and twenty minutes later, her aunt's aging skin was pink and glowing. She was back to looking like any other normal geriatric. No reasonable person would ever suspect that just a short while ago her auntie was walking around with tassels pasted to her boobies.

"Maybe if I had me some hormones, my girls wouldn't hang so low," her aunt said. She was staring at her nakedness in the mirror and she had her water balloon-shaped breasts cupped in her hands. She hefted them to the middle of her chest, like before. "What do you think?"

Bailey let her mind float away to her favorite daydream... counting the grains of sand on a beach in the Caribbean.

"I bet it's the hormones that keep Lea Townsend looking so perky," Aunt Fiona continued.

Bailey quit counting grains of sand. "Lea's on hormones?"

"Yep. She's been getting a boost from yam cream for years now."

Bailey sat there feeling clueless. She'd been so caught up in her own drama that she had no idea what was going on with anyone else. She put a towel to her auntie's head and gently rubbed her hair. "Lea may be perky, Auntie, but she's not nearly as loveable as you."

Aunt Fiona smiled. "I love you, too, cupcake. But what about Elvis? You still think he's loveable, right?"

"I do," Bailey said. She bit her lip, stifling tears.

"Will he be going home with us?" Aunt Fiona asked.

"Carter has to stay here and take care of business." Bailey finished towel-drying her aunt's hair, then got up and went over to her aunt's bag. "Let's get you some fresh clothes." She took out a clean white blouse and a pair of sky-blue polyester pants—old lady clothes.

Aunt Fiona narrowed her eyes and smushed her lips around some. "It's that Frank Zoopa fellow, isn't it? I told you, someone needs to teach that rat-fink not to interfere in other people's lives."

"It's not Frank Zoopa. Carter doesn't remember me, and we can't stay here forever, waiting until he does." Bailey looked around the room one last time to make sure she hadn't forgotten anything. The place looked clean, so she clicked both of their bags shut. The only thing left to do now was check on Liza and the twins. Bailey looked at her watch. If they got themselves downstairs in the next ten minutes, they would have no problem making their flight. That would give Liza nearly half an hour to stop at various slot machines on their way through the casino and out to the taxi line.

"I'm going over next door to see how Liza and the twins are doing," she told her aunt. "Please don't do anything but sit right there and wait till I get back." She pointed at the chair.

"Don't you worry about me," Aunt Fiona said. She sat in the chair and clasped her hands in her lap, looking like an obedient child. But Bailey knew better. She didn't dare leave her auntie alone for more than just a brief minute.

She stepped into Liza's room and was happy to see all three of her friends in the process of getting ready to leave Las Vegas. She helped Liza locate her cell phone, which had somehow ended up in the ice bucket, and then she returned to her room. But the room was sans one old lady wearing blue polyester.

Bailey was frantic. She raced to the bathroom to see if her aunt was there. No aunt. She opened the door and checked the hallway. Nothing. She couldn't believe it. She'd left her auntie alone for barely a minute. How could an old lady move so fast?

She ran back to the other room. "My auntie is gone! She's escaped!"

Liza and the twins looked at her, and didn't even have the good sense to look concerned, which didn't help at all. Bailey felt a panic attack coming on. "We have to go find her! Now!"

Liza finally took action. She went over and checked one of

the dresser drawers. "Hmm," she said, rustling through it.

Bailey's heart skipped a beat. In her opinion, it was never a good thing when someone *hmm'd* in a situation like this. "Hmm, what?"

"I think your aunt may have another gun."

"Sweet," Mark said.

The hair on the back of Bailey's neck prickled. "What gun? Carter has all of my aunt's guns. Even the one she stole from the exhibit in Sam's Town."

"Sweet," Mark said again, and Bailey shot him a shut-the-hell-up look.

Liza grimaced. "Not *all*. She had one more and she gave it to me for safekeeping. She told me not to tell you… said you wouldn't understand."

Bailey felt her knees buckle. "Are you *insane*? Of course I wouldn't understand." She began pacing. It was becoming a regular routine. Back and forth, back and forth, back and forth.

"Jesus," Liza said. "Calm down. It's not like it's a *real* gun."

Right. Tell that to Carter. Bailey stopped pacing. "We've got to go find her."

Grudgingly, Liza and the twins filed out of the room. Bailey followed and they all took the elevator down to the casino floor. Bailey sent Mark and Brian to the forum shops—they hated shopping, so no chance they'd get distracted—while she and Liza headed out to search among the rows of slot machines. But their search for her auntie came to a halt when they rounded a corner and ran into Mike Shur. He stood arms crossed, looking like he meant business.

"I saw you on the monitors," he said. "Without your bags. Boss told me to make sure you make your flight."

Bailey frowned. "I don't think so. I'm busy at the moment."

"It's not a request."

Of course it wasn't. She pressed her lips together, thinking. Mike wasn't going to make this easy. He'd left her no choice. "Have you told Carter about our kiss?"

Mike's face paled and he stepped aside.

Bailey gave him a friendly pat on the chest. "Thanks. I owe you." And she and Liza were on their way.

"What was that kiss business all about?" Liza asked. She looked back over her shoulder at Mike with a sigh. "And why didn't you introduce us?"

"We kissed. In the back of a taxi. And you don't want to get involved with him. He lives here and you live in Seattle."

Liza didn't say another word, but Bailey knew further explanation about the kiss would be required later.

Fifteen minutes into their search of the gaming floor, the twins appeared. They'd had no success finding Bailey's aunt, and Bailey was growing ever more frantic that if her friends didn't leave for the airport right then, they'd never make their flight.

"You guys go. I'll see you when I get back to Coupeville." If she and her auntie didn't end up in jail and have to spend all eternity there. No telling what kind of trouble her auntie was getting into right this very minute.

"We can't leave you. You need us," Liza said.

"Yeah, Peaches, you need us for moral support," Mark said, and he slung an arm around her shoulder and squeezed her tight against him.

Bailey didn't have the energy to be upset with Mark for calling her Peaches, or for using this as an opportunity to cop a hug. She was upset enough with her aunt. "I'll be fine," she told her friends. "Please, go. Carter will be upset enough that I'm still here. I'll call you as soon as I get back home."

Reluctantly, Liza and the twins left her standing there in the middle of the gaming floor. Bailey watched them disappear into the crowd. She wanted to scream.

Chapter Twenty-Two

Carter held a chair out for Nikki at the front of his desk. "I wanted to thank you again for what you did for me," he told her.

"You mean the kiss? Sure, baby. Anytime," Nikki said.

"If you really mean that, I was wondering if you'd consider doing a little more pretending."

Nikki's eyes sparked. "You know you can count on me. I'm all yours."

The door opened and Twinkie swept into the room. She was dressed in a skirt that was too short and a blouse that showed too much cleavage. Carter didn't like it, but this was Las Vegas and his sister was part of the landscape.

Twinkie's face twisted into a sneer at the sight of Nikki. "Why am I not surprised? You're like one of those damned scavengers out in the desert. Soon as you see any signs of road kill, you swoop in to get your share."

Nikki returned Twinkie's sneer with one of her own. "I wouldn't exactly call Carter road kill. As you can see, he's very much alive."

Twinkie stuffed her hands on her hips. "How about you

make yourself scarce? I need to talk to my brother. *Alone.*"

Nikki *tsk tsked.* "Poor Twinkie. You've lost your man and now you have too much free time on your hands. Whatever will you do? I could give you a few suggestions."

Carter bit back a laugh. As entertaining as it was listening to his sister and Nikki spar, he thought it wise to hide his amusement.

"Are you going to let her talk to me like that?" Twinkie asked.

Carter held up his hands. "Leave me out of this. You two need to work out your own problems." He shuffled some papers around on his desk. "Nikki and I were in the middle of a meeting. Did you need something?"

Twinkie moved closer. Carter kept an eye on her. Another inch and he'd be forced to do something. The last thing he needed was for his sister and Nikki to go at it right there in his office. Someone could get hurt. Most likely him.

"What did you do to Bailey?" Twinkie asked.

"I have amnesia," he said. "Bailey has a problem with that."

"Yes, but what did you *do* to her?" Twinkie tossed a hand in the direction of the control room. "I just saw her, and she looks like hell."

"I told her to go home."

Twinkie's eyes were like fire. "You're an ass."

He paused, not wanting to say something he might regret, but he was getting exasperated with the name calling. "What would you have me do, *pretend* I know Bailey?"

"Yes! You're good at pretending. Every time you sing, you make women believe you're Elvis. Why can't you make Bailey believe you love her?"

Carter spread his arms. "I have no control over what women believe. They hear me sing and something goes haywire in their brains."

"And something must have gone haywire in *your* brain for you to be keeping the company of this one." Twinkie cut her eyes to Nikki. "Honest to God, Carter, can't you see that she's using the situation to get close to you? For crissake, open your eyes."

Nikki snuggled up to Carter and fingered the opening of his shirt. "Carter, honey, make her go away. You don't need all this drama. You're still recuperating from what that nasty Frank Zoopa did to you."

Twinkie's lips pinched tight and her nostrils flared. Carter thought she looked like she was about to combust. "All right," he said. "I've heard enough from the both of you." He looked at Nikki. "Why don't you go powder your nose?" Then he looked at Twinkie. "You need to leave. Now!" He nudged her toward the door.

"What's up with you two, anyway?" Twinkie asked. "Are you doing it? Is that what Bailey walked in on? God, Carter, how could you?"

"Whether or not Nikki and I are doing 'it' isn't any of your business."

She turned and poked him in the chest. "I say it is. Bailey is about to become my sister-in-law."

He frowned. "I don't have time for this. I have a mess to clean up."

"What mess? You mean the mess with that lady losing her kidney to some maniac?" She shuddered. "So awful. Have you found out who's responsible? Frank's never gonna let this rest. We'll all have to go into hiding."

"Let me worry about Zoopa. Speaking of hiding, I thought you were afraid to leave your room."

"I got bored."

"Bored is better than dead." He nudged her out the door.

"Fine, I'll leave," she said. "But don't blame me if Bailey moves on. And do yourself a favor, get a rabies shot as soon as that she-creature scurries back to her cave."

Carter shut the door behind her and locked it. Women. As much as he loved them, he was sure glad to have been born a man.

Nikki reappeared, and he tucked a finger under her chin. "Thanks for going along with me on this. If everyone believes you and I are involved, Bailey will be that much safer. If there's anything I can ever do for you in return, just ask."

"Oh, I will," Nikki assured him. "The way I see it, you owe me big time, having to deal with your sister. In fact," she trailed a finger down his chest, "I can think of a few things you could do for me right now."

He arched an eyebrow. "You do understand that this is all pretend, right? That you're not really my girlfriend?"

Nikki pouted. "Way to spoil a mood, Carter."

He crooked a smile at her. Better to be a mood spoiler than an ass.

Chapter Twenty-Three

Bailey looked again between every row of slot machines, checked every gaming table, and looked in every window of every shop. She found no one who even remotely resembled her aunt. It was like she'd vanished. Then, just as Bailey was about to give up and go back to the room, she saw Twinkie standing outside the nightclub Zero Gravity. Twinkie was wearing a handful of blue sequins and matching stiletto heels, and she was with a handsome fellow in a well-tailored suit. Bailey rushed over to her. "I can't find my auntie. Have you seen her?"

"No," Twinkie said, showing genuine concern. "How long has she been missing?"

"I don't know that she's missing, per se. I just can't find her."

Twinkie looked over at her date. "This is my brother's fiancée. I think I should help her search for her aunt."

"No," Bailey said, shaking her head. "I'm sure she'll turn up. I just can't imagine where she might have gone all by herself. It's not like she knows many people here. You and Carter are about it. The only other person I can think of is that old guy my mother has been texting. But I just saw him over at one of the roulette tables and my auntie was nowhere in sight."

Twinkie looked thoughtful. "My grandmother used to disappear, and we'd all be crazy with worry. But then we'd find her and everything would be fine. Something would have upset her and she just needed to go off on her own to think. Was your aunt upset about anything?"

Bailey let out a short, terse laugh. "Frank Zoopa. She thinks someone needs to teach him a lesson."

"Don't we all?" Twinkie said.

Now that she'd mentioned it, a cold chill ran through Bailey. Could her auntie have possibly gone to see the notorious Frank Zoopa?

"I really hate what's happened between you and Carter," Twinkie said. "I went up to his office a while ago and tried talking some sense into him, but that predator Nikki was with him and he wasn't in any mood to listen." She pressed her lips together. "Sorry, I did the best I could."

"Thanks," Bailey said. She looked around, still in search mode for her aunt. She couldn't do anything about Carter right now. That situation had to work itself out on its own. "I really can't talk anymore. I need to go. Enjoy your date," she told Twinkie, and she headed for the front of the casino to get in the taxi line. She was going to pay Frank Zoopa a visit. It was a long shot that her aunt would go there, but she had no other ideas about where to look.

Nervous that she might run into Carter, or that he might see her on one of his monitors, she hurried through row after row of slot machines. She was approaching the large check-in lobby where, just outside, a long line of taxis awaited their next fare. She was almost home-free. But then the worst possible thing happened. Carter stepped up beside her, keeping pace and asking questions. "How's it going? Going somewhere? *Miss your plane?*"

Bailey was dumbstruck. How did he *always* find her?

"Carter," she said, by way of stalling for time. She had no

175

idea what to say to him. He'd given her several chances to do as he'd asked and each time she'd done just the opposite. She could see the frustration on his face.

"Bailey," he said back. But he wasn't stalling for time. He was grinding his teeth. "Why are you still here? I told Mike to make sure you got on your plane. Do I need to fire him?"

"Leave Mike out of this. My aunt and I are just heading to the airport."

Carter looked at his watch. "Cutting it close, aren't you? Airlines typically want passengers to check in two hours before take-off." He looked around. "And where, exactly, is your aunt?"

Bailey did a quick look over her shoulder. She spied a hole in the wall that had a Ladies' sign posted above it. "There," she said, pointing. "She had to make a pit stop."

Carter leveled his gaze at her, looking like he doubted every word that came out of her mouth, and she didn't blame him.

"You're gonna be on that plane," he said. "I did all the work for you, made your flight plans, even arranged for Mike to give you a ride to the airport. Yet, here you are."

She scoffed. "You made my flight plans because that's what you do. You decide something, and then you make it happen, whether the other party likes it or not. Twinkie's right. You're a bully."

Carter stiffened. "I'm not a bully. I don't go out of my way to say or do anything that would hurt anyone, just for the simple fun of it. I care about what happens to people who are important to me and I'm a no-nonsense kind of guy. That doesn't make me a bully. And if you really think that, why would you want to marry me?"

"Hey, Bailey, I've been looking all over for you." A man sidled up to her and slipped an arm around her waist. He looked at his watch. "We gotta get a move on, if we're going to make our show." He turned to Carter and offered him a hand. "Hi, I'm Dave."

Carter ignored Dave's hand. He looked like he wanted to kill Dave.

Bailey was taken aback. She had no idea who the man was. But then she realized it was Twinkie's date. But why was he standing next to her, pretending to be *her* date?

"Do you know this man?" Carter asked.

"Him?" Bailey said. She wanted to say no, but a muscle beneath one eye was threatening to twitch and she was afraid that if she told one more lie, it might go into full-blown convulsions. "Of course… he's… he's…"

"Your date," Dave supplied, grinning. "We should be going, Koo Koo."

Carter raised both eyebrows. "Koo Koo?"

"It's a nickname I gave her," Dave said. "She's my little Koo Koo girl." He leaned in, and Bailey thought he was going to whisper something to her, like Twinkie was waiting for him, so he had to hurry and get back. But, instead, he did a quick tongue flick to the inside of her ear.

Eew! Bailey's gag reflex engaged and she slapped a hand over her mouth. She looked over at Carter, thinking maybe he might be willing to slug the guy on her behalf. But instead he turned a nice shade of rage, and then walked away.

"Have a nice date," he said over his shoulder.

Bailey felt like crying. She'd finally broken Carter. He was leaving and never coming back. She turned to Dave and shoved a hand into his chest. "What the hell did you do that for?"

Dave fell backward into a crowd of roulette players and everyone got upset. Then a big burly guy shoved Dave back over to her. He was like a giant pinball.

Finally, Dave found his footing. He grinned wide at Bailey. "You're feisty," he said. "I like that."

Brother. That's all she needed was another Mark Jefferson.

"What's going on over here?" Twinkie asked, stepping up beside Dave. He was straightening his suit coat.

"He licked me in my ear," Bailey said, and her gag reflex engaged again.

Twinkie glared at Dave. "I told you to come over and pretend to be her date, not give her a tongue bath."

"I was improvising," Dave said.

"Well, how about you improvise your ass right outta here," Twinkie told him. She grabbed Bailey by the arm and steered her away from Dave and his tongue, and after a minute, they both broke out laughing.

"Wow," Twinkie said at last. "A guy buys you a drink, and just when you think he might be normal, he proves you wrong. Honest to God, I'm beginning to question my taste in men."

Bailey compressed her lips, keeping her feelings on that subject to herself. She had no room to talk.

"Sorry about that," Twinkie continued. "I saw you were trapped by Carter and I thought I could help you escape."

Bailey reached out and gave Twinkie a hug. "Thanks. I think I've escaped." Forever. She'd never seen Carter so mad.

"Hey," Twinkie said, "since I've lost my date, I'll help you find your aunt. Just give me a minute. I need to pay a visit to the little girl's room."

Bailey nodded, but she had no intention of waiting. As soon as Twinkie was out of sight, she headed for the taxi line. She appreciated Twinkie's offer to help, but if she told her where she was going, all she'd get is resistance.

Carter could feel steam building under his scalp as he stood waiting for the Security elevator. *Koo Koo?* Who the hell calls a woman Koo Koo and lives to tell about it? He slammed a hand into the wall, wishing he'd done the same to Bailey's so-called date.

Just as the elevator door opened, he got a call on his cell phone. A guest in one of the high roller suites was requesting to see him.

He switched courses and went to the elevator that would take him up to the top floor. He punched the UP button. And then punched it again... just because. While he waited for the elevator to arrive, he glared out over the casino floor and saw the guest everyone referred to as Old Elvis. He was standing at a roulette table with a woman who looked young enough to be his granddaughter.

Carter remembered something new. Before his injury, Bailey had asked him to check the old guy out. She'd been worried about her mother and Old Elvis becoming too involved. Carter hadn't seen it as a problem, and he'd laughed it off, telling Bailey that her mother was a grown woman and should be able to have a man-friend. But Bailey had been adamant that something about the old guy just wasn't right.

Delving into a guest's private life wasn't something he usually did—keeping up with gamblers who were hell bent on cheating the casino was his job—but he'd promised to check Old Elvis out when he had the chance. It never happened though, because he'd ended up out in the desert with a knock on his head.

Maybe he'd still find the time. Maybe now, if the elevator didn't show up. He looked up at the floor indicator light. It seemed to be stuck on the eighth floor, not moving at all. He surmised the likely cause was probably some couple that had decided to join the I've-had-sex-in-an-elevator club. *Tourists.*

He looked back over at Old Elvis. Other than a remarkable resemblance to what would have been an aging Elvis Presley, he'd done nothing to attract any attention to himself. There was no reason to suspect him of any wrongdoing. It was understandable that he enjoyed Bailey's mom. She was somewhat younger than him, still attractive, and probably fed his aging male ego. Though for his age, he still looked to be in pretty good shape. Didn't have a pot on him like most older men. Plus, he had a head full of his own hair, with sideburns to match. His clothes were subtly flashy, yet tasteful and expensive. Whatever the old guy's game was, money didn't appear to be an issue. In fact, Carter's one-minute expert assessment of the old guy was that he was a harmless soul, not looking to cause anyone any grief. And the majority of women, young or old, would likely find him damned attractive.

But who was the young woman standing by Old Elvis's side? Maybe Bailey did have cause for concern.

Carter watched the activity surrounding the table where Old Elvis and his lady friend were seemingly chummy and having a good time. After a minute, she leaned in and said something to him, then tore herself away and headed for the women's restroom.

Carter looked back up at the indicator light. It still hadn't moved. Whatever was going on up there on the eighth floor, he didn't want to know. And he was tired of waiting. He wandered over and stood close enough to Old Elvis that they could talk and hear each other over the din of voices and dinging slot machines.

"You a local?" Carter asked the old guy. It was a good enough conversation starter. Not too personal, something anyone might ask.

Old Elvis glanced at Carter and chuckled. "No. Seems like it, though. I've been here more times than I can remember."

"I could comp you and your wife a nice room to show our appreciation," Carter said. He was fishing and he could see on the old guy's face that the old guy knew it.

"I'm not married," Old Elvis said. "Was once. To a woman many years younger than myself. Long time ago. Didn't work out. My wife was possessive and couldn't take the hours I worked. That's the trouble with young women. They want you all to themselves." He chuckled and looked straight ahead into space, as though he was reliving a particular memory.

"Yet, you're seeing a woman many years younger now," Carter pointed out.

Old Elvis eyed him thoughtfully. "I suppose I am. But it's not the woman you just saw me with. She's the daughter of a friend."

Now Carter was truly curious, and he had to ask, "Anyone ever tell you, you look like the King of Rock and Roll?"

The old man got a wistful look on his face, but it was gone in a flash. "You strike a resemblance to the man yourself. You sing, too. I've seen you. You're good. The women love you, the same as they once loved..." He was quiet for a minute, then, "Don't let that go to your head, son. Those women only want one thing from you."

Carter cocked an eyebrow. "And that would be?"

"Your body. What else?" The old guy laughed, and then jutted a thumb over his shoulder. "That pretty lady you were talkin' to earlier, she's different. She wants the whole package. Don't lose sight of that. In the end, if you let her go, all you'll have are your memories."

The young woman returned from the restroom, and she and Old Elvis went back to playing roulette.

Carter headed back to the elevator, satisfied that the old guy meant no one any harm. The elevator door finally opened and he rode up to the top floor. When the door opened again, a raven-haired beauty met him and welcomed him inside her suite. She smelled of lily of the valley... and gin. "Can I help you?" he asked her.

"I have no air-conditioning," she said. "It feels like the desert in here." She let her creamy white robe fall off one shoulder. Her skin had a moist glow and her chest was sprinkled with freckles.

"I can get maintenance up here right away," Carter said. He reached for his cell phone.

The woman placed a hand on his wrist, stopping him. "I thought maybe *you* could check it out for me."

Carter knew women. He was pretty good at spotting a come-on, and this woman was definitely coming on to him. Likely, she'd seen him perform, and then had also seen that he worked security and decided to find an excuse to need his services... even if that service had nothing to do with keeping her or her belongings safe. No harm done. It'd take but a minute to check out the room's AC unit.

"I can take a look, can't promise anything," he said. He went over to the far wall and stood in front of the AC control box. It was fairly straight-forward, something even a woman who'd been drinking should be able to figure out. He pushed a button and turned a dial and that was that. Cool air began flowing into the room.

"All better," he said, turning back to the woman. He wasn't surprised in the least to see her robe lying in a fluffy pile at her feet.

"I couldn't wait," she said. "I was burning up."

"Give it a minute," he told her. He ignored the heated reaction in his groin and moved toward the door. "It should be cooler in here in no time."

The woman wrapped her arms around herself. "*Brrr.* You're right. It's already cooling off."

"You *are* naked," he pointed out, refusing to be drawn in.

The woman's lips primped into a pretty smile. "How observant of you. So, tell me, do you like what you see?"

"I'm a man. You're a beautiful woman. What's not to like?"

She crossed over to him, slipped her arms around his neck, and looked up at him through heavily mascaraed lashes. "You're a handsome man," she remarked. "Has anyone ever told you how much you look like Elvis?"

"Elvis who?" Carter asked, keeping a straight face.

The woman burst into laughter. "You've got to be kidding. Elvis! The King of Rock and Roll, for crying out loud!"

"Oh... him. Never," he said, shaking his head. But he couldn't resist giving her his much-practiced lip sneer.

She laughed again and touched a finger to his bottom lip. "Oh, that's good. I like that." And then she raised herself up onto her toes and kissed him.

It's not that he didn't enjoy her kiss. Her lips were soft, and the warmth of her body was tempting. He could easily bed her, and then be on his way. But it wouldn't be right. And, too, there was Bailey. He pulled the woman's arms from around his neck and nudged her back a few inches. "You don't wanna do this," he told her.

"Oh, to the contrary. I think I very much want to do this."

He didn't want to be rude, or insulting, but his patience was wearing thin. "I have a rule. I don't sleep with a woman until I at least know her name."

The pretty drunk gazed into his eyes and gave him a curious look, like she was trying to figure out whether he was being serious or not. "My name is Hollie," she said at last. "Hunter. Only it's Hollie with an 'i-e,' instead of 'y'. I think my mother just didn't know how to spell it." She giggled and tipped to one side.

Carter caught her and held on to keep her from falling. "Okay, Hollie with an 'i-e,' I've done all I can for you. Maybe you should call it a night."

Hollie didn't budge, just hung on his shoulders with her eyes closed, swaying slightly. Carter listened to her breathe for a moment, then told her, "I need to go, ma'am. If there's nothing more…"

"I think I need to lie down. In there, please." She pointed a dark-red manicured finger nail toward the bedroom door. "Would you help me? I'm afraid I've had a bit too much to drink."

Her motives were obvious, but Carter thought it was probably best that he help her to her bed. If she got sick, she'd be closer to the bathroom and it'd save housekeeping the chore of having to clean up after her. And if she didn't get sick, well, maybe she'd sleep through the night and avoid taking a fall. He swung her up into his arms and carried her into the bedroom, not bothering to turn on any lights. He deposited her on the bed and stood looking at her for a moment, lying there in the milky glow of the light from the other room. Her face was pale and eerily beautiful.

Her eyes fluttered open. "Tuck me in?" she beckoned, smiling sweetly.

Carter tossed the covers over her and then pushed a small wastebasket over next to her side of the bed. That was it. His job was done. He'd have one of the women from housekeeping check in on her later.

He rode back down to the casino floor to take the Security elevator up to the control room. When the elevator doors opened, Twinkie was standing there, flapping her arms, looking like she was about to take off.

"Where the hell have you been?" she asked. "I've been looking all over for you. Do you even bother to check your messages?"

He pushed past her. "I was helping a guest. That's my job."

"That's right. And Bailey is one of your guests. You need to go after her. I think she might be in trouble."

"I just saw her not too long ago. She's fine. She's got a date." Carter started down the hall toward the control room.

"Jesus, Carter. Would you just stop and listen to me for a minute?"

"What?" He spread his hands.

"Bailey hasn't got a date."

"Okay. Whatever you want to call it, she was with a man."

"You're an idiot. He was *my* date."

Carter gave her a hard look. "Great. Good taste. First Zoopa, now some ass who goes around sticking his tongue in women's ears." He moved again toward the control room and Twinkie hurried to keep up.

"Okay, let's not make this about me and my taste in men," she said.

"You have none."

She hopped in front of him and stuffed her hands on her hips. "Are you gonna take this seriously, or not? Bailey is in trouble."

He paused, irritated and concerned all at the same time. "What kind of trouble?"

"I think she's gone to see Frank. I saw her get into a taxi."

"Why would she go see Zoopa?"

"To find her Aunt Fiona. Evidently, she wandered off. I offered to help Bailey search for her, but she took off when I went to use the bathroom."

"Don't jump to conclusions. Just because Bailey went off

somewhere in a taxi doesn't mean she's on her way to see Zoopa."

"Nor does it mean she isn't," Twinkie said. "I have a bad feeling. Bailey told me her aunt made some comment about someone needing to teach Frank a lesson."

"That's crazy," Carter said.

Twinkie tipped her head to one side. "Well."

Carter swore and turned around. His insides were rolling like thunder, like all hell was about to break loose. He should have taken Bailey and her aunt to the airport himself. He got back on the elevator and stopped Twinkie from following. "You stay here. I don't need to be worrying about *three* crazy females."

"I take offense at that," Twinkie said.

"Take all the offense you want, but you're still staying here." He pushed the DOWN button and was on his way.

Chapter Twenty-Four

Bailey's taxi got buzzed in without question at the gate in front of Zoopa's mansion. She took that as a sign that her aunt was indeed there and in all likelihood making Frank Zoopa wish someone would come and get her.

The taxi driver pulled up the drive and stopped just long enough for Bailey to pay him and get out. Then he sped off. Bailey surmised he probably had other fares to pick up... either that, or he didn't enjoy being in such close proximity to the one house in Las Vegas that was most likely to erupt in gunfire.

Bailey paused to take a good look at the mansion that had once been Carter's childhood home. Undoubtedly, Zoopa's ownership helped fuel the on-going animosity that existed between he and Carter. Even so, she wasn't at all nervous about being there. In fact, on one rare occasion when Carter and Zoopa had called a cease-fire, Carter had brought her there to attend a gala event at which Zoopa had announced plans to build a new casino. It was one of the most magical evenings of her life—a chance to see luxury living at its finest.

Only now, it didn't look so luxurious. It looked lonely. And neglected. Probably Zoopa was too busy interfering in other people's lives to take care of the home he'd practically stolen out from under Carter's parents.

Mindful of why she was there, Bailey made her way along the front walkway, noting how the hedges needed trimming and how the flowers—mostly roses—needed tending. She bent to smell one pink rose that was just entering full bloom. Its scent was delicate and fruity and it reminded her of home. She couldn't wait to get back to Coupeville, but leaving behind the man she loved was about the hardest thing she'd ever had to do.

She moved on, stepping up to the mansion's double doors. They opened before she could even knock, and a woman, dressed appropriately in a black and white uniform, stood in the doorway before her. "Mr. Zoopa has been expecting you," she said. She neither smiled nor frowned. She was all business, and business didn't look like it gave her much to get excited about.

Bailey followed her inside and they ended up in a room with walls that were lined with bookshelves filled with hundreds of books. The library.

The uniformed woman gestured toward a chair and told Bailey to make herself comfortable, but Bailey was more comfortable staying on her feet. The woman left, and Bailey's gaze circled the room. It was a reader's dream, to be sure. Her eyes were drawn to a section of books that looked enticing and old, and she read their spines. They were classics—*Pride and Prejudice... The Picture of Dorian Gray... Great Expectations.* She traced a finger along the shelf, smiling, remembering one high school English assignment where she was required to do a report on one such book. Forced reading, but well worth it.

She moved over to the center of the room, where a large desk and an expensive-looking chair sat, as though on display. She couldn't imagine a man like Zoopa doing anything as mundane as sitting and reading, yet there was a book on the desk with a marker holding a page. Other than that, the desk was neat and orderly—just a few papers and a small wooden box that piqued her curiosity.

She flipped open the box. Cigars. Cuban. Of course.

She was about to open the book, but the door on the other side of the room opened and her aunt paraded in, escorted by Frank Zoopa and two gorilla-looking guys, whom Carter would probably refer to as hired thugs. Everyone was laughing and chatting and acting like they were old friends catching up on old times, but Bailey saw no reason to laugh.

She snagged her aunt's arm and dragged her away from Zoopa and his men. "What are you doing here? I've been worried sick about you!"

"I came to have a *tete-a-tete* with Mr. Zoopa," Aunt Fiona said. "If he wasn't such a badass, I wouldn't mind dating him." She gave Bailey the eye. "What are *you* doing here?"

Bailey frowned. "Looking for you. Obviously! And FYI, you can't have a *tete-a-tete* with a man like Zoopa. Nor would I *ever* let you date him."

Aunt Fiona crossed her arms over her chest and *hmmfed*. "I guess I'm old enough to make that decision for myself."

Bailey turned on Zoopa. "What have you been doing with my aunt?"

Zoopa chuckled, and so did his goons. "Nothing. I promise. She showed up on my doorstep, and I let her in. We had a nice visit. I showed her my garden... she gave me some tips to keep my roses insect-free, and then we had some iced tea. It was all innocent." He passed around behind Bailey, allowing his hand to graze her back. She shivered in response.

"Auntie, will you please wait for me outside? I'd like to speak to Mr. Zoopa alone for a minute."

"I've seen the garden, so I think I'll go check out the rest of the house," Aunt Fiona said. "Send out a search party if I'm not back in ten minutes. A person could get lost in a place this size."

"Want me to go with her?" one of Zoopa's henchmen asked Zoopa.

"No need. But you two can leave me and Davis's fiancée alone," Zoopa told him. He gave his henchmen a make-yourself-scarce nod, and they did, shutting the door behind them. Then he turned to Bailey. "What can I do for you?"

"I'm just here for my aunt," she said. "But now that I know she's safe, I'd like to make a request. I want you to leave Carter alone."

Zoopa opened his arms. "Do you see him here? I'm doing my thing, he's doing his." He spread his lips and showed a lot of teeth. "In fact, I could show you what Davis is up to right this very minute. Care to see?"

She was always curious about how Carter spent his time, but she didn't trust the evil Mr. Zoopa. She narrowed her eyes at him. "What do you mean?"

Zoopa shrugged. "Plain and simple. I can show you what your sweetie has been doing for the last hour."

"You're spying on him?"

"I like to think of it as keeping an eye on him," Zoopa said. "Someone's been causing problems that are slowing down the construction of my new casino, not to mention a guest over at the Phoenix recently lost a kidney. Damn fine surgery, I'll admit, but not very good for business." He paused. "I have a pretty good idea who's behind it, but it's always best to be sure, when contemplating a move to even the score."

Bailey laughed a nervous laugh. Carter was talented at carving a piece of meat, but surgery? *Please.* Even she, with a chunk of medical training behind her, couldn't perform a major surgery that involved removing someone's kidney. She could use a needle to dig a sliver out of a toe, or immobilize a broken bone with whatever might be handy, but that was about it.

"You're crazy," she told Zoopa. "You need to stop looking at Carter every time something happens in one of your casinos."

"Probably," Zoopa said. "But for some reason, I always seem to find Davis at the end of the trail whenever something goes wrong. Let's see what he's up to now, shall we?" He moved around behind his desk and pulled out a gadget that looked like any normal remote control. Bailey suspected it had a multitude of uses—phone, iPod… gun.

Zoopa pushed one of the buttons on the controller and a large flat screen dropped from the ceiling on the opposite wall. He pushed another button and two images appeared. It was Carter with some woman.

Bailey swallowed. She wasn't at all sure she wanted to see what he was up to at the moment. The woman was definitely not familiar. But the plain truth was there were probably thousands of women Carter spent his time with that she didn't know, or had ever seen.

"She's quite a beauty, don't you agree?" Zoopa asked. "It looks like she and Carter are holed up in a suite at The Oasis."

"It means nothing," Bailey said. She refused to let Zoopa see he'd upset her where Carter was concerned. "In case you didn't know"—and she knew darn well, he did—"Carter hasn't been himself lately. And just because he's in a suite with some woman doesn't mean he's up to no good."

"How about we watch and see," Zoopa said.

Bailey stared at the screen. The voices were muted, but she could clearly see that Carter was simply helping the woman with her AC unit. Even with Carter's memory lacking, she knew he would never do anything so monumental that it would end their relationship. He knew he was engaged, even if he wasn't ready to remember or admit it.

In an instant, the scene changed. While Carter had his back turned, the woman dropped her robe and now it was down around her ankles. Bailey's heart thumped wildly, waiting to see what happened next.

It wasn't anything good. The woman, seemingly intoxicated, put her arms around Carter's neck, and then she kissed him. Bailey prayed that Carter's response would be to turn and leave, but he didn't. He picked the woman up and carried her to the bedroom.

Searing pain filled Bailey's chest. She stumbled back and caught herself on the edge of Zoopa's desk. Her world was spinning out of control. First Maria, then Nikki, and now some strange woman in a hotel room. It was too much. "I don't need to see any more," she told Zoopa. She wanted to run away, just go home and never see Carter again. "I need to go find my aunt."

"Sorry you had to get hurt in all this," Zoopa said, "but I thought you deserved to know what kind of man you were about to marry." He moved toward the door. "I'll help you locate your aunt."

Zoopa guided her out of the library and Bailey was only faintly aware of his hand on her arm. They crossed a large foyer, over to a wide staircase and climbed for what seemed like forever, until they reached the top. She was numb with pain as Zoopa continued guiding her along, opening doors and poking his head in room after room in search of her aunt. Every room was empty. Her aunt had done a good job of disappearing. But then they came to the last door on the left. It was ajar. Zoopa pushed it open, and there was Bailey's Aunt Fiona, perched on a thick-cushioned window seat, looking out over the back of Zoopa's property.

"He's even got a swimming pool," Aunt Fiona said. "We shoulda brought our swim suits."

Bailey saw a tree outside the window, its branches old and thick, hanging over the roof like some great beast taking a rest. She suspected the room used to be Carter's. She looked around and saw nothing to suggest he'd ever occupied the room, but the tree was a giveaway. Twinkie had told her about it, and about how Carter had made good use of its branches to climb out his window during the night and get into all kinds of trouble with the neighbor girls.

Some things never changed.

"I'll let you two have a moment," Zoopa said. He pointed to a door at the side of the room. "You'll find tissue in there," he told Bailey, and then he disappeared.

"Don't worry, sunshine. Mr. Zoopa ain't no threat." Aunt Fiona waved a dismissive hand. "He and I had a long chat. It seems Carter's parents and Zoopa had a big misunderstanding way back when and it's been a sore that's been festering for years. Carter needs to chill."

Right, Bailey thought. Carter did need to chill... kissing other women, that is. But right now, she wasn't going to worry about what Carter did or didn't do. She needed to set her aunt straight about Zoopa. "Listen, your friend, Mr. Zoopa, swindled Carter's parents out of this big, beautiful house. So I'd say the odds of Carter chilling are about a gazillion to one." She pointed to the bathroom. "I'm going to use the facilities and I expect you to be here when I come out. Then we're leaving."

Bailey closed herself inside the bathroom, and immediately yanked a tissue from a gold ornate box that was probably worth more than her entire bathroom back home. Maybe even her entire cottage. She sat on the edge of a large soaking tub and dabbed at her eyes repeatedly, trying not to end up like she had before, looking like a raccoon.

She let out a heavy breath. If anyone needed to chill, it was her. Only she couldn't, because she'd just had her heart broken. She swung her eyes to the ceiling, wondering how much heartache one woman should be expected to endure. Evidently, a lot.

She sat quietly for a long time, trying to resign herself to all that had happened. She finally came to the conclusion that finding the perfect man was more like a fairy tale than reality. Especially when it came to Carter. He was no white knight on a horse. Dark prince was more like it... and she was a naïve young princess to have ever believed their fairy tale would end in anything but disaster.

If only Zoopa had left them alone. If only she could have found a way to make Carter remember her. If only...

Tears formed in her eyes, but she was determined to keep them at bay. She put the tissue to her nose and blew, hoping that would do the trick.

"Did I ever tell you what happened three days before my wedding to your Uncle Rex?" her aunt spoke through the door. "We was planning on a real doozy of a ceremony, but then the preacher got struck by lightning and was laid up in bed for a solid two weeks. His hair even went curly. Me and your Uncle Rex thought it might be a sign we shouldn't get married." She paused. "Maybe you and Elvis shouldn't get married."

"Okay, Auntie," Bailey said through the door to her aunt. "I'll give it some thought." She sniffled quietly into her tissue, doing her best to pull herself together. She and her aunt needed to get to the airport. They'd missed their flight, no doubt, but being that it was late, maybe they could get seats on another flight. If not, she didn't know what they'd do. Certainly, they weren't going back to The Oasis.

"I'm sorry you and Elvis couldn't work things out," Aunt Fiona continued. "I thought if I came here and gave Mr. Zoopa a good talking to, it might help. But I think Elvis has issues that stem from his childhood, and he might need therapy."

Bailey swung the bathroom door open. "You can't *talk* to Zoopa. He's a *bad, bad* man. He doesn't understand talking. He understands blowing people up and burying them in the sand and cutting off their fingers. And if Carter has issues, it's because of that bad man."

Her aunt *hmmfed*. "Mr. Zoopa wouldn't cut off an old lady's fingers. He might do *some* things, but I've got something for him if he tries." And she pulled a big gun from her purse.

Bailey cringed and took a step back. She was never going to get used to the sight of her aunt holding a gun. Then she remembered what Liza had said. That her aunt had gotten herself another fake. Even so, she touched the barrel to make sure. It was a fake all right. Hard rubber.

"For the love of God, Auntie, you didn't pull that on Zoopa, did you?"

Her aunt pursed her lips. "I was tempted. A girl has a right to protect herself. But Elvis told me no more guns. And now that I've met Mr. Zoopa, I don't think I'll need to use it."

"Too bad," Bailey said. And she meant it. Too bad, too, that the gun was only made of rubber. "And, *please*, stop calling him mister. He's not a mister anything. He's a snake."

"Okay, cupcake," her aunt acquiesced. She walked over to the window and tossed the gun out. "There. I promise, no more guns. But look on the bright side, if Elvis'd had you thrown in jail, you could have requested congenial visits."

Bailey placed a hand over her chest. Yes, congenial visits would have been nice, but *conjugal* visits would have been even better. "That's a nice thought, Auntie, but we don't have to worry about going to jail. We're going home." She took her aunt's hand and led her to the door.

It wouldn't open. They'd been locked in.

Chapter Twenty-Five

"Don't tell me, we've been kidnapped!" Aunt Fiona exclaimed. She was all wide-eyed and beaming. "Maybe if Mr. Zoopa asks for a ransom, Elvis will come and rescue us."

Bailey sighed. "I'm afraid that might be wishful thinking, Auntie. Carter is too busy at the moment to be worried about us." Too busy doing God knows what with that woman back at the hotel.

She checked the door again. Still locked. She looked around the room, over to the window. No bars. In fact, the window was wide open and a nice breeze was blowing through the room.

Certainly, if the window was open, they weren't prisoners, Bailey reasoned. The door was obviously defective. She walked over and looked out to see if climbing down the tree might be an option. It wasn't. Nearly all the lower branches had been removed, which meant if they chose that route, they'd have to slide part way down the tree's trunk. Definitely not an option.

She turned back and looked around the room for something she and her aunt might use to lower themselves to the ground.

Drapery, sheets, anything that could be tied together. But all she saw was yellow and pink everywhere. This was so not a teenage boy's room.

Bailey sat on the end of the bed to do some thinking. Beneath all the fluff of yellow and pink were sheets. Okay, so maybe they were pink, too, but it was worth considering. Though it would be a shame to disrobe such a beautiful bed to use the linens to escape the madman's mansion.

She went to the closet to look for an alternative. The closet was empty, except for a couple of boxes marked Private. She considered what could possibly be in them. Might be an interesting way to pass the time, should they happen to be stuck there for a while.

"Do you think they'll feed us?" her aunt asked.

"I don't know, Auntie. I suppose they might." Bread and water, and a dish of maggot soup on the side.

"Technically, they didn't kidnap me. Technically, I was a trespasser," Aunt Fiona said. She pressed her lips into a thin line. "I read that in some states shooting trespassers is legal."

Bailey did a mental eye roll. That certainly made her feel better.

"Do you think they'll give us a room ticket, where we can check our meal choices and hang it on our door before one a.m.?" her aunt asked.

Bailey looked at her aunt and wondered how anyone could live so long and maintain such optimism. If only there was a pill.

She crossed back over to the window and reached out, grabbing one of the old gnarled tree branches. A chunk broke off in her hand. The tree was definitely past its prime. Even if there had been branches all the way down, she wouldn't trust them to hold any weight.

She sat on the window-seat and closed her eyes against the bright sun. It felt good to just sit and let it warm her skin. No telling when she would feel heat like this again. Six months was her guess. That is, if she ever made it back to Coupeville alive.

A minute passed, and she looked out over the blue aquamarine pool that sat below the window. A smile lit her lips as she reminisced about being out there with Carter the night of the party, kissing him and falling in love. Yet, now he was in some hotel room, kissing some *other* woman.

Her throat constricted. She didn't want to cry again, so she forced herself to think about something else. Her babies. Oh, how she missed their beautiful furry faces. Tucker and Maggie May were the best dogs ever, and she couldn't wait to give each of them a big hug. Tucker would be so excited to see her that he'd spin in circles until he fell over from dizziness, and Maggie would toss her snout in the air and warble until she got a treat.

Bailey sighed with longing to see her dogs.

"Maybe I should call for room service right now," Aunt Fiona said. "You look like you could use some food."

"I'm fine," Bailey said. "I just want to go home." She stood and did some pacing to pass the time. No telling how long they'd be stuck in this room. Until Zoopa saw fit to check on them, she supposed.

After only a minute, she got tired of pacing, and sat back down. She felt like she could use a nap, so she lay back and closed her eyes and imagined being home, where she belonged. But then her stomach began to feel queasy. Maybe she did need some food.

The longer she lay there, the queasier her stomach became. Finally, she got up and made a beeline for the bathroom. She closed the door and stood in front of the toilet for a long minute, sure that she was going to be sick. Nothing happened, same as before. It was another false alarm. And frustrating. Not that she enjoyed being sick, but she also didn't enjoy feeling this way with no results. She splashed some cold water on her face, and then went back into the room. Her aunt gave her a *knowing* look. "You're wrong," she said.

"I don't think so. I think there's a cookie in the cookie jar."

Bailey shook her head. "It's just stress." She shoved a

finger to her eye to stop it from twitching.

"You just barfed," her aunt pointed out. "That's a sign of morning sickness. Course, a lot of diseases cause barfing. Food poisoning, for instance. You haven't been to the buffet, have you?"

Bailey shook her head and sucked back a whimper. All this talk about barfing and eating at the buffet was not helping matters one little bit.

Her aunt sat beside her and patted her belly. "Isn't this exciting? A baby in the family... and it isn't Mark Jefferson's."

Gawd. Bailey's eye twitched double-time. She turned to her aunt. "Listen, you can't *ever* say anything like that again. I mean it. Not to me, and especially not to Mom."

Her aunt nodded. "Gotcha. She might really move to Kalamazoo."

For sure.

Aunt Fiona looked thoughtful. "If it's a boy, you could name him Elvis. Course, seeing as your mom's boyfriend is Elvis, too, we'd have to figure out how to keep each of 'em straight. I once heard that Elvis's mafia boys used to call him 'E'. We could call them Big E, Little E, and Baby E. Or how about Old Elvis, Young Elvis, and Baby Elvis?"

"Enough!" Bailey held up a hand. "There is no baby. And I don't want to hear anymore about it. Let's just find a way out of here."

Chapter Twenty-Six

Carter ran into Maria on his way out of the casino, and she talked him into letting her go with him to Zoopa's. It didn't take a lot of talking. He wasn't in any mood to argue. Besides, she was a big girl. She could handle herself in just about any situation. She might even come in handy, should anyone need medical attention.

After commandeering one of the casino's Cadillac Escalades, he and Maria headed down Las Vegas Boulevard. Twenty minutes later, they'd only made it two blocks. Carter craned his neck and looked out the window to see what was going on. A block up from where they sat, traffic was even gnarlier, at a near stand-still. From what he could tell, four of the five lanes heading out of town were blocked, and an officer was busy threading cars and pedestrians through a tangled mess that looked like a cab had been involved in an accident. Probably with one of the pedestrians. It happened all the time. Tourists were so eager to get to their next destination that they failed to yield to traffic and counted on cab drivers to stop for them. But cab drivers waited for no one. Time wasted was lost revenue.

Carter drew his head back in the window and punched off the stereo. The background noise was clutter he didn't need. "There's an accident up ahead. It'll take forever to clear," he said to Maria.

"Turn here," she said. She pointed to a side street.

Maria was right. They would come out past the mess down the street. Carter swung the Escalade off onto the side street and maneuvered it along the backside of a new casino under construction and another one that had long been there. When they emerged, and turned back onto the Strip, they were just past the accident site. On their way again, Carter relaxed only slightly. "I'm surprised to see you're still in town," he said to Maria. "Why?" he asked. Though he didn't really expect a straight answer.

"I thought you might need help."

"Haven't you helped enough?"

She laughed quietly, offering no response.

A couple of young men darted out in front of the Escalade to cross the street against the Walk light, and Carter laid on the horn. "Dumb asses," he yelled out the window to them, but all they did was laugh and flip him off. Maria joined in by shouting a curse and adding a hand gesture of her own. This time, the men offered no retaliation. They were on a mission. Carter quickly saw what it was when the men ran up close behind a couple of young women in short skirts and painted-on tank tops. Evidently, hooking up with a couple of cuties was worth getting killed for.

Carter shook his head, though it wasn't that long ago when he would have reacted the same way in the presence of a hot woman. That was before he met Bailey. Bailey had somehow managed to tame him. He had to get to her.

A few more agonizing minutes in traffic and, at last, they were clear of the Strip. A scant twenty minutes after that, he rolled the Escalade to a stop just down from the gate that permitted entry onto Zoopa's property. He wanted to avoid alerting Zoopa and his men of his arrival. He needed to think about how to proceed. Rushing in, guns blazing didn't seem a wise choice. Someone could get hurt. He would take no chances where Bailey and her aunt were concerned. He couldn't say the same for Maria. She was fidgeting in her seat, eager to move.

"Are we going in?" she asked. "Or we gonna sit here and make out?"

Carter gave her a cross look. "This isn't a game. Lives could be at stake here."

"That's what I've always liked about you, *amor*. No games." She tossed her hair over one shoulder. "Tell me, do you never think about us anymore?"

Carter checked the clip on his gun. This was one of those trick questions. If he answered no, then he might be in for a discussion that was more complicated than he cared to have at the moment. If he said yes, then... hell, he saw no reason to even go there. They were over, and he and Bailey were getting married—if she'd still have him after he finished his business with Zoopa.

"We need to stay focused." He got out of the Escalade, pressing hard on the door to close it, rather than slamming it shut.

Maria got out after him. She sidled up next to him and gave him a soulful smile. "Are you saying you lose focus when you think about me?"

"I'm saying I don't want to get killed because I'm not paying attention. This isn't the time for us to be discussing what or who I do or don't think about."

"Do you think Bailey will want us to stop being *amigos* once she learns of our history?"

He regarded her, wary of her motives. "I wasn't going to give her a detailed account. I'd like it if you didn't, either. What's past is past. Let's leave it there."

Maria pouted. "Okay, *mijo*, though my silence will cost you." She smiled. "But don't worry, it will be painless... mostly."

Carter ignored her threat, preferring to keep his mind on the task at hand. He wasn't concerned with what she wanted for her silence. Right now, he had a woman to rescue.

He looked around the area and saw security cameras everywhere. He had no illusions. They'd already been seen. And that was probably only fair, being that Oasis cameras caught Zoopa from every angle, whenever he entered the casino. Zoopa couldn't drop a piece of lint without someone reporting it back to the control room.

"Problem?" Maria asked.

"Nothing I didn't anticipate." Carter moved along the drive, staying hidden among the foliage. Maria shadowed him. A few minutes later, he stopped and crouched behind a bush at the back of the mansion. Maria followed suit.

Carter paused, seeing the sun glint off the water in the swimming pool. He remembered the night he brought Bailey there to a party. He'd suggested they go for a swim, but she didn't have a suit and didn't like the idea of skinny-dipping. She was such an innocent back then. Full of ideas about how love could conquer all... or something like that. Until he came along and hurt her and made her forget all that nonsense. That was something he had to fix.

"Something on your mind?" Maria asked.

"Nothing I care to share." He turned his focus to the back of the house. "Once we're inside, you follow my lead. Got it?" he said. His tone was gruffer than he intended, but he wasn't about to apologize. He wanted no mistakes where Bailey was concerned.

Maria laughed softly. "Okay, tough guy."

Carter moved around behind a bush with big white flowers that smelled of oranges. His mother had planted it way back when. He could never remember what it was called, so he'd always just referred to it as the orange bush—though it never bore any fruit, orange or otherwise.

He hadn't expected so many memories to jump out at him. They were everywhere, making his head feel like it might explode.

"You okay, *mijo*?" Maria asked.

He nodded. "Fine." He would be, anyway, just as soon as he knew Bailey was safe and out of that house. He repositioned himself and the toe of his shoe hit something. He looked down at the ground. Damned if it wasn't a gun. He picked it up, and then smiled. It was a gun, all right. Fake.

He shoved the hunk of rubber into his pocket. He couldn't be sure about Bailey, but the gun confirmed that at least her aunt was here, probably inside causing Zoopa all kinds of grief.

The French doors at the back of the mansion swung open, and two of Zoopa's men came out. They each lit a cigarette and blew toxic smoke up into the still air. One of the men moved into the shade and took off his blazer. Then he pulled his tie from around his neck and tossed it over the back of a wrought-iron chair. Carter recognized him. His name was Rikko, Zoopa's top dog. They'd clashed on more than one occasion.

Both men sat. They seemed in no hurry to finish their smokes and get back inside to the air-conditioned comfort of the mansion. They were waiting.

"Let's go," Carter said over his shoulder to Maria.

"With Zoopa's boys out there?" she asked.

"Zoopa's made us. No point in hanging around out here in the bushes."

"So, what?" she asked. "We're going in with guns drawn?"

Carter grinned. "You've been watching too much television, honey. Just follow my lead." He started to leave the cover of the orange bush, but Maria caught him by the arm.

"Wait, *mijo*," she said. "You know as long as you're alive, that sonofabitch will not rest. He is like a dog that cannot sleep, because he knows if he does, that is when you will strike. Game over. You win."

Carter had no idea what she was getting at. "And?"

"I just want to make sure you have thought this through."

Thought this through? Hell. "Don't worry about me," he said. "Just remember what I told you. We do this *my* way."

"First things first, *amor*." Maria pulled him to her and let her lips languish on his in a slow sensual kiss.

"Are we good?" Carter asked when she finally let him go.

"We're good. Let's go get your girl."

Chapter Twenty-Seven

Bailey sat by the window, needing some fresh air. Instead she got a whiff of cigarette smoke. She looked down for the source. Two of Zoopa's men were on the patio. But then a movement in the bushes caught her eye. She zeroed in and saw a man. He looked familiar.

Carter?

Joy, like a fountain of fireworks, burst in her chest. Her man was there to rescue her! She looked up and thanked God. But when she looked back down, Carter wasn't alone. A woman was crouched at his side. Was that Special Skills Maria? Bailey focused hard, squinting into the sunlight, and saw that it was. But it didn't matter, because of course Carter and Maria were *both* there to rescue her and her auntie.

Oh, double joy! Bailey was feeling all kinds of happy. Even her stomach was happy. And her eye had stopped twitching. In another minute, Carter would race up the stairs and he'd find her and take her in his arms and they'd kiss and, *OMG*! He must have gotten his memory back!

She jumped to her feet, spinning around. "Carter's here, Auntie! We're going home!"

"Where?" Aunt Fiona moved over to the window and looked out. "You mean down there, kissing that woman?"

"What!" Bailey rushed back over to the window and took a look. She gasped and practically fell off the window seat. She had to be seeing things. But she wasn't. And now she knew Carter wasn't there to rescue her, after all. Probably he had more business to take care of with Zoopa.

Aunt Fiona craned her neck to see. "Say, isn't that the woman you've been calling Special Skills Maria?"

Bailey was desperate to get away... to anywhere Carter wasn't. She moved across the room, over to the door. If it was still locked, she was going to kick it down. Or maybe just scream. That would get someone's attention.

Stupid, stupid, stupid! That's what she was. Zoopa had shown her that live feed of Carter with that woman at the hotel and she'd all but forgotten about it in her excitement. And now he was outside with Maria? Unfreakingbelievable!

Just as she was about to check the door, it opened and Zoopa stood there looking all fat and smug.

"You!" Bailey poked him in the chest. "Why did you lock us in here?" Her voice was shrill and she was practically hysterical.

Zoopa's brow drew tight. "No one is stopping you from leaving." He swung the door wide. "You're free to go anytime you want."

"Are you here to torture us?" Aunt Fiona asked, hitching her chin. "If so, you might wanna start with my niece, 'cause you won't get anywhere with me. I'm old and it's likely I'll die soon, anyway."

Zoopa laughed. "Now, why would I want to torture two beautiful women? I'm just here to see how you're doing."

"Not good," Bailey said. "We need to go home. And now we've missed our flight."

"No problem," Zoopa said. "One of my men will drive you to the airport. You'll be back home in time to get a few hours' sleep before daybreak."

Great, Bailey thought. Not that she'd be able to sleep after a day like this. "What about our bags? We left them at the hotel."

"My men have already picked them up," Zoopa told her.

She narrowed her eyes at him. He'd been waiting for this moment. She'd bet on it. He probably had a hidden camera out there in the garden and knew Carter was in the bushes, kissing Maria. It had probably been his plan all along to keep her and her aunt there until Carter came to the rescue. In fact, it wouldn't surprise her if Zoopa was using her as bait.

She thought about that for a minute. Bait or not, he couldn't possibly have known the kissing scene in the bushes would happen. Could he? Probably. He was just like Carter. They both seemed to know everything that was going on in Vegas before it ever happened.

She did a mental head shake, knowing she was being ridiculous. But all this spying and sabotage and threats was just too much. This wasn't normal life. She needed to get back to baking pies and taking her dogs for walks and fighting off Mark's advances. Scratch that. She'd prefer not to ever again have to fight off Mark's advances. He needed to go make advances on some other girl.

And, too, she needed to get her auntie home. If they stayed in Las Vegas much longer, her aunt might be in danger of becoming a full-fledged gun moll.

"Let's go," she told Zoopa. "Come on, Auntie." She grabbed her aunt's hand.

"In case you're thinking of having your men make a detour out into the desert," Aunt Fiona said, "I think you should know my niece is pregnant. That would make three victims you'd be responsible for."

All eyes turned to Bailey.

"Well, well, all the better," Zoopa said.

For who? Bailey wondered. Not her. She opened her mouth to once again deny the pregnancy rumor. But why? What did it matter if the bad guy thought she was carrying Carter's baby?

A big linebacker looking fellow appeared in the doorway. He whispered something to Zoopa and they both stepped out into the hallway.

Bailey's heart raced. What was going on out there? And what if, when they were making their getaway, they ran into Carter? That would be a disaster. As mad as she was at him, if she looked into his eyes, it'd be all over. She'd go all gooey inside.

"You okay?" Aunt Fiona asked.

No. "I'm fine, why?"

"You moaned."

"Did not."

"Did so."

Zoopa and his men stepped back into the room, and Aunt Fiona looked over at them. "Didn't she moan?"

All three men nodded.

Great. Of course, Zoopa had the room bugged. He'd probably heard everything they'd said in that room. Bailey felt her blood pressure rise. Here she was suffering with a broken heart and these people had no respect for her pain.

"Your boyfriend is here," Zoopa said.

Bailey's stomach did a little flip. "I don't want to see him."

Zoopa nodded at one of his men. "Derek here will take you down the back staircase."

Well, that was easy. And that was how life was supposed to be, right? People were supposed to fall in love, buy a house, live their lives. Not that adjustments wouldn't need to be made along the way, and to be sure, life with Carter would have been an *extreme* adjustment—he was a complicated man, after all. But that didn't mean they couldn't have had a normal life together, with mortgage payments, children, and college expenses.

If he'd only stop kissing other women!

Down the back stairwell they raced, and all Bailey could think about was how she'd never really known Carter. Her only excuse was that passion and chemistry had been ruling her head. But no more. As of this very moment, her love trip with Security Guy was officially over.

With their hands raised in casual surrender, Carter and Maria left the cover of the orange bush and walked toward Zoopa's men. The difference in temperature from shade to sun made it feel like they'd just walked into hell.

Zoopa's men looked up in feigned surprise, but they were swift to react. Their weapons were drawn in an instant.

Carter lowered his hands and spread them wide. "No need for all that. I'm just here to pick up a couple hotel guests."

The men chuckled. Rikko gave Carter a nod of respect, though he and Carter were nowhere near being friends. Ever since Rikko had run his hands up Bailey's legs in search of a stolen diamond, it was all Carter could do to keep from making Rikko an amputee.

"You know the rule, Davis," Rikko said. "Check your weapons at the door."

Carter unholstered his 9 mm and handed it over. "That's all I have. And I expect to get it back in working condition," he told Rikko.

Rikko acknowledged nothing. He turned his attention to Maria. "Gun?"

Maria wasn't so obliging. She huffed in anger at the request.

"I'd be careful if I were you," Carter told him. "She's a mean one."

Rikko ignored Carter's warning. He reached to pat Maria down and things went from bad to worse. Maria reacted with a knee to Rikko's crotch and a fist to his face. He all but went down to his knees, holding his boys with one hand and his nose with the other. He did some hard blinking, like he might be close to tears, but he managed to hold it together. "*Sonofabitch*," he said, doubling over. "Fucking bitch." Red liquid squished between his fingers, and sweat beaded on his forehead. His face was one big grimace.

"Told you," Carter said.

Rikko glared up at them from under his sweat. "She broke my nose."

Carter spread his hands in supplication. "The lady doesn't like to be touched."

Rikko continued holding nose. "Give me your fucking gun," he told Maria.

Maria smiled and handed over her piece. "Sure, all you had to do was say '*por favor*.'"

Rikko stuffed Carter's gun into his waistband and tossed Maria's at Zoopa's other watch dog. They led the way inside, but Rikko kept a close eye on Maria, making sure to stay well out of her reach.

Carter didn't think Rikko needed to worry. Maria had done a little damage and she was happy for the moment. If not, Rikko would find out about it soon enough. If there was one thing he knew about Maria, when she wasn't happy, she let it be known. Which was why he probably shouldn't have let her tag along. Her hatred for Zoopa, curious as it was, was as palpable as his.

He looked over and tried to get a reading about what was going on inside her head. Impossible. She was the picture of cool, not giving anything away. He knew better, though. It wouldn't take much to push her over the edge. And no matter how many times she'd agreed to let him handle things, she had a tendency to do as she damn well pleased, which could be dangerous for everyone concerned.

Immediately inside the door, Rikko stopped them. He waved a wand down their fronts, then down their backs, and seemed satisfied they had no more weapons. "In there," he said, nudging them along.

Carter led the way, and then stopped when they were standing inside a large foyer at the bottom of a staircase that he and Twinkie used to enjoy zipping up and down when they were kids. Memories. They sucked sometimes. This was one of those times.

Zoopa appeared at the top of the stairs. "Davis," he spread

his arms in a welcome gesture. "To what do I owe this pleasure?" Then he zeroed in on Maria. "I see you've brought along your sidekick."

Carter heard Maria huff and he slid her a look. Her face was a nice shade of angry and she had a vein pulsating in her neck. In a mere thirty seconds, she'd gone from cool to red hot. Her Southern Miss half had been taken over by her kick-ass-now, ask-questions-later half, and he didn't like it one little bit.

"You're not gonna make me regret bringing you here with me, are you?" he asked her, lowering his voice.

She didn't say a word. Her eyes were focused on Zoopa.

"You hear me?" Carter urged her to respond. "I don't want Bailey caught in the middle of some vendetta you have against that rat bastard."

She shot him a look and spoke quietly. "Take your head out of your ass, *mijo*. That man means to kill you."

Carter looked at Zoopa. Zoopa's eyes were red with rage. Maria was probably right. Not that he hadn't figured that out a long time ago. In fact, at this very minute it was likely Zoopa was pondering whether or not he wanted to make another trip out into the desert. But spending one more hour out in that heat wasn't part of Carter's plan. Not unless he was already dead.

"I'm not here to see you," he told Zoopa. "I'm here for Bailey and her aunt."

Zoopa chuckled and started down the stairs. "Ah, Bailey. You just missed her. Traffic can be a bear sometimes, huh? She gave me a message for you, though. Said she never wanted to see you again. Too bad. I thought the two of you made such a cute couple."

Carter clenched his jaw. Hearing Zoopa say Bailey's name only fueled the fire that made him hate the man. And the fact that Zoopa somehow knew he and Maria had been stuck in traffic didn't surprise him in the least. Creating a snarled traffic mess to ensure he'd miss seeing Bailey was just Zoopa's style.

When Zoopa got to the bottom of the stairs, he continued on into the library. Carter and Maria followed, and Zoopa gestured for them to sit. They didn't. Carter wasn't there to have a whiskey and shoot the shit.

"Where's Bailey?" he asked.

Zoopa pulled a cigar from the wooden box on the desk. He snipped the end of the cigar and lit it. A ceiling fan swept most of the smoke up and away, but the smell lingered. Premium quality. "Derek took your girl to the airport. It seems she doesn't like it here anymore. Can't say as I blame her. See, here's the thing. Women don't like it when they catch their man cheating. It takes all the air out of a relationship."

"My relationship with Bailey is none of your business," Carter said.

"You're right," Zoopa said. "But I have to tell you, you should have seen the look on her face when I showed her what you were up to with Ms. Hunter." He put the cigar to his mouth and puffed hard. Smoke curled around him. "I've been meaning to ask, how're things going with the Elvis act?"

Carter remembered Ms. Hunter was the woman with the AC problem. That Zoopa had had a hand in that too was no surprise. "You think you have it all figured out, don't you? Well, you don't know Bailey. She's never going to believe anything you say. She may be mad right now, but she'll think about it and realize you were just setting me up."

Zoopa shrugged. "Maybe." He puffed a little more on his cigar. "You know, I like Bailey. That's why I gave her a free pass. But you?" He compressed his lips and shook his head. "Not so much. What is it with you, anyway? Every time I leave you for the buzzards, someone comes along and saves you. Then you end up causing me even more trouble."

"He's goddamn Superman," Rikko said, laughing.

Zoopa gave Rikko a stony glare. "Or maybe you're stupid, and I need to hire me some new help."

Rikko shut his trap and stared at the floor.

"You know what they say," Carter said, spreading his arms,

"only the good die young."

Zoopa was non-committal. He turned his cold, unblinking eyes to Maria. "And what am I going to do with you? First, I catch you cheating in my casino, and now here you are again, trying to do who knows what. I think you might be more trouble than Elvis here."

Carter looked at Maria. "Cheating?"

"He lies," she said. "He kicked me outta his casino, 'cause I won a little money. He was afraid I was going to clean him out." She smiled sourly. "Only thing is, I left behind some of my chips. I think I would like them back now, *por favor*," she told Zoopa.

The hair on the back of Carter's neck bristled. He'd underestimated Maria's objective. Not only had she hoped to reconcile with him, by hurting Zoopa financially, but she was in revenge mode because Zoopa had humiliated her by asking her to leave his casino.

Zoopa chuckled dryly. "You're getting nothing. You were cheating and you got caught. You're lucky I didn't call the cops on you."

Carter held up a hand. He needed to stifle whatever was about to happen. "I don't care what's going on between you two. You can settle that later. Bailey is my only concern right now."

"Give it up, Davis. Bailey's done with you," Zoopa said. "Now answer me a question... what did you do with the kidney you stole from my guest? Sell it on the black market? Jesus, I wish I'd thought of that. I'd be one rich sonofabitch. You wanna come work for me? We'd make a great team." He drew hard on his cigar and tilted his head back, blowing another cloud of smoke up toward the fan.

"He didn't take the kidney. I did," Maria said. She smiled a smug smile.

Zoopa shrugged, casually. "I know. I just wanted to hear you say it." His eyes were like cold black stones. "You surprise me, Ms. Cruz. I wouldn't have thought some back-water tramp would have the brains to pull something of this magnitude off."

Jesus. Carter felt all hope of things going smoothly slip away. Both Maria and Zoopa were out to even a score, and if Zoopa thought he'd rendered Maria harmless by having her gun checked at the door, he was a fool. She didn't need a gun. As long as she had her hands, she was good to go. She was one tough bitch.

"You are lucky I do have brains," she told Zoopa. "Otherwise, your guest who lost her kidney might be a corpse right now."

Zoopa regarded her with a nasty sneer. He waved a hand at Rikko, motioning for him to remove her from the room. Rikko hesitated. It was likely he hadn't forgotten about what had happened a few minutes earlier, when he'd attempted to search her.

"What the hell are you waiting for?" Zoopa bellowed. "Get her the fuck outta here."

Rikko stepped forward, but Maria wasn't about to be taken anywhere. She side-jabbed him, and then went for Zoopa's throat. Hitting her mark, Zoopa's eyes were bulging from their sockets before either of his men could react. He gasped for air like a man suffering from emphysema.

Zoopa's men scrambled to help. Rikko tried prying Maria's hands from Zoopa's face, and Zoopa's other dog grabbed Maria around her waist. Their effort to rescue their boss was futile. Maria's grip on Zoopa was firm. She had both her thumbs dug deep into the flesh over his eyes and she wasn't wavering.

"How do you like me now, you fat bastard?" she screamed. "I bet you didn't expect a back-water tramp like me to get the jump on you with your boys standing right here, did you?"

Carter was impressed. He wanted to pat her on the back and praise her lavishly, but he knew the outcome was still up in the air, and not likely going to be good, even though at the moment, she seemed to be winning the war.

Rikko finally pulled her away from Zoopa, and Zoopa was left squinting and sputtering, trying to get his eyesight back.

He'd dropped his cigar on the floor and it was lying there smoldering. Carter toed it out. No sense in letting the house burn down.

"You'll pay for that," Zoopa told Maria. He nodded at Rikko, and this time Rikko didn't hesitate. He manhandled Maria over to the door, making sure to keep clear of her feet.

Carter's mind went into overdrive. If he let Zoopa's men take Maria out of the room, it might be the last anyone ever saw of her. That wasn't in the plan. He might not want to run off to Charleston with her, but it didn't mean he wanted her dead, either. He fingered the gun in his pocket. Granted, it was made of rubber, but Zoopa and his men wouldn't know that. Not at first, anyway.

"Leave her be," he told Rikko. He pulled the gun from his pocket and held it close, adding a silent prayer that no one would notice its lack of authenticity.

Zoopa's eyes assessed. He shot Rikko a sharp glare. "I thought you checked them for weapons." His face was still red from being choked and he looked as though he might be on the verge of having a stroke.

Rikko pulled Carter's 9 mm from his waistband. "This is all I found on him. I even used the wand." The blood from his nose had dried, and though he'd done his best to wipe it off, some of it still remained, dark and crusty around his mouth. He looked almost clownish and it was hard to take him seriously. For sure, Zoopa wasn't.

"Well, the wand's broken! What do you call that?" Zoopa shouted.

In the moment it took everyone to look at the gun in Carter's hand, Zoopa slid open his desk drawer and came out with his own weapon. He fired off a round in Carter's direction, but Maria was ready. She dove in front of Carter, taking the impact of the bullet with her own body. It dropped her to the floor.

Carter didn't waste any time. He took two steps and knocked his gun out of Rikko's hand. It fell to the floor, and he

and Rikko both slid across hard wood, grabbing for it. Carter
got there first. Rolling over, he kicked Rikko in the chest, and
then he fired off a round at Zoopa.

Zoopa's eyes opened wide, like he couldn't believe he'd
been shot. Then he dropped his gun and stumbled forward. He
hit his head on the edge of the desk on his way down to the
floor. He didn't budge, just lay there lifeless and crumpled,
with his eyes blinking up at the ceiling. Finally, he groaned
and it was lights out.

"Jesus," Rikko said. "You killed him."

Carter felt for a pulse. It was weak, but there. "Wishful
thinking," he told Rikko. "He'll suffer some, probably have a
monster headache, but he'll live."

Maria was still on the floor. Carter crouched next to her. He
didn't need to feel for a pulse. She was a survivor. Plus, he
could see the rise and fall of her chest.

She opened her eyes and smiled a half-assed smile. "You
owe me, *mijo*."

"I didn't need this complication," he told her. "You were
supposed to let me handle things."

"You know how stubborn I can be," she said, the sound of
her voice quiet and low.

"You're the stubbornest woman this side of the Grand
Canyon," he agreed.

"Nobody has to know you were here," she said. "Go to
Bailey."

Carter glanced over at Rikko.

"I never saw you," Rikko told him.

Chapter Twenty-Eight

Carter stared at the picture of Bailey that sat on the corner of his desk. Having it to look at had been the only thing keeping him sane these last couple of weeks. Time couldn't pass any slower. And he couldn't explain to Metro what had happened to Zoopa any better than he already had. It was self-defense, everyone had agreed. Even so, the powers that be had insisted he stay put until there was an official announcement that attempted murder charges wouldn't be filed.

If he'd known it was going to take so long, though, he'd have gone to Bailey right away. He needed to fix things with her. Screw the consequences. He could have dealt with them after he and Bailey were back on track.

He turned his attention to a pile of folders stacked on his desk. Several new employees were scheduled to start security training this week. All that was required of him was to sign on the dotted line.

He pulled the first folder out and signed the new-hire papers, then the next, and the next. He was just about to sign the last one when his office door swung open. It was Mike Shur. "Got a minute?" he asked.

Carter waved him in, and then scribbled his signature on the last new-hire's paperwork.

Mike kept quiet and just stood at the front of Carter's desk, looking like he had fire ants chewing on his leg.

"You got something you want to say, or you just going to stand there and sweat?" Carter asked.

"I got something I need to tell you," Mike said, shifting his weight from one foot to the other.

"Okay." Carter tossed his pen aside, sat back in his chair, and folded his hands behind his head. "Let's hear it."

"It's about me and Bailey."

Carter cocked an eyebrow. "I didn't know there was a *you-and-Bailey*." He snatched up a pencil and began working it between his fingers.

"There isn't. Not like that, anyway." Mike rubbed a hand over the back of his neck. "This isn't easy, so I'm just gonna say it. Me and Bailey, we kissed. No, that's not right. She didn't kiss me. *I* kissed her."

Anger swelled inside Carter's chest. Adrenaline shot through his body, making his heart race. Of all the things he could have imagined Mike might need to say, this was the last thing he expected. "Did I hear you right? You kissed Bailey?"

"Yes, sir. But don't be mad at Bailey. She was in a vulnerable place and I was just trying to comfort her. It wasn't planned, or anything. It just happened." He swallowed. "I thought you should know. It's been bothering me."

Carter stopped working the pencil and snapped it into two jagged pieces. He did some mental cursing, but so far, so good, he'd managed to keep from putting his hands around Mike's throat. "Is that why you've been popping Tums? Here, I thought it was all the cheeseburgers you've been eating." Mike had no response, which was just as well. Carter had heard enough. "Get the hell outta here," he told Mike.

Mike did as he was told, and Carter remained sitting at his desk, stewing. Bad enough he had to worry about the likes of Mark Jefferson going after Bailey, but now one of his own employees had a thing for her? He gripped the edge of his desk so hard his knuckles turned white. He wanted to pick his desk up and throw it, but he settled for snapping another pencil. They were cheap and he had plenty.

The door opened again and this time it was Detective Mark Forester. He and Carter had been friends for some time, but right now Carter wasn't looking at him as a friend. Forester was likely there on business. He'd been keeping Carter apprised of what was going on with the Zoopa case.

"I hope you have some good news for me," Carter said.

Detective Forester chuckled and settled into a chair at the front of Carter's desk. "Bad day?"

"You have no idea."

"Maybe I can help," Forester said. "The DA has decided not to press charges. I guess that means you're going to have to marry Bailey, after all." He shook his head. "Shame. She's such a homely thing."

Carter frowned. "Watch what you're saying about the woman I love."

They both laughed.

"Have you talked to her?" Forester asked.

"Tried calling. Either she's never home, or she's just not answering. Can't say as I blame her. I put her through a lot."

"No way to leave a message?"

"Her answering machine is off. She's making it hard for me."

Forester nodded. "Women have certain rules. Thou shalt not kiss other women, or get caught giving them foot rubs."

Carter rubbed a hand alongside his jaw. "Yeah, I know. I have a lot of making up to do. I just hope she'll at least give me a chance to explain."

Forester looked at his watch. "If you leave now, you can be in Seattle by dinner time. You could take Bailey to a nice restaurant—stop and get her a gift, first—then get down on your knees and beg. Women like begging. Makes 'em feel like you can't live without 'em." He grinned. "I forgot. You're not the begging type. Guess that means you'll have to count on charm." He shrugged. "Do your Elvis thing. That always seems to work."

"*Used* to work," Carter said. "She's wise to my ways, now." He reached and pulled a small box from his desk drawer. "I already got her a gift." He opened the box, revealing a sparkling diamond ring in a white gold setting, complete with one large, flawless diamond, plus, a row of smaller diamonds on either side. Simple, yet elegant. Just like Bailey.

Forester gave a low whistle. "Is this in addition to the other ring you gave her?"

"I figure if she has to plan a new wedding, she deserves a new ring."

"Makes sense." Forester stood. "Good luck, my friend. I hope it all works out for you and Bailey this time."

After Forester was gone, Carter sat at his desk, looking at the ring and thinking about how he'd almost let his need for revenge cost him the best thing that had ever happened to him. Never again, he vowed. At last, he and Bailey could be together, and nothing was going to stop them from getting married. Unless she refused to forgive him. If that was the case, maybe he *would* beg.

He tucked the ring into his pocket and stacked the new-employee paperwork at the side of his desk, with a sticky note on top, telling whoever saw it to go ahead and begin the new-hire orientation process. He'd get to know the new members of his security team when he got back from Seattle.

He made a quick phone call and checked in with Mike who was off seeing to business on the gaming floor, and then he was on his way. But as eager as he was to get to Bailey, he needed to make just one stop on the way to the airport. He didn't know how much time Rosa had left and he wanted to sing for her once more and let her know he was thinking about her.

Chapter Twenty-Nine

Bailey was a few blocks up from her cottage, on her way back from picking a late crop of berries she'd discovered on one of her morning walks with Tucker and Maggie May. Tucker and Maggie were trotting by her side, keeping her company, but she was beginning to feel the need for human company. After what she'd gone through with Carter, she'd been taking some time to herself and hadn't seen much of anyone since she'd gotten back from Las Vegas. She'd told herself that she was happy in her routine of baking pies during the day and spending quiet evenings at home alone with her pups. But she suspected the truth was something else entirely. Because, really, how could she be happy? Right now, she and Carter were supposed to be on their honeymoon. But they weren't. And with each passing day not hearing from him, it seemed more and more certain they were truly and completely over.

With Carter out of her life, it was reasonable to expect she'd begin dating again. Though she might have to cross the water and check out the dating pool in Seattle. Pickings were slim to none in Coupeville. It was mostly retirees who were looking for a slower pace. The only eligible bachelors she could even think of were Brian and Mark. And being that Brian was still involved with Liza, that left Mark as *the* most eligible bachelor in all of Coupeville.

Scary.

It wasn't that Mark was *so* bad, but he was bad enough that it would make her mom cry if she thought Mark might become part of the family. In her mom's eyes, Mark was nothing more than a grease-monkey with an out-of-control libido. For the most part, Bailey agreed... about Mark's libido. But he was also a good friend who was always willing to work on her car for free. That was something. She just didn't think she'd ever again see him as someone she'd want to hook up with.

She sighed, pushing all thoughts of Mark and Carter from her mind. For now, she just wanted to enjoy her walk. She continued on the well-traveled path through a piece of property that was forested with madrona trees. Tucker's and Maggie's paws crunched on the peeling bark, and the sound made her think of a time when, as a young girl, she'd spent an entire afternoon tumbling in huge piles of maple leaves that her Uncle Rex had raked together. It was a nice memory.

The path ended, and so did the crunching, and Bailey headed down the street in the direction of the twins' auto repair shop. Tucker and Maggie knew the way and they were eager to get to their favorite pit stop. As soon as the auto shop came into sight, they took off running for a planting bed where a variety of shrubs and flowers grew, despite being watered by every canine in town.

Tucker arrived first and immediately hunched over to do his business. But Maggie, true hunter that she was, spied a mound of dirt and went at it like a rototiller with both paws, looking to turn up some hidden critter. Bailey laughed, watching her.

Tucker had finished his business and was now doing his part to make sure every bush got watered. Bailey didn't bother checking her pockets for doo doo bags. She hadn't brought any. The way she saw it, leaving Tucker's poo for the twins to scoop gave them something to do during off-hours. She was a good friend that way.

When both dogs seemed satisfied with their visit to the planting bed, Bailey looked and saw Brian through The Auto Shop window. He was helping a customer. If it had been Mark, she might have continued on home. But Brian was slightly less annoying and a lot easier to handle than Mark, so she decided now was as good a time as any to get back into socializing with friends.

"Let's go get a treat from Uncle Brian," Bailey said to Tucker and Maggie. Both dogs reacted to the word "treat" and ran ahead to wait for her at the door. They danced on all paws, eager to go inside.

Bailey caught up and pushed through the door, and Brian tossed Tucker and Maggie each a Milk Bone.

"You gonna clean up after your dog?" he asked.

"Huh?" She looked at him in all innocence, and he returned to his customer, a woman Bailey had never seen before.

Gretchen Carlyle was there, too. She was sitting over in the corner on an orange plastic chair, circa sometime in the 70s, waiting, and looking smart in a familiar floral dress that was cinched at the waist with a wide belt.

"Hi, Mrs. Carlyle," Bailey said to her. "Nice dress."

Gretchen smiled. "Your mom gave it to me. She said she was cleaning out her closet and getting rid of all the clothes that made her look like a frumpy old housewife. I guess it don't matter if I wear old housewife clothes. I *am* an old housewife."

Bailey did a mental head shake. She sure wished she could figure out what was going on with her mom. Genetic or menopause, either way, she wished it would just be over, so that things could get back to being semi-normal again.

Once Brian finished with the stranger, he motioned to Gretchen, and she moved over in front of the counter. "Let me finish with Mrs. Carlyle, then I'll be with you," he told Bailey.

"Oh, that's all right. I just stopped by to say hi. So, hi," she said and she went back out the door. That was enough socializing for one day.

Tucker and Maggie immediately ran back over to the planting bed. Tucker watered a couple of bushes, and Maggie dug up a freshly planted flower bulb. She took a bite out of it, but quickly realized it wasn't food and spit it back out. She was a dog with discriminating taste, whereas Tucker ate things that made Bailey gag at the very *idea* that he'd even put them in his mouth.

"Hey, Peaches," a voice called to her.

Bailey looked. It was Mark. He was eyeing her and leaning against the side of one of the open car bays, rubbing grease from his hands with a rag that was already so black with grease it was beside the point. She gave him a quick hand wave.

He dropped the rag and made his way over to her. "Haven't seen you around much," he said. "Glad to see you made it home." He grinned. "You hear from Sideburns yet?"

"No." And she didn't care to talk about Carter, or any other part of her Las Vegas adventure with him. "He's been busy."

"You wanna do a little crying on my shoulder?"

She frowned. "Do you see me crying? I just stopped here to let my dogs take care of business." She nodded at the large brown pile Tucker had made. It was next to a nice rhody—a Grace Seabrook, one of her favorites—that bloomed blood red every spring.

"You gonna scoop that up?" Mark asked.

"I could," she fished around inside her pocket, just for show, "but, sorry, I seem to be fresh outta bags."

"I have some," Mark said. He pulled a couple out of his cover-all pockets and grinned, handing them to her. "This I gotta see."

"One will do. Thanks." She snatched one of the bags from his hand, but made no move to pick up Tucker's leavings. It was a disgusting job. If Mark were a gentleman, he'd offer to do it. She waited to see if he would.

"It's a big pile," Mark commented. "Plus, there are a few

more over there." He pointed to an area where there were *several* more piles. "Would you mind?" His eyes flashed with amusement. He was enjoying this. So much for being a gentleman.

Bailey appraised the piles. Some of them were *huge*. "My dogs didn't leave those," she said. "The small ones probably belong to Lea Townsend's Yorkshire terrier, and I don't know about the rest. Anyway, I'm not scooping any other dog's poo piles. They could be diseased."

Mark laughed. "That's your aunt talking. When did you ever hear of anyone getting a disease from dog poo?"

She thought about that for a minute. She'd never actually heard of anyone contracting a disease from dog poo.

Still.

"Besides," Mark continued. "Those piles weren't left by a strange dog. They were left by *my* dog. I figure after all the work I've done on your car, the least you could do is scoop some poop for me."

"Nice try. My car is new. You've only worked on it once, when the top wouldn't go up. Besides, you don't have a dog," Bailey reminded him.

"Do so. I just got him. Name's Chandler." He turned and gave a short whistle. Two seconds later a big dog, glistening black fur from head to tail, bounded out from inside one of the car bays. He stopped beside Bailey and shook, leaving a deposit of *wet* all over the front of her.

She backed away. "Gross!"

"He's not gross," Mark said. "It's hot out. He's got a lot of hair. I just hosed him down. I took him down to the water, but he doesn't seem too interested in swimming. He mostly seems interested in sleeping."

Bailey stepped closer and rubbed Chandler's dark coat. He wasn't so gross, after all. His fur was silky and shiny in the sun and he looked well taken care of. But not by Mark. She didn't believe for one minute that he was Chandler's owner. "Hey, boy," she said, stroking Chandler's back. "Where'd you come from? Where's your mom and dad?" Chandler looked up at her with big brown eyes that sparked with quiet energy. He might not be much of a swimmer, but he sure seemed like a nice dog, and with all that hair looked to be part retriever, part Newfoundland.

Surreptitiously, she checked to see if Chandler was wearing a name tag. He was, and it did indeed say Chandler.

"Where'd you get him?" she asked Mark.

Mark shrugged. "He just happened along."

"You found him?"

"He found me."

Bailey rolled her eyes. "Okay, *he* found *you*. Are you doing anything to *find* his owner?"

Mark nodded at the shop. "I put up a sign, says Big Black Dog, inquire inside."

Bailey rolled her eyes a second time. Obviously, if this poor dog was going to make it home to his *real* owners, she was going to have to take part in the operation. As she stood there contemplating what to do, Chandler ran over to Tucker and sniffed his rump, but Tucker had privacy issues and he quickly scooted out of range. Maggie, however, was more accommodating. She allowed a three-second rump sniff. But that was it. Any longer and things might turn violent. She'd been attacked a couple of times by delinquent dogs and was quick to go into defense mode. Plus, she tended to be wary of anyone, human or otherwise, that came anywhere near her mommy.

Bailey nervously awaited the eruption that was sure to come. Surprisingly, it never did. Instead, Maggie went into full wag mode. She heartily approved of Chandler's sniffing.

Love at first sniff, perhaps?

Impossible. Tucker was the only boy dog for Maggie May. She'd been smitten with him ever since she'd first latched onto his neck with her sharp puppy teeth, and the feelings were mutual. At the moment, though, Tucker didn't seem concerned that another dog was moving in on his turf. He was busy watering all the bushes in the planting bed.

"Looks like they're gonna get along fine," Mark said. He nodded at the brown piles again. "Seeing as Chandler's almost family, do you mind?"

"That would be a definite no," Bailey said. As soft and beautiful as Chandler was, she wasn't about to scoop his poop. "Look at it this way, one day you'll have kids, and this will prepare you for what you're gonna see in their diapers."

Mark got a gleam in his eye. "Are you saying what I think you're saying? That you want to have my baby?"

Bailey felt that *eew* feeling in her stomach coming on again. She hoped it was another false alarm.

Gretchen Carlyle appeared. She'd finished with Brian and was on her way to her car. "Are you all right, dear?" she asked. "You don't look so well. Shall I call your aunt? I think she's a better doctor than Doc Russo ever was. I pricked my thumb on a rose thorn and it got all red and throbby, and your aunt came over and fixed me good as new."

"I'm fine, Mrs. Carlyle, thanks," Bailey told her. The *eew* feeling had passed.

Gretchen got into her twenty-year-old Plymouth and was on her way. Then Bailey and Mark were alone again. They stood side-by-side watching the love birds, Maggie and Chandler get to know each other. Tucker had made himself scarce. He'd slipped back inside The Auto Shop to beg for another dog biscuit from Brian.

Mark nodded at Maggie and Chandler. "Maybe they'll have a family," he said. "Like us."

"No. *So* not like us," Bailey said. "If I have a family, it'll be with my husband... which won't be you." She poked him in the chest.

Mark wasn't ready to let up. "I think you might be in denial, Peaches. Elvis doesn't remember you." He wrapped a sympathetic arm around her shoulder. "And if you are thinking about having a family, I wouldn't wait too long. Tick tock, tick tock."

Bailey jabbed him hard in the ribs and moved out of kicking range before she did something to render Mark incapable of fathering children.

"Ouch! Okay," Mark said, grabbing his side. "So, you're not ready to have my baby. But I know you've been lonely, so how about if me and Chandler come over later, and we can all watch a movie together. I could borrow *Marley and Me*, or maybe *Old Yeller* from my mom."

Bailey looked at Mark and contemplated his offer. It was hard to believe he even had a mom. But everyone has a mom, right? And now she was feeling bad about jabbing him and hurting another woman's child. Plus, it was highly likely she'd gone insane even thinking about letting Mark come to her house for the evening when she was feeling so needy and vulnerable. The last time she felt this way, she was in Carter's office and she and Carter had ended up with their clothes in a heap on the floor. But that was then, and this was now, and she really could use some friend time.

"Okay," she relented. "I'll see you later."

Mark eyed her for a long minute. "Really?" he said at last. "You're not just messing with me?"

She nodded. "Really." Though she questioned her judgment in agreeing to watch a sad dog movie. The last thing she needed was another reason to cry.

Tucker had gotten his treat from Brian and came happily trotting back. Bailey hooked Tucker and Maggie to their leashes and she turned toward home, not looking back once. She didn't need to. Knowing Mark, it was likely he had a string of drool hanging from his bottom lip.

When Bailey got home to her little white and blue cottage that overlooked Penn Cove Bay, she saw her neighbor, Old Man Winston, sitting out on his front porch, watching the world go by. Old Man Winston was a crusty old soul. He had sea blue eyes that were watery with age and a smile that was seldom seen. He was a war survivor, and word was he had an arsenal big enough to protect the entire island. Most people were afraid of him and not many dared to enter his domain. Bailey wasn't afraid, though. Living next door, she knew him better than anyone, and beneath his crusty exterior, Old Man Winston was really a sheep in wolves clothing.

"Hi, Mr. Winston," she said, her smile wide and genuine. She and Old Man Winston hadn't had a conversation in forever. "I couldn't find enough for a pie, so I thought maybe you'd like these." She handed him her pail of berries.

Surprise lit Old Man Winston's face and he even attempted a smile. He took the pail from Bailey and gave her a thank-you nod, and then he retreated back into his cave, a cottage that was similar to hers.

Bailey's heart felt lighter knowing she may have brightened the old man's day. Probably no one had ever given him a pail of berries. She scratched the top of Tucker's head. "I guess maybe he won't be shaking a stick at you anymore for tinkling on his bushes."

She walked through her front door, feeling better than she had in days. Until she saw her mom sitting on her sofa, looking frazzled.

Chapter Thirty

All of Bailey's good feelings fizzled. Not too many reasons would have her mom dropping by for a visit without calling first… etiquette and all. "What's happened?" she asked her mom.

"Either I'm having a hot flash, or I've got Typhoid," her mom said. She ran a hand across her forehead. "That's according to Fiona, anyway, and I suppose I have to take her word for it, now that Doc Russo is gone."

Bailey gave her mom a doubtful look. "You're not really going to take anything Aunt Fiona says seriously, are you?"

Her mom sighed. "No. And that's not really why I'm here. I wanted to talk to you about something. Your aunt says you haven't been feeling well."

Gawd. Obviously, her auntie had opened her mouth to her mom about the possibility there might be a baby on the way. Bailey waved a dismissive hand, hoping she was being paranoid. "I'm fine. I'm sure it was just stress from planning the wedding and what was going on with Carter."

"Are you sure? Your aunt says differently."

Bailey gave her mom an I-don't-know-what-you're-talking-about look. She saw no reason to have a might-be-pregnant conversation. "I'm positive. But now that you're here, would you like to stay for a cup of tea? I have green, black, and peppermint." She'd purchased the peppermint after having read that it helped settle an unsettled stomach.

Speaking of unsettled, both of her babies were looking out the front window, and Maggie's tail commenced wagging. Bailey knew it couldn't be Mark. As eager as he was to spend time with her, it was too early for his arrival. She looked and saw a crowd of women gathering on the sidewalk. Front and center was her own auntie. Some of the women were carrying brightly-colored packages that were adorned with plenty of curly ribbon. They waved excitedly when they saw her.

"What's going on out there?" Bailey asked her mother. She smiled and waved back at the crowd of women.

"I should have warned you. Your aunt has put together a shower... of sorts. It's good to have a support group at a time like this, you being unwed and all."

Bailey groaned. This pregnancy business had gotten out of hand. Once and for all, she needed to set her auntie, and now her mom too, straight. Later. Right now, she didn't have time. "Mom, you have to send all those women away. I'll come over tomorrow and we'll talk. And, frankly, I'm surprised you're not having a hot flash over this."

"Well," her mom said, "I probably should. But I'm just trying to be supportive."

"No need. I promise." She looked at her clock on the living room wall. "I don't think I even have time for a cup of tea. I need to take a long bath. Mark is coming over tonight and we're going to watch a movie."

"Mark? Jefferson?" her mom asked.

"Yes, Mom. Mark Jefferson."

"But... what about Elvis?"

"Elvis doesn't remember me. We can talk about that later, too."

"But what about..."

Bailey guided her mom over to the door. "Thanks for

stopping by, and tell Auntie I'm especially looking forward to talking to *her* later." She nudged her mom out the door, and then she heard Tucker's tail thumping on the floor. He was looking up at her with his smiley dog face that seemed to be saying *I feel your pain.* She scratched behind his ear. "You're a good boy, Tucker. At least you understand my plight."

The phone rang, and it was Liza. "Let's go to the street fair over in Oak Harbor tonight and, afterward, we can get shit-faced," she said.

"Sounds good to me," Bailey told her, and meant it. But then she got to thinking… What if she really was pregnant? It wasn't out of the realm of possibility. And if she was—which she wasn't—it might be better if she skipped the getting shit-faced portion of the evening.

"Great," Liza said. "Wear something fun. I'll send Mark over to pick you up." Then she disconnected.

Bailey stared at the phone. Mark? What about *Marley and Me*? And *Old Yeller*? She shrugged it off. It was just as well. She wasn't really up for a night of fighting off Mark's advances.

She went to her room and stood in front of her closet, staring inside, looking for something "fun" to wear. She raised an arm and sniffed. Probably Liza expected her to shower, too. There went her leisurely bath.

After a good ten minutes of standing under lukewarm water—she really needed to have Uncle Rex come over and check her water heater—she heard her front door open, and then Mark and Chandler appeared in her bathroom doorway. They were both wearing smarmy grins and looking her up and down like she was tonight's dinner. Chandler decided he was thirsty and he made a beeline for the toilet, nudging it open with his nose. He stuck his head in and slurped loudly, making a mess all over her bathroom floor. Mark didn't even try to stop him. He was too busy ogling her.

Bailey spoke through clenched teeth. "In case you haven't noticed, I don't have any clothes on."

"I noticed," Mark said. He gave her his smarmiest grin.

"Do you mind?"

"Not at all."

"*I* do. Out!" She snagged a towel off the rack and covered herself.

Mark didn't budge. He looked disappointed she'd covered up. "Is that any way to treat a house guest? Can't I have just one little peek?"

"You just had one. Get. Out!" She shoved a finger toward the door.

"How about two peeks... seeing as you owe me."

She glared at him, her anger so runneth over she couldn't form words. She slipped past him and made it to her bedroom without incident—meaning he didn't "accidentally" pull off her towel. "I owe you nothing," she said at last.

"I say you do."

"How do you figure?"

"I let it slide when Mr. I've-got-a-squirrel-in-my-pants broke into the shop last summer and tried to steal a valuable piece of merchandise."

She scoffed. Carter had more than a squirrel in his pants. He had a rocket. But Mark didn't need to know that, and she wasn't about to argue details with him. "That piece of merchandise didn't belong to you," she reminded him. "It belonged to a very bad man, and you're lucky Carter took it. Otherwise, that bad man might have come looking for it at your shop. Carter probably saved you. And, anyway, that happened so long ago the statute of limitations has run out. Like I said, I owe you nothing."

Mark shrugged and flopped down on her bed. He pulled a small amber bottle—peach schnapps—out of his jacket pocket and waved it at her. "Want some?"

The devil's elixir. "No!" she said, and she gave her head a vigorous shake. "I don't even want to smell it."

"You sure? It's good for what ails you. Your aunt gave it to me." He put the bottle to his lips and tossed back a few gulps.

Bailey's jaw dropped. "You told my aunt about the night

we drank peach schnapps together?"

"Nope," Mark said. "She read all about it in *Coupeville's Own*." He picked up the remote and clicked on the 12-inch TV Bailey kept in her room for nights when she couldn't sleep.

"When? That happened eons ago."

He shrugged. "News travels slow here."

She wasn't buying it. "I think you should leave." She grabbed the remote and clicked the TV off.

Mark didn't budge... except for the movement it took to draw another swig of peach schnapps.

"Now!" she said. She glanced over at her dresser, at a bottle of leftover doggy tranquilizers, and wondered how many it would take to almost, but not really, kill Mark.

Maggie May wiggled into the room to see what was up, and Bailey spent a moment cooing to her to let her know Mommy was okay. Tucker didn't show his face. If she wasn't bleeding, he wasn't concerned. And Chandler was lying on the floor with his eyes rolled up in his head. He was already bored with sniffing Maggie's heinie.

Just like a man.

"I thought we were going to the street fair," Mark said. "Liza will be disappointed if you've changed your mind."

Bailey did a mental groan. "Fine. Just, *please*, get out of here, so I can get dressed."

To her surprise, and for the first time ever, Mark actually did as he was asked. He slunk out of her room without another word. Maybe there was hope for him yet. On the other hand, maybe the key to controlling him was to keep him liquored up with peach schnapps.

Ten minutes later, she walked into the living room, dressed for "fun" in a red polka dot dress, a pair of barely there sandals, and an extra coat of mascara. Her skin still had a nice glow from her time spent in Las Vegas, and for the first time in weeks, she had a spring in her step. Maybe there was hope for her, too.

Mark's eyes lit up when he saw her. "You look sweet

enough to eat, Peaches." His compliment was followed with a little tongue maneuver that had her reconsidering the entire evening.

"Dammit, Mark, I've asked you to stop calling me Peaches at least a million times. And get your foot off my coffee table." Frustrated, she raised one of her strappy sandals to Mark's leg and gave it a good shove. His shoe scraped along the surface of the table, and they both stared down at the piece of furniture that had been handed down to her from at least a century past. His shoe had left a mark.

Bailey's mouth gaped open. "Look what you've done! This was my great, great... great grandmother's, and you've scratched it."

Mark stared at the table. "I had nothing to do with that. You're having major PMS or something." He turned and faced her. "You need sex. Elvis has dumped you, and you need someone to replace him." He got up from the sofa and inched over close, saying, "I think that someone is me."

Bailey could feel his heart beating. It made her have thoughts that she had no business having. She shoved him away. "My sex life is none of your business. *Carter* hasn't dumped me. He's just having memory problems at the moment. So, *please*, for the love of God, stop calling me Peaches."

"Why? Sideburns isn't here. And if he doesn't remember you, I doubt he cares what I call you. You and I are free to resume our relationship."

"You and I have never *had* a relationship."

"Once," Mark corrected her. "We had a relationship once."

Bailey ground her teeth until they were on the verge of shattering. "Okay, once," she acquiesced.

A quiet beat passed between them, and Mark stepped close to her again. He wove his hand through her hair. "You used to like it when I called you Peaches."

Bailey was missing Carter so much that it was easy to imagine it was *his* hand in her hair. "That was a long time ago," she whispered, closing her eyes. "Things are different, now. I'm engaged. Almost married."

"Elvis has left the building," Mark said. "It's just you and me now, Peaches." He pulled her close and his lips grazed her cheek.

"Let me go."

"I could make you forget all about Elvis."

"I'll scream."

"I like it when you scream," Mark said.

Jeez. She tried to push him away, but he held on tight. "Aren't you and Liza doing it now?" she asked. She knew they weren't, but it was worth a shot.

"Liza and I are over. She and Brian are going at it."

So delicately put.

He grazed her temple with his mouth. "And more than likely, Sideburns is doing it with every woman in Las Vegas."

Bailey bit down on her lip to keep from crying. "Leave Carter out of this." Carter may very well be doing *it* with another woman, but she didn't need to hear about *it*. That was too painful to think about. Him kissing other women was one thing. But *it*? She'd be like Humpty Dumpty. No one would ever be able to put her heart back together again.

"He tossed you away like an old jock strap." Mark continued. "That's something I'd never do." He held her even closer.

Her nose wrinkled. "That's disgusting. I'll thank you not to compare me to a filthy piece of material meant for holding a man's Willy Wonka."

"My Willy Wonka wants you."

She'd heard enough. So much for getting back to socializing with friends. "Out!" She jammed a finger toward the door. "Now!"

"What about the street fair?"

Oh. Right. The street fair. "You can wait out in your car until Liza gets here." She shoved him out the door and slammed it shut. He had to jump back to avoid losing his foot.

"I'll be out here if you change your mind," he yelled to her through the door.

She thumped her forehead on the wall a couple of times, and then turned and rested her back against it. Maggie May circled through her legs, whining and looking worried, probably wondering if she should kill something. Tucker lifted his head and yawned. He saw no reason to get excited.

Then there was Chandler. He was sitting so perfect and sweet and looking at her like he wanted something. A treat was her guess. Wait—Chandler! Jeez, Mark had forgotten his dog.

Lucky dog.

She went to her doggy-treat drawer and took out a box of Milk Bones. When she turned around, all three dogs were eyes focused on her.

"Don't worry," she told Chandler as she handed him his Milk Bone. "You're safe now."

Chandler looked up at her with his big brown eyes that seemed to say, *Thank you for rescuing me from that idiot.*

She rubbed the top of his head affectionately. "You're welcome."

She read his name tag again. It still said Chandler, but she wondered, Chandler Who? He had to have a mommy somewhere who was missing him very much. If one of her babies were to go missing, she wouldn't be able to rest until they were found.

She made a mental note to take Chandler over to Coupeville's Veterinary Hospital and have them check to see if he'd been micro-chipped. If so, Doctor Joy could make sure Chandler made it back home, where he belonged.

The thought of sending Chandler away gave Bailey a moment of sadness. Though she'd only known him for a few hours, he was already growing on her. Any dog that could get along with her Maggie was a rare find. But as nice a dog as Chandler was, she couldn't keep another big dog in her small home. And she certainly couldn't see Mark keeping Chandler. If it didn't roll on four wheels and go from zero to sixty in five seconds flat, Mark would surely lose interest.

Speaking of... she wondered if he was still outside, waiting. He could wait forever, for all she cared, after taking that sneak peek of her in her birthday suit. But since he came with tonight's package of fun, she would forgive him that transgression this one time. After all, it wasn't anything he hadn't seen before.

She took one last look at herself in the full-length mirror and decided against the sundress and barely-there sandals. Something more conservative would be better—safer. She didn't want to give Mark any further encouragement.

Five minutes later, she had on a pair of Victoria's Secret skinny-leg jeans, white Tommy Hilfiger tennis shoes, and a white no-name boatneck T-shirt that hung off one shoulder. That was "fun" enough. A quick swipe of Clinique's Silvery Moon lipstick and another layer of mascara and she was good to go. Except for one last thing... She wrote a quick note to whoever might find it, that she was headed to Oak Harbor with Liza and the twins. Just in case.

When she opened her door, Liza was just coming up the walk. She was looking rosy in a pale pink thermal V-neck sweater, with a pair of matching heels, and a cream-colored skirt. She'd been in a pink phase for a while now and wasn't showing any signs of letting up. Bailey thought it was possible Liza had stock in the color pink.

"What's this?" Liza asked. She gave Bailey's outfit an appraising look. "I told you to wear something fun."

Bailey spread her arms. "This *is* fun. I'm even wearing fun underwear." She stepped outside and saw Old Man Winston on his porch, gathering his daily paper. She waved, and he growled. All was well. Probably he'd already forgotten about the berries she'd given him.

She approached Mark's '67 Plymouth Barracuda and caught Brian staring at her.

"You look way sexy," he said.

Mark's eyes gleamed at her from the driver's seat of the car. He kept his lips zipped. Not even 'Peaches' came out of his mouth, which meant he was on his best behavior. But Bailey wasn't falling for it. The evening was young and she knew he was just biding his time.

She leaned into Liza. "If either one of them touches me, I'll have them arrested. Not only that, but I don't want to read about tonight in tomorrow's newspaper."

Liza gave the twins a sharp look. "You heard her. Both of you keep your hands to yourselves." Then she smiled sweetly. "Or on *me*."

"No harm in telling her how sexy she looks," Brian said. "It's good for a woman in her condition to hear that kind of thing. It shows sensitivity."

Bailey ignored Brian's remark. She was having a hard enough time convincing her aunt she wasn't in any particular condition.

Everyone piled into the Barracuda—Liza and Brian in the back, and her in the front, riding next to Mark. It wasn't ideal, but how much trouble could Mark get into while he was driving? The real challenge would be for him to behave himself once his hands were free.

The Barracuda rumbled down the street and Bailey was surprised at how good it felt to be out and about. Even if it was with Mark Jefferson.

Chapter Thirty-One

The sky was blue and the air cool when Carter's plane landed at Sea-Tac airport. It wasn't cold, but coming from near triple digits made it seem so, and he was glad he'd worn a light jacket. Though, really, the weather was the last thing he cared about. He intended to spend every waking minute indoors, and in bed, with Bailey.

If she'd have him.

If she'd forgive him.

If she hadn't moved on.

Now, he was just over-thinking the whole damn mess. Of course, Bailey hadn't moved on. His hand went to his pocket and he felt the rigidness of the small box that contained the new ring he'd purchase for her. And, of course, she would forgive him. That is, if the car he'd arranged to have pick him up ever got there.

He craned his neck, looking down a long stretch of pavement for any sign his ride was en route. It was shuttles and taxis everywhere.

A long ten minutes later, a black town car pulled up to the curb, and two hours after that, the car deposited him on the cement walk in front of Bailey's cottage. His stomach was tied in knots and he'd worked himself into a mindless wreck. But he couldn't help it. He needed to see her... hold her... kiss her. He needed to look into her eyes and see the look that told him he was the only man she ever wanted to be with. Only then would he be satisfied that she was still his.

His mind went briefly to what Mike had told him, that *he'd* kissed Bailey. Carter didn't understand it, but he was certain it was a one-time thing. The same as the kiss he'd shared with Nikki.

He drew deeply of Puget Sound's salty air, staring at Bailey's front door, preparing himself for what he wanted to say to her. If all went well, later that night, he anticipated they'd sit out on her one-man, two-dog deck gazing at the moon's reflection on Penn Cove Bay. Bailey would tuck herself in his lap, and Tucker and Maggie May would curl themselves around his feet. For a while, they'd just sit and listen to the waves lap gently against the rocks below her cottage. Then, when he worked up the perfect proposal, he'd once again ask her to be his wife.

It seemed like an easy thing. But seeing the hurt in her eyes while he tried explaining the things he'd done might be the hardest thing he'd ever had to do. He didn't want to consider that they might not get back together. He needed a chance to make up for all the pain he'd caused her.

It was time. He raised his hand to knock on her door, but then he saw the curtains stir in the window at the next cottage over. It was Old Man Winston, spying on him. Carter chuckled. The spying was a welcome sight. Old Man Winston was just doing his job, keeping an eye on things.

The old guy poked his head out his front door. His white hair danced in the breeze as he gave Carter a guarded look. "She ain't home," he said. "She and some other kids took off in an old hot rod."

"Would that hot rod be a Barracuda?" Carter asked.

"That it would," Old Man Winston said. And then he disappeared back inside his cottage.

Carter bristled. He knew who owned that car. But he also knew that Bailey had no interest in Mark Jefferson. Even so, he didn't like it.

He took off down Main Street, in the direction of Bailey's mom's house, glad he had his memory back, else he'd have a hell of a time finding it. If anyone knew where Bailey might have gone, it would be her aunt.

He made his way toward the center of town, garnering plenty of friendly smiles, along with some stares. A man and a woman across the street waved hello, and he waved back. He recognized them, but couldn't remember their names.

Half way down the block, just as he approached Penn Cove Gallery, a swarm of women rounded the corner. They saw him and moved forward as a single unit, waving their hands and squealing like they'd just spotted the real thing—the King of Rock and Roll.

One woman called to him, "Oh, *yoohoo… Elvis.*" And she raised the hem of her dress, exposing the full length of her knee-hi support stockings. She had a Looking Good Salon apron hanging from her neck and curlers sitting in tidy rows along her pink scalp. She was waving an old Elvis LP high above her head, shouting, "I didn't get your autograph when you were in town last, and I'm not about to let you get away this time without signing something for me."

Carter smiled. All the faces, the sights and smells, even the sounds of some of the women's voices were a welcome memory. Everything was coming back to him in a rush. He wasn't at all surprised at how many people already knew he was in town. Coupeville was small and news spread fast among the locals.

He stopped where he was and waited for the women to come to him. They were in such a mad rush. Another woman scuttled around the side of the building. It was Mavis, manager of the Looking Good Salon. She had a curler in one hand and was giving chase to the woman in the apron. "You get back here, Audrey. I won't be held responsible if your hair doesn't set properly."

Mavis was in a dead run and her screaming got the rest of the hive stirred up. In seconds, the entire crowd swarmed around him. One of the women, who was more spry than the rest, elbowed her way to the front. It was Lea Townsend, the woman who was known for dressing her Yorkshire terrier and pushing it around town in a baby buggy.

"Remember me, Elvis?" Lea asked, squeezing up close, until they were chest to chest. She wasn't shy about letting him know she had designs on him. "I once threw my leopard print panties at you. Did you keep them? I bet you did." She gave him a sly wink.

Carter's mouth lifted at one corner and he went into Elvis mode. "I remember your panties, honey. You're looking real good. Haven't aged a day since I last saw you."

Lea giggled like a fourteen-year-old and put a hand to her lips. Her face flushed pink and it mixed well with her rosacea. "I might be up late tonight, till at least nine o'clock, if you'd like to come by for some herbal tea," she told him.

He took one of her hands and kissed the back of it. "I'll keep that in mind, honey."

"Get in line, Lea," a woman named Macy Drew screamed. She was standing just behind Lea, and she grabbed Lea's arm, propelling herself forward. "Back off. I owe this boy a big fat kiss. Business at The Knead & Feed has doubled since he licked Bailey's face. Our marionberry pie sells out nearly every day. It's even been written up in the Sunday edition of *The Seattle Times.*"

Carter grinned as the memory of that day came rushing back. It was his first time to Coupeville and Bailey had taken him to The Knead & Feed for lunch. After they finished the best turkey and cranberry cream cheese sandwich he'd ever tasted, they each ordered a slice of homemade marionberry pie, baked by none other than Bailey herself. It was delicious beyond compare.

He'd cleaned his plate, but Bailey had stopped after only a

few bites, claiming she was full. Though when he was up at the register paying, he'd seen her sneak just one more bite. And when he returned to the table and saw a trace of purple berry on her lips, it gave him the perfect opportunity to lean in for a kiss. By the time evening rolled around, everyone in Coupeville was talking about how their very own Bailey Ventura had been licked by Elvis.

He chuckled. That was one memory he wanted to keep.

The swarm closed in even tighter around him, until he could barely move. But Carter felt no concern for his safety. This wasn't the typical Vegas crowd, where clothing and even body parts were up for grabs. These women wanted nothing more from him than an autograph or to share air space with him. And he was happy to oblige. He took a piece of paper from one of the women and scribbled his name, then another and another, all the while smiling to himself. He was giving these women a thrill, and their husbands would thank him later tonight when their libidos were in high gear.

"What's going on here?" a voice beyond the sea of women called out.

Carter looked up and over the top of a dozen gray heads. "Is that you, Fiona?"

"You're darn right it's me. Is that you, Elvis?"

Carter gently nudged the women directly in front of him to one side and held out his arms. Fiona stepped forward and he drew her in for a hug. She wasn't alone. She had three dog leashes in her hand, but only two dogs—Tucker and another he'd never seen before.

Tucker rushed up to him, and Carter crouched to pet him. The other dog stood nearby receiving his own share of attention from all the women.

After Carter was finished with Tucker, he stood and faced Bailey's aunt. She looked him over good, squinting through a burst of sun that had peeked through a few gathering clouds. "I should have known it was you. Only one thing gets these women amped up, and that's a hot man. I thought I might be hallucinating from those mushrooms Olivia put in the meat loaf last night, but hearing your voice, I know it's really you."

"It's me," Carter said.

"You're a sight. Too bad Bailey isn't here to see you." She glanced down at his black boots. "I betcha they wanted to pry the heels off those at the airport. It's a likely place for a bomb. Did you get frisked?"

"No, can't say as I did."

"Too bad," Aunt Fiona said. "Let's walk. I gotta get these dogs back home."

Carter nodded at the empty leash in her hand. "Where's Maggie?" He glanced down at the black dog. "And who's this? Did Bailey get another dog?"

"Nah," Aunt Fiona answered, patting the strange dog on the back. "This one here is just a visitor." She squinted, looking up the street. "Maggie saw a squirrel and backed right outta her collar. She's a wily one. Not like Tucker. He likes to sleep all day."

Carter looked and saw Maggie at the base of a big tree with her paws propped high. She was barking and giving a squirrel her two cents worth. But as soon as Carter whistled to her, she broke from the tree and came a runnin', with her tail and hind quarters wagging in full-out joy at the sight of him.

He and Fiona and the pack of dogs all continued on their way. "About Bailey," he said. "How is she?"

"She's good. Been keeping to herself a lot."

"Do you know where she's gone?"

Fiona clucked her tongue against the roof of her mouth. "I could take you to her, but I'm not sure I should trust you. Just when my niece has me convinced you're not a punk, you go and get yourself a girlfriend."

"I'm not sure what you mean," Carter said.

"I saw you kissing that woman outside the window at Frank Zoopa's house. She's slinky. Wears black like it's painted on. What do you have to say for yourself? You gonna give up the slinky one and marry my niece, or what?"

He laughed. This was exactly the kind of talk he expected to have with Bailey's aunt. His only concern was whether or not she might be carrying a gun.

"I love Bailey," he told Fiona. "And I want to marry her. Beyond that, I can't say what will or won't happen. It's up to her."

"Sounds good to me," Fiona said. "I heard from Liza and she told me she was taking my niece over to Oak Harbor. Plus, the Jefferson twins are tagging along." She grabbed Carter's hand. "We'd better hurry. The evil twin means nothing to Bailey, but I hear he's been practicing his Elvis act, and word is he's gotten pretty good. The show is at six. I think you should sing 'Rock-A-Hula *Bailey*,' seeing as that's the song that made her fall in love with you in the first place. She always felt you wrote that song just for her. We'll take the Nova."

Carter stopped in his tracks. "Bailey's gone to an Elvis impersonator competition?"

Chapter Thirty-Two

"Are you going to kill the evil twin?" Fiona asked Carter as he pointed Olivia Ventura's 1974 banana yellow Nova in the direction of Oak Harbor. Olivia was taking up space in the back seat. She didn't want to miss seeing Elvis perform.

"Do you *want* me to kill him?" Carter asked.

Fiona pressed her lips together and looked as though she might be giving the idea some serious thought. But then she shook her head. "You wouldn't be any good to Bailey if you went to prison."

"Lord. All this talk about prison and killing people," Olivia said. "Can't we just have a nice conversation?"

"All right, Olivia," Fiona said. "What would you like to talk about? Your boyfriend? You know those long distance romances never work out. Too bad for you. I hear sex helps with hot flashes."

Olivia groaned from the back seat. "That isn't the kind of conversation I had in mind."

Fiona turned the conversation in another direction. "You can go after Fred Sweeny," she told Carter. "He can't sing a lick and he ain't got no hair, but he's still got some movement in his hips."

An hour later, Carter and his two passengers rolled past the "Welcome to Oak Harbor" sign. Carter paid an elderly couple twenty dollars to park in their front yard, and then he herded Olivia and Fiona two blocks down to where a street fair had been set up in a large pasture of dry grass. Why it was called a "street" fair was anybody's guess.

Booths lined one side of the pasture, where vendors sold local homemade wares, such as jewelry, artwork, and food. On the other side, carnival callers beckoned passers-by to toss away their hard-earned money on a slim-to-none chance of winning some cheap stuffed animal.

Each end of the pasture was set up for entertainment purposes. On one end, it was a collection of thrilling rides for both kiddies and adults. On the other end was a stage. Carter assumed this was where all the beer-filled men, and maybe even a woman or two, would be allowed to live out their fantasy of playing King of Rock and Roll for a day.

The only fantasy Carter had was to make Bailey his bride.

He guided Olivia and Fiona down one side of the pasture, past several refreshment stands, where he offered to buy them something to eat or drink. Both women declined. Carter suspected they weren't too keen on the idea of having to use the portable facilities.

"Now, when we get to the stage," Fiona told him, "you go on ahead to the back and wait with the rest of your fellow performers. Olivia and I will be out front. We'll find seats near Bailey and Liza."

Bailey and her friends had "done" the street fair. They'd ridden on rides, had some refreshments, and lost some money playing stupid games for prizes. Bailey was eager to sit when Liza suggested they take a break and check out the evening's entertainment. They found seating in front of a large stage, where Bailey sat between Liza and Brian. Mark had made himself scarce. Bailey figured maybe he had an issue to work out with one of the on-site Honey Buckets. She made a mental note to tell him to keep his grubby hands off her when he reappeared. Not once had she ever heard of a Honey Bucket that had a sink with soap and running water.

After several minutes, and Mark was still missing, she got a creepy feeling in her stomach. Something wasn't quite right. She looked around and saw a man walking from one end of the stage to the other. He was checking cables and microphones and looking not bad in a white jump suit that made her think of Elvis.

Elvis?

She snapped her head around and glared at Liza. "Where's Mark?" she asked Liza.

Liza gave her the ol' innocent look. "What do you mean?"

"*Mark*," Bailey said. "You know, Brian's twin brother?" She looked over at Brian. He was preoccupied, looking at a couple of young women who were both wearing sweaters that clung to their bosoms like glue.

Liza mumbled something unintelligible, and then glanced toward the stage.

The creepy feeling in Bailey's stomach grew exponentially. "Don't tell me... you brought me here to see Mark sing in an *Elvis* competition?"

"Relax. Jesus. No reason to freak out."

Bailey felt herself going into hyperventilation mode. "Why would you do this to me?"

Brian squeezed one of her knees. "Don't worry. Mark's been practicing. He's pretty good now."

Bailey swung her head around to Brian. "FYI, I don't care how good he is." She dropped her head into her hands and contemplated getting some new friends—ones who hadn't heard of Elvis. Which was totally ridiculous. She'd have to go all the way to Mars.

"Oh, honey," Liza said. "Just wait. It'll be fun."

Bailey felt like her eyes might bulge right out of their sockets. "*Fun?* You think it'll be *fun* for me to sit here and watch a bunch of balding, middle-aged men waddle around a stage, pretending to be Elvis?"

"Mark's not middle-aged. Or bald. He even dyed his hair. It's so black it's almost purple," Brian said.

Bailey shot him a shut-the-hell-up look, and he promptly zipped his lip. And, yes, she knew Mark had dyed his hair. She'd sat next to him on the ride over, *for crying out loud!*

"I never want to have fun again," she told her friends. "I'm all *funned* out. And if I was going to have fun, it certainly wouldn't be here in Oak Harbor… at an Elvis impersonator competition! In case you don't remember, Carter broke my heart. *He's* an Elvis impersonator. Get it?"

Liza gently took her hand. "I do, and I'm sorry for your loss. But would it be so bad to stay and listen to Mark sing a song or two? Like Brian said, he's been practicing for weeks. For you."

Bailey cringed. The last time Mark tried his Elvis act out on her, she'd acquired the nickname Peaches. And try as she might to get him to let it go, he refused. *Aargh!* Her head was on the verge of imploding.

"I don't want Mark doing anything for me," she said. "And I don't want to do anything for him. He always manages to turn it into something more." Something sleazy.

"Okay," Liza said. "Then how about doing it for me?" She batted her lashes and gave Bailey the big doe-eyes.

"Forget it," Bailey said. "The eyes don't work on me."

"Please," Liza said.

Bailey contemplated Liza's request for all of a second, giving consideration to the fact that Liza was her best friend. But was that enough to submit to torture? Maybe. "Fine. I'll stay for one song," she told Liza. "But it means nothing." She sank down into her chair, crossing her arms over her chest, determined to *not* enjoy the show.

Brian tossed an arm over her shoulder and gave her a good

squeeze. "We understand, Peaches. I'm sure it's been hard on you, being alone and all. Could be you need a new boyfriend." He dropped his hand lower, until his fingertips lightly grazed the top of her left breast.

Bailey stiffened at the unwelcome touch. If she didn't know better, she'd think it was Mark sitting next to her. "If you want to continue working on cars, you'd better move your fingers," she said. "And P.S., aren't you dating Liza? And P.S.S., I am *not* lonely."

Brian removed his arm from her shoulder, but now all Bailey could think about was how lonely she really was. She'd seen several men shuffling around behind the stage and they were all wearing some sort of Elvis attire, which only reminded her of Carter. He was everywhere.

Except with her.

She pulled a tissue from her purse and sniffled into it.

"Why the tears?" Liza asked. "You haven't even heard Mark sing yet. And I promise, if he's that bad, we'll leave. But at least give him a chance. You never know… he might end up being the Elvis impersonator of your dreams."

Bailey felt like screaming. She'd jump off the Tacoma Narrows Bridge before she'd let Mark have that distinction. If she and Carter were really over, she wanted nothing more to do with *any* Elvis impersonators. And especially not Mark. Period. He may have fooled her once, but she wasn't about to let him fool her again.

Now she was just plain mad. She shouldn't even be here. She stewed for another minute, and then jumped from her seat. "I can't do this. I need to go home."

Liza grabbed her by the arm. "What? Why?"

"Because." Bailey flapped her arms at her sides. "Because" seemed like a decent enough reason.

"But you said we could listen to one song. How do you think Mark will feel when he comes out and none of us are here to see him perform? You may not want to copulate with him, but he is a friend. Don't you care about his feelings?"

Unfortunately, Liza had a point. Bailey sat back down in a huff, and a man appeared on the stage. It was show time. The man said a few words, giving a short history on Elvis, and how there were now more than eighty-five thousand Elvis impersonators walking the earth... and if the current growth rate continued, by 2019, a third of the world's population would be Elvis impersonators. This announcement led to much cheering and hand clapping, but Bailey was just glad she didn't have to sit through hearing them all sing.

The show started with each Elvis wannabe swiveling his or her hips across the stage, doing their best to entertain the audience. Bailey recognized one of the men—Fred Sweeny. He was from Coupeville. But the rest were strangers who probably lived right there in Oak Harbor. A few of them had real moves, but most of them couldn't sing a lick. Even so, they were all good enough for a simple show on a Saturday afternoon when you wanted a reason to get out of the house. None of them, however, even came close to being able to pull off "Elvis" the way performers such as Donny Edwards, Ben Portsmouth, or even her very own Security Guy could.

Bailey soon felt her eyes *and* her ears glazing over.

At last it was Mark's turn to wow the audience. Bailey's seat was prime real estate. She could see each performer as they stood awaiting their turn to be announced. Mark was there now, and she sat up, not wanting to miss a thing. She was eager to hear if he'd improved since the last time he played Elvis. He certainly looked the part. His hair was styled ultra cool Elvis, circa 1968, and he was wearing black slacks and a silky blue shirt that was unbuttoned to mid-chest, showing just enough chest hair to stir a woman's libido. He also had a silk scarf draped around his neck that he probably intended to toss her way. Not that she intended to take it.

The entire audience watched and waited while Mark shifted the mic from one hand to the other. He looked nervous, like he wasn't sure what he'd gotten himself into. Bailey almost felt sorry for him. But then the MC called his name, and he swept out onto the stage like he knew exactly what he was doing. He made his way over to where she was sitting and stood directly in front of her. They locked eyes for a quiet moment. She had no idea what to expect. But then Mark opened his mouth, and the words to "Can't Help Falling in Love" flowed like silk over his lips.

Bailey was in awe. She felt heat all the way to her toes.

"I've never seen the evil twin looking so hot," someone whispered in her ear.

"Auntie?" Bailey couldn't believe it. "What are you doing here?"

"Me and your mom came to see Elvis," Aunt Fiona said. She motioned for Brian to scoot down, and then she settled into the chair next to Bailey. Bailey leaned and saw her mom there, too.

"Mom?" Bailey was nonplussed. She couldn't imagine either one of them driving to Oak Harbor.

Bailey's mom sat next to Liza. She looked at Bailey and no words were spoken, but the warning was there. *Don't even think about getting involved with that Jefferson boy, or I'll jump off the Deception Pass Bridge.* But Bailey wasn't worried. Her mom was afraid of heights and being that the Deception Pass Bridge stood a couple hundred feet above water that was deep enough to sink the Space Needle, she didn't see her mom's threat as ever becoming reality. Her mom wouldn't even get close enough to the rail to jump.

"Isn't this fun?" Aunt Fiona said. "We're all out on a date together."

The music changed, and Mark made a smooth transition into "Got A Lot of Livin' To Do." His eyes were still fixated on Bailey. She folded her arms across her chest and ignored him, but he was oblivious. He went down on his knees and slid to the edge of the stage, until he and Bailey were practically nose to nose. She wasn't impressed. Carter was a master at that move. It drove women wild... when Carter did it.

Bailey slammed her eyes shut, hoping against hope that when she opened them, Mark would be nose to nose with some other woman. Unfortunately, that wasn't the case. Once again the gods had seen fit to deny her wish. Mark was still just inches away. And he had the entire audience backing him. Everyone was on their feet, chanting, "*Kiss her, kiss her, kiss her.*"

Mark jumped down off the stage and got real close, like he was actually going to do it. And he did. Plus, he threw in a little tongue action… until Bailey pushed him away.

"That's it. I'm leaving," she said.

"I'll drive you. My job here is done," Mark told her. He reached into his pocket and pulled out his car keys, dangling them from one finger.

"I'd rather hitchhike," Bailey said.

"Hitchhiking is dangerous," Aunt Fiona piped in. "If it were me, I'd take my chances with the evil twin."

Bailey's mom nodded. "I hate to say it, but I agree."

Mark's lips slid into a smarmy grin. "I think I'm beginning to grow on your mom."

Like toenail fungus.

Bailey gave him a cold glare. "Let's get something straight. Even if you *were* to grow on my *mom*, you don't have a chance with me. Been there, done that. Won't be doing it again."

Bailey's mom gasped and put a hand over her mouth.

"But, Peaches, I love you," Mark said. He looked genuinely hurt. "Won't you just give me another chance?" He was using his best Elvis voice, pulling out all the stops.

A collective sigh sounded throughout the audience. Bailey was dumbfounded. She looked around. Every man, woman, and child had their ears tuned in to hear her response. She turned in her chair, facing them all. "You don't *know* him."

Mark pulled her close. "They know enough. C'mon, Peaches. I've still got that bottle of peach schnapps under my front seat. How about we ditch Liza and Brian, and go sit under our madrona tree? I'll make you forget all about Elvis."

The audience—a bunch of troublemakers—cheered Mark

on, so he kissed her again, and this time, he threw in a little hip grinding for emphasis. When he was finished, he whispered in her ear, "Does that bring back any memories?"

"Not a one," Bailey said. Though if she were being honest, she did feel a little weak in the knees. But that was only because his hip grinding reminded her of Carter.

The crowd continued cheering, and the music started up again. It was time for the next performer to come out on stage. But Bailey had heard enough. She'd taken her mind to her favorite beach in the Caribbean. She was eyes closed and ears deaf to everything but the sound of surf meeting shore. That is, until the next Elvis wannabe began to sing. Of all songs, he could have chosen, it was "Rock-A-Hula Baby." Only he had it wrong. He was actually singing "Rock-A-Hula *Bailey*."

Bailey caught her breath. Only one man she knew would make that mistake. She opened her eyes and Carter was microphone in hand, looking straight at her.

"Carter?" She wasn't at all sure.

"Imagine that," Aunt Fiona said.

Carter moved over to the edge of the stage and jumped down, right in front of her. They were face to face. She touched him, and he stopped singing. "You're really here?" she whispered.

"Like I never left you," he said. And he put a finger to her chin and kissed her.

It was much too good to be true. Bailey felt like her heart might bubble over with joy. But the moment didn't last. A bloodcurdling scream came out of nowhere and it was lights out.

Chapter Thirty-Three

Bailey slowly opened her eyes. Her lids were heavy and she felt as though she'd been tackled by one of Carter's rabid fans. She was lying on the sofa at her mom's house and Carter was at her side, holding a cloth to her forehead. He hadn't been a dream, after all.

The rest of her family was there, as well, along with Liza and the twins. They were all standing around, looking concerned.

"What happened?" she asked.

"You got cold cocked," Aunt Fiona said. "A woman flew over two rows of seating to get to Elvis. She wanted to beat you to that scarf he had around his neck."

Bailey looked at Carter. "It's really you, right?"

Carter nodded. "It's me."

That night, everyone sat down to a feast of spaghetti, sourdough garlic bread, and salad greens topped with homemade Ranch dressing. Even the twins had been invited. Bailey guessed her mom saw no problem in breaking bread with Mark and Brian, so long as they didn't consider it an invitation to join the family.

Bailey looked around the table, beaming. This was a happy day. Carter remembered her, she'd survived a run-in with one of his fans, and now here they were ninety-nine percent back together. The remaining one percent would happen after Carter explained a few things... like Nikki, Maria, and the woman in the hotel room. Those were all the women she'd seen him kissing. Plus, she had some of her own explaining to do. It was time she told him about what'd happened between herself and Mike Shur. No problem. After all they'd been through, it was but a minor glitch. Nothing to stress about. So where had her appetite gone?

"Aren't you going to eat?" her mother asked. "Here," she said, and she offered Bailey a piece of garlic bread.

"I'll just have a little salad," she told her mom. She passed the bread down to her auntie, who had only a small mound of salad greens on her plate, as well. Her auntie was all about watching her girlish figure. She took a piece of bread and passed the plate down.

Once everyone was ready to dig in, Aunt Fiona cleared her throat and waited for a break in the activity. "I'd like to give thanks before we eat," she said. And she dropped her head in prayer mode. "Thank God we haven't had a first frost yet," she began. "My dahlias hate the frost."

Bailey couldn't help but smile. She never knew what to expect from her auntie.

Aunt Fiona continued, "And thank you for not letting the buzzards peck my niece's fiancé's bones clean when he was splayed out, belly down, out in the desert. I bet a man like him has some tasty meat."

"I'm sure no one wants to hear that kind of talk at meal time," Bailey's mom said.

"I wouldn't mind," Mark said, and Bailey kicked him under the table. She cracked an eye at Carter. His lips were turned up, though he was doing a fine job of keeping his amusement to himself. He was a good man that way.

"Isn't it funny how things work out?" Aunt Fiona went on. "Girl meets boy, boy gets amnesia, boy remembers girl and finds out she's pregnant."

Everyone went quiet, and all eyes were on Bailey. Even her Uncle Rex had his eyes—both of them—laser-fixed on her. It was the first time ever. Probably he was waiting for some kind of explanation.

Carter placed a hand on her knee, giving it a reassuring squeeze. It was exactly what she needed at that moment.

"I have a great idea," she said. "Let's eat dinner before it gets cold."

Uncle Rex was on board with that idea. He forked some spaghetti into his mouth, and then some more, until everyone else seemed satisfied that it was okay to do the same. Bailey was ever so grateful. The discussion about whether or not she was pregnant—which, for the last time, she wasn't, because while dinner was being prepared, she sneaked out and took a test and it was negative—wasn't something she wanted to have with her entire family and the twins. She and Carter could talk later, when they were alone.

Dinner went quick, and then Bailey's mom disappeared into the kitchen and returned with a fresh-baked marionberry pie. It was devoured in less than two minutes.

Olivia got up again and opened a cabinet behind the table. She took out a bottle of Chambord and poured herself a flute, downing it in one gulp. Then she refilled her glass and drank it down, too. Bailey felt her left eye begin to twitch. No telling what was coming next, what with her mom's out-of-whack hormones ruling the roost.

Sufficiently lubricated, Olivia cleared her throat, and then tapped a butter knife against the side of the nearest dish—which was totally unnecessary, being that she was already the main attraction. "My baby's getting married," she began.

"Amen," Aunt Fiona said.

"To... an Elvis impersonator," Olivia continued.

It was an OMG moment for Bailey. She couldn't believe

her mom had finally gotten it right, that she was marrying an Elvis *impersonator*, and not *Elvis*.

"Amen," Aunt Fiona repeated.

Olivia bit into her bottom lip. "And now she's going to take my grandchild all the way to Las Vegas, where I can't even be a grandmother."

Oh boy. Bailey looked around, hoping someone would put a stop to her mother's derailment. No one did, so Bailey sank low in her chair, feeling lower than low. Now that her mother had said it, it didn't seem fair that she was about to move away and take her mother's grandchild with her.

Wait—she wasn't even pregnant!

A tear rolled down her mother's cheek as she poured herself another glass of Chambord. She drank it and looked straight at Bailey. "Honestly, do you think a mother raises her child for nearly thirty years, to then have that child move a thousand miles away?" She tossed her arms out, sending what remained in her glass splattering on the forget-me-not wallpaper. A few drops of Chambord hit Mark in the face, but he just wiped it away and licked it from his fingers.

Bailey sank even lower in her chair, until she was nearly on the floor. Everyone had their eyes on her, looking at her like she had some nerve to make her mom cry. She made a mental note to never let her mom have more than one drink. Ever.

Aunt Fiona grabbed the Chambord bottle and poured her own glass of devil water. She downed it in one gulp, and then went for seconds. But Carter was quick. He snagged the bottle from her just in time.

Aunt Fiona gave him a hard look. "I knew you were a punk, wearing all that black. And now you're gonna take our girl away, where we'll never see her *or* her baby."

All eyes were on Carter, now, like this was all *his* fault. Even Mark was giving him a scowl. But being that he saw Carter as competition, his opinion didn't count.

Bailey couldn't believe what was happening. She opened her mouth, ready to defend her man against the evil twin and everyone else, but Carter squeezed her hand under the table, letting her know he could handle things. He wasn't at all intimidated by the things her family was saying.

"Only one question left to answer, I suppose," Aunt Fiona said. "Are you *absolutely positive* your baby doesn't possess Jefferson genes?"

Bailey felt the muscle beneath her left eye go into full-blown convulsions. She looked over at her mom, and her mom looked like she might be contemplating the big jump. Carter didn't look much better. His eyes were dark, and it wasn't the good kind of dark, like when he was lost in lust. They were murderous dark, and he was looking straight at Mark. Bailey thought she might have even heard him growl.

Mark held up both his hands, going into defense mode. "Hey, leave me outta this. I ain't touched her. Not since we shared a bottle of peach schnapps up in the madrona tree." He jutted a thumb over his shoulder in the general direction of the living room, where there was no madrona tree, but everyone got the gist.

"You stuck your tongue down my niece's throat, earlier," Aunt Fiona pointed out.

Carter turned to Bailey. "Peach schnapps? Is that why he calls you Peaches?"

"It was a long time ago," Bailey told him. "*Waay* before you and I—"

"Dude, it wasn't that long ago," Mark said.

Brian nodded in agreement, and he and Mark high-fived.

This time, Bailey definitely heard Carter growl.

Liza was quick to jump in. She jammed an elbow into Brian's side. "The man carries a gun on his chest and a knife strapped to his leg. I suggest you guys keep your yappers shut, unless you have a death wish."

"Amen," Aunt Fiona said.

Bailey chewed her lip. The situation had taken the worst kind of turn. No telling what Carter was thinking of doing to Mark. Especially, after seeing him kiss her at the Elvis show in

Oak Harbor. She had to do something to get everyone back on track. She laid a hand on Carter's arm, hoping he could sense how much she loved him. "Mark and I are only friends. I promise."

Carter didn't look convinced and, anyway, it was too late. Maggie May was upset at all the ruckus and she scrambled out from under the table, howling loud enough to fill every corner of the house, and probably every corner of Coupeville. It was unbearable.

Uncle Rex had had enough, too. He slammed his hands down on the table and scooted his chair back. He had one eye on Bailey and the other on the door. "I can't take this racket. I'm going out for a drive in the Viper."

"Oh no, you don't," Bailey told him. "You're going to stay right there." She pointed at his chair. Her adrenaline was flowing, her head was throbbing, and she had no idea what might happen next, but it wasn't going to be pretty if everyone didn't just calm down.

She stood and screamed, "Everyone, stop and listen to me! Once and for all. I. Am. Not. Pregnant. Not by Mark, and not by Carter. Especially, not by Carter. He and I aren't even having sex! He only remembered me today!" Though there was the time in his office a couple of weeks ago.

Everyone sat in stunned silence, and Bailey wondered if she'd gone too far, telling them about her sex life.

"That's a shame," Aunt Fiona said at last. "I read in *Cosmo* that having regular sex can add years to a woman's life." She pursed her lips and looked squinty-eyed at Rex. "I also read that when some men reach a certain age, they don't even *want* sex anymore. Course, when a man carries on with a shameless hussy, I suppose it could dampen his appetite for what he's got at home."

All heads swiveled in Uncle Rex's direction, and Bailey's mom got up from the table. She said something that rhymed with duck, and she pushed through the kitchen door.

Bailey followed after her.

"I can't take it anymore," her mom said. She sniffed and grabbed a tissue. Then she pulled a small amber pill bottle from her pocket and handed it to Bailey. "You'd better keep these. I might be tempted to empty the entire bottle into your aunt's morning cup of tea."

"Do you think Uncle Rex is really having an affair with Lea Townsend?" Bailey asked.

Aunt Fiona pushed through the door. "I heard he was hanging out over at the salon when we were in Las Vegas, talking to all the women. Could be he's turning into a swinger."

Bailey's mom groaned. "For heaven's sake, Rex is not having an affair with Lea. He's been planning a birthday party for you, you loon." She threw up her hands. "There. Are you happy? Now you've ruined your birthday surprise."

Aunt Fiona clucked her tongue on the roof of her mouth "I didn't ruin it. You're the one." She grinned. "I guess this means the dry spell is over. And now that I know Rex isn't cheating on me, I guess tonight I can bring out those tassels I brought back with me from Las Vegas."

Bailey's mom sniffed into her tissue. "Great. That's just great. Everybody'll be having sex but me." She shook her head. "I'd rather drink arsenic than go without sex for the rest of my life. I'll turn brown around the edges. My petals will fall off."

Brother, Bailey thought.

The door opened and Carter stuck his head in. "Everyone has left. You ready to go?" he asked Bailey.

Her hero.

Chapter Thirty-Four

The rest of the evening was a breeze. When Bailey and Carter got back to her cottage, she took him out to her deck, where they settled into a cozy huddle for some serious conversation. She didn't want to go near the bedroom until she'd explained about the kiss she and Mike had shared. Carter was in good spirits and their talk was easier than she anticipated. He completely understood and forgave her—and how could he not, when he'd been caught kissing at least *three* other women? She didn't ask if there were more. Some things were better left unknown. The important thing was that they were finally back together, and he was more than willing to talk marriage.

Only one other subject needed discussion. Whether or not she was really pregnant. When she brought up the subject, Carter silenced her with a kiss. He told her no explanation was necessary. He'd already assumed it was her auntie's imagination run amok.

And now that they had all that craziness out of the way....

Epilogue

Bailey and Carter went on to have three beautiful children—a boy named Ryder, and two girls named Gabrielle and Violet. They divided their time between Las Vegas and Coupeville, where Bailey opened her own award-winning bakery. Her specialty was marionberry pies. Bailey came to realize Coupeville wasn't such a bad place to live… so long as she was able to take regular vacations to exotic locales. Carter eventually won the title of World Champion Elvis Impersonator. He also became half-owner of The Oasis resort and casino.

Olivia Ventura and Old Elvis began living together in Coupeville, and Olivia never again spoke of the real Elvis Presley making a comeback.

Aunt Fiona and Uncle Rex bought a condo in Las Vegas and they, too, split their time between Coupeville and Sin City. Aunt Fiona never did become a showgirl.

Mark Jefferson married an Ann Margret impersonator, and they had a couple of cute little red-headed girls, who they named Annie and Margret.

Brian Jefferson never married. He continued working at The Auto Shop, until he eventually opened a museum for classic restored cars.

Liza Blair went on to be a toothpaste ad model. She married and had one child, a little girl named Madison who had blond hair and the same dazzling smile as Liza.

Twinkie Martinson married into wealth, and she and her husband bought back the house where she and Carter grew up. Her husband partnered with Carter and became the other half-owner of The Oasis resort and Casino.

Maria Cruz went back to South Carolina. She married another doctor, and they bought a home adjacent to Briar's Creek Country Club, where they spent their weekends golfing.

Mike Shur married Nikki Amsterdam. He took over as head of security for The Oasis Resort and Casino after Carter became half-owner.

Tucker and Maggie May lived a long joyful life. They spent their days swimming and hiking and begging for treats.

Chandler's true owners were found via a microchip in his neck, and he went back to a loving home, where he spent his days dreaming about Maggie May.

Frank Zoopa continued to rot in prison for a very long time.

THE END

ABOUT THE AUTHOR

Alexa Darin makes her home in Washington State, where she is surrounded by nature and spends most of her leisure time hiking in the Alpine Wilderness with her two beloved Yellow Labrador retrievers. She believes that every romance writer should have a survival kit that contains dark chocolate, red wine, and tissue. Readers can learn more about Alexa and her upcoming books at:

www.alexadarin.com

Made in the USA
San Bernardino, CA
02 September 2015